INVASIVE SPECIES

Weapons of Choice Book 6

Nick Snape

For Gloria
Whose tireless energy keeps us all going

CONTENTS

INTRODUCTION

Each of the Weapons of Choice Novels can be read in isolation with a little background information. If you have read the previous books, then please skip to the prologue if you don't require any reminders. If you do wish a revisit of past events and characters, I have provided further information on my website. Either click the link below or type in the address:

www.nicksnape.com/about-6

PROLOGUE

Khoikhoi Atoll, Planet Stratan, Stratan Solar System

(300 Hundred Years Ago)

The huge engine booster glistened in the bright sunshine, the black outline contrasting against the snow-laden foothills and jagged mountains that tore into the deep blue sky on the mainland, far beyond the volcanic island's edge.

!Nias stroked the metal shell of the outlet port, imagining fire erupting as the fuel ignited on the count of *zero,* the chemical rocket urging the huge weight of their last hope skywards, and towards the orbiting Sail Ship.

Only forty light years to travel across an empty void. Three hundred years frozen in time. And at the end of it? A forlorn hope that the planet we seek holds the key to our future.

No pressure then.

!Nias scratched at the scabbed tattoo under his left eye, the spiral matching the first he received just a year ago when first assigned to the mission. Breaking off the last scab, he glanced into the reflective metal surface of the rocket booster, briefly admiring the matching set signalling his rank as Senior Technician for his squad of Marines.

His wide nose flaring as he breathed in the frigid air, *!Nias* adjusted his armoured suit at the pinch point round his neck.

Come tomorrow, he'd be wearing cryotube kit, with tubes and needles keeping him alive, his body entering the long stasis he may never wake up from. A lab experiment just two years ago. Now he, and the fifteen other Stratan Marines, were to be the real test specimens.

Only a projected 40% failure rate to worry about. And when they say projected, they mean we don't have a clue.

Across from *!Nias*, the briefing chairs were set out around a large temporary platform, the roughness of the scaffolding reflecting the speed at which the programme had been accelerated over the last few weeks, as the world spiralled towards chaos. In an hour's time, the world's press would descend on their little patch of technological paradise, eager to hear about the Seed Cache Project that *!Nias* and his fellow team members had sworn to keep secret. But during recent months, the construction of the planetary laser systems to complement those in orbit had set the Minoas' government on fire. The country's leaders seeing the new equipment as a direct threat, a new weapon in the escalating war of words between them and anyone their ever-increasing paranoia regarded as aggressive.

The Stratan Council immediately brought the project forward by half a year, desperate to send a sign of hope into the void, something the people of the planet could believe in. With the Minoas pathogen increasing at an alarming rate, the rapid increase in male sterility had swept the world. The reality had sunk in, the emotional and psychological impact outrunning the physical decrease of the available gene pool. Violence and crime had quadrupled in the last few months, from the already high rates sweeping the Council countries over the last few years. Society was on the edge of collapse.

!Nias' nose flared, the warm breath condensing in the frigid air as he walked away from the platform and down the stone steps towards the swirl of the sea. His booted feet crunched across the crystal beach, the countless shards reflecting the light

back in broken rainbow patterns. A wonder that hadn't existed just twenty years ago, but now one source of hope amidst the potential disaster the world faced.

On reaching the water's edge, he dipped his hand within the swirl of crystals that pervaded the seawater, the suspended rock crystals shifting with the eddies he created against the slow-moving waves. *!Nias* smiled, his thin lips stretched across his face as the patterns whirled into the familiar rainbow wheel and curved lines that so fascinated the scientists.

"Isn't nature wonderful?" he said. "When we work with it, rather than trying to adapt it to kill our own *!ke*."

"Hey, *!Nias*. Are you playing in the water again?" The shout echoed around the small cliffs of the bay, the nesting bird life rising as one cloud of green and blue flickering wings in jittery response. *!Nias* let out a long, wistful sigh, his large eyes drinking in the multi-coloured spiral fading in the waves before turning to face reality.

"Yes, *Aeka*. You finished chopping fruit with that sword of yours?" he replied, eyeing the woman's tattooed face. The fresh claw marks through her eyeline and down her cheeks, a sign of her promotion to squad leader for Deti, the first Marines likely to step on Earth. He eyed the dent in her head, the result of a vehicle crash when she was younger and emphasised by the cut of her hair. *Aeka* never hid from any challenge, and though her drive for discipline and order set his teeth on edge, he admired the ferocity with which she commanded respect.

"All done. You'll be glad of it when we make Earth. You can never have too many weapons. Life is unpredictable enough on this world, never mind our place of origin."

!Nias snorted in agreement, nodding as he did so, "Yes, if the people, the *!ke*, of Earth are as angry as ours it may come in useful. Are you attending the media session?"

"Got the short straw. First on the planet means I'm the star of the show. I don't mind. They see me as a freak as it is." *Aeka* bent down to the water, swirling three or four patterns in the lazy waves, the rainbow wheels merging then separating into singular forms. *!Nias* watched as she spun three more, forming into a complex, interlinked matrix. *Aeka's* senior technician had been born within the volcanic atoll and spent hours demonstrating the complexity of forms she could create within the sea. It was the only time *!Nias* witnessed *Aeka* relax. Her eyes flickering between intricate forms as she took deep breaths and fiddled with the red gemstone pierced through her left ear.

"You'll do well. All steel and determination, just what the people need right now. The self-destruction of the SeedShip has fed the paranoia even further. They need leadership and hope, you can provide that," said *!Nias*, his foot digging into the glittering beach.

"Yeah, well, there's no choice otherwise, is there? They know my dad is in hospital after the riot in Kabbo City. Can you imagine the questions that'll come flying about that? Hero police officer and all – can his damaged daughter live up to his expectations, etc, etc." *Aeka* ran her hand through the intricate water pattern, dissipating the beauty with an angry swipe. "Come on, we have a briefing. Apparently, it's quite dangerous sleeping for three hundred years in a cryotube and flying across forty light years of space. Fancy that."

!Nias shifted his back, easing into the orange gel as it wrapped around him, welcoming the Stratan Marine into his cryotube. He glanced across the Sail Ship's lower life support room, the eight coffin like boxes sealing one by one as the future hope for humankind prepared for the long sleep. *!Nias* conjured up the image of the huge sail ranging outwards from the ship, its dual role to capture as much solar energy as possible, while the lasers from Stratan and orbit pushed against it. Slowly accelerating

out of the Stratan System, on a direct heading for Earth and the longed-for Haven genetic knowledge it may contain.

"Senior Technician *!Nias*, it is time for you to merge with the cryotube interface. The cryogenic system requires your biochemical and nutrient needs to be analysed for a fourth time before you enter stasis."

"Yes, Ship. On it. Ready for check four," he said, easing back the final few centimetres as the gel entered his ears and, with a momentary panic, his nose and mouth.

I just hope check four is accurate.

PART ONE

CHAPTER 1

Leaving The Tiqsimuyu System

The approach to the Node was as smooth as always, the Explorer Ship easing into familiar navigation patterns when nearing the transfer system. The absence of light as the ship slipped closer, always a sure sign they were on the right trajectory, and the signal for Yasuko to batten down the spacecraft's systems to ensure their integrity. It was also the starting point for rising panic. Her awareness of the organic components in the Explorer Ship's systems enabling Yasuko to recognise emotions that had previously roamed data banks unheeded. And these were easy to label. The mix of anxiety, stress, fear and excitement that she measured so clinically in her human crew, obvious to her now.

What will I face on the other side? Now S'lgarr has shown me what they are, am I able to resist, or will it heighten an inner species' desire to join them?

Yasuko had debated across her systems about engaging Smith's help. In the end, embarrassment, another recognisable but subtler emotion, prevented her from asking. That, and how would he react if he recognised the mix of jealousy and lust emanating from the creatures roaming the space between the Nodes? Would he see that in her? How could he not?

The nanobots ensured Noah and Zuri slipped into unconsciousness, Finn drifting off last as the needle delivered drug took effect. A sliver of relief shivered across Yasuko's mind, her friends and crew safe from whatever lay beyond the nodal gate. The bow of the ship slipped through, and Yasuko braced for the onslaught.

And there was silence.

Absence.

A void depleted of the howling hunger, empty of envy.

Yasuko's mind spiralled, the expectations and walls tumbling under the emotional power of the barren expanse.

Where? Where have they gone? Has S'lgarr done something? Or have they consumed him, taken his life force, and left? I don't understand.

But the abyss did not answer. The space between the stars lay silent.

CHAPTER 2

Entering The Stratan Solar System

"How much longer?" asked Noah, stretching the mechanised foot out, wriggling each of the blue metal toes in turn as Yasuko watched on.

"The neural links need further fine tuning. I'd say with three more days of the exercise routines I set, you will have those fully functional and the whole lower leg will operate within normal parameters. Of course, you could just ignore those exercises, like you have been, and we'll be talking about a month," replied Yasuko, engaging her best hard stare upon Noah.

"Oh, come on Yasuko. There's work to be done. It's not as if I'm actually avoiding them, more like getting distracted. Finn wants the new developments for the body suits in place within the next few days for testing." Noah's eyes flickered up to Yasuko, checking her facial expression before returning to the toe flexes. The resultant sigh told him all he needed to know.

"I set the exercises in a timetable for you," Yasuko pointed to the wall above Noah's workstation, a colour-coded schedule emerging from within the metal and sitting squarely in his eyeline. "Follow it, or I'll let Zuri know you have been deliberately going against my advice."

Noah baulked; Zuri had been on the warpath for days after leaving the Tiqsimuyu System. She knew the next stop was Stratan and had been playing over her memories of their first encounter back on Earth. Losing Bhakshi, Kapoor, Cillian and others sat heavily on her. Even their brief time with Corporal Lumu, who'd given his life in the pursuit of the Stratan Marines, gnawed at her heart. And when Zuri fretted, those around her suffered too. *!Nias,* whose body lay in cryostasis in Yasuko's lab, took away her certainty with just a few words when they had first opened Yasuko's ship.

Noah swallowed deeply. "I'll do them. No need to disturb Zuri right now. I've been through enough pain as it is."

"Yes, you will," said Yasuko, spinning on her heel and striding away from Noah and on towards her next problem. The aftereffects of facing off against S'lgarr had left the ship depleted of resources, and the appetite to hang around the Tiq system after so much death had been so low, they'd left in a hurry. The ship required a variety of base metals and minerals and, according to the information from the Data Storage lab, there was a possibility Stratan's singular moon had everything they needed. Her initial scans picked up repeating radio signals from its rocky surface, and going by the content, they would find an old moon base. After recent events, she just wasn't sure how well the squad would take it. The alternative, a planet with a thick, hydrogen rich atmosphere and a small rocky core, would require a much longer timescale to mine, with the ore spread across the vast planet's crust at much deeper depths.

Got to face up to the reality at some point. And we need that conversation about the Node transfer.

Finn watched the spear spin between the nanobot trainer's hands, the blunt, soft rubber tip a blur as it ran through the movements designed to distract. The mesmerising speed and fluidity drew him in, and the trainer spun, rolling and aiming to bring the tip to a full stop in front of his face. Finn, instantly aware of the new danger, ducked, bringing up the shaft of his own spear to knock it away. He moved to sweep the nanobot, with stiff joints still recovering from the trials on Nutu Allpa arguing about his choice. The nanobot lifted its foot, avoiding Finn's laboured movement with ease.

This is going to hurt.

The spear surged forward, the tip hitting him in the rib plate and sending him flying backwards to crash into the hull. The trainer stood back, its program paused as Zuri gracefully rose from the couch and stood by its side, her eyes and amused smile grating at Finn's pride.

"Not a word," he said. "It's only my fourth session. I'd much prefer a punchbag and a big gun."

"You need to add some fluidity to your choices, Finn. A more subtle approach. Besides, it was Yasuko's analysis that led to this, not mine. We took a battering on Nutu Allpa, and you hate normal recovery exercises. This is the most beneficial method where you can learn something at the same time. You've already improved, and you won't always have your armour or a gun to hand. We've gotten lazy, depending on Yasuko to provide everything."

"I'm all about power, not grace. Grace is your thing."

"You practice enough, and you can have both."

Zuri rubbed at her hip while walking over to the weapons rack, removing the same training spear Finn was using. The nanobot trainer turned as Yasuko called its next program, Zuri taking her preferred stance and eyeing Finn until he matched hers. With the bot moving through a basic kata, or 'form', in front of them, they both mirrored its movements. Zuri from memory, Finn copying the movements as his eye and brain attempted to coordinate his lumbering body into the correct passage and flow from each position.

With Finn sweating, and Zuri stretching out her hip joint again, they stopped as the *form* ended. The nanobot trainer merged into the floor with Yasuko appearing on the couch, her eyes serious and virtual body stiff. They both knew she was only just starting the journey towards understanding who, and what, she truly was, and subsequently much harder to read, but the signals were obvious. There were decisions to be made, and Stratan was on everyone's mind.

"Maybe we could talk?" Yasuko said.

"After a shower, and with everyone together," said Zuri, her mood switching. The pleasure gained from exercise, forgotten. "If that's okay?"

"Yes, of course. I'll make sure Smith knows."

"Are you there, Smith?" asked Yasuko.

"Sure am. How's my feathered one doing today?"

"I'm fine. Though I am worrying a little about what's coming. We are meeting in about an hour to discuss Stratan and other things. I wondered if …?"

"I'd made a decision?" Smith let out a virtual sigh. "Yes, and no. I am not ready to go back to a real body. At least, I don't think I am. I can't face trying and then finding myself hating it. What would I do then? Abandon the body, leave it to die? Or maybe go insane, not cope mentally with being wholly human again. The loss of … of …"

"Connection? To interact instantly with the data stream, or have full knowledge of what's going on around you? Being … limited."

"Yes, that's it. Have you been thinking about this too? Since, you know, you found out you were…are…alive?"

"Of course, though I have no qualms about trying the other side out. I think I am a hybrid and therefore have no fear of being one or the other. I am curious, and it may well be when we have returned you to Earth that I can explore options. Besides, I have you as my test subject."

"Ah, a lab rat, am I? So, what do I do? Stay virtual or inhabit a powered suit like our copies? I don't think I can stomp around in those huge armoured units all the time, either."

"We could design you a smaller version, more human sized. Give you a physical presence. Would that help your thinking? If you wanted, I think I could closely mimic your appearance."

"Would I get an input, you know, in the design?"

"Of course. Though be warned. I won't be turning anything up to eleven."

"There you go, spoiling all my fun. You going to spill the beans about the Nodes? The space between?"

"Spill the beans? Ah, yes. You mean tell people, what a strange idiom. Yes, they need to know. Did you see?"

"No. I took on board the caution you advised. I don't think you know how scared you sound every time you mention it. Smith was definitely not at the wheel."

"Hah. Yes, you would probably have thought I was quite mad if you had. It was empty, Smith. They have gone, and I don't know where. The only thing I can think of is that S'lgarr's awakening has dramatically changed things. And with our luck, and his history, it won't be for the better."

"Okay, here's another thought. If they've gone, can humans stay awake through the Nodes now?"

"Possibly. Why?"

"Because sometimes they see what we can't."

CHAPTER 3

Within The Stratan Solar System

"It is slightly smaller than Earth's moon, probably quite similar to the one around Nutu Allpa. Rocky, no real atmosphere and no life as far as the sensors can pick up," said Yasuko, her eyes roaming across her crew. "It provides a gravitational force that affects Stratan, so the oceans have tidal movement, though likely of a lesser level than Earth."

"And there's a base? A moon base?" asked Finn, a grim set to his face, half an eye on Zuri, whose attempts at a relaxed pose on her couch were failing.

"Yes, Noah. Do you want to explain?"

"We've analysed the auto-repeat radio signal from the moon. It's hard to tell exactly, but it must have been running for about eighty years, having cross-referenced the time stamp with the few planetary signals. It's not an exact process, however, because the standards have changed. The message calls for a rescue by the Stratan Council. They were running out of food after a meteorite strike on their hydroponic farms," said Noah.

Zuri shifted position, searching for some comfort in the familiarity of her couch. But the usually calming feel of the cushions provided little relief. Her emotions were tumbling over, her nerves brittle, and thinking subsequently muddled. Over the last few days, she had sought peace in exercise routines and training, but now she was forced to consider the possibility of contact with *!Nias'* people, his *!ke*. And she genuinely did not know how she felt about it. She buried herself deeper into the couch, dragging cushions over her stomach, hugging them tightly, well aware Finn was watching her.

"This place ... is it a mining operation?" asked Smith's hologram, fully formed and standing next to the central dais.

"Very likely, or at the very least, a viability study," said Yasuko. "And exactly where I need to go. All the ores and minerals are within a few kilometres of that central space. It's logical for us to land there. It'll save at least a week's time over the alternative planet and the lack of atmosphere will make logistics easier. I'm sorry, I know that somewhere like this is the last place you want to land after our encounter with S'lgarr." Yasuko dipped her head briefly, then started again. "But if speed is important, then it's the best option."

"We can track Stratan from there, though, is that right?" said Finn. "We have a few demons going round in our heads, Yasuko. They killed our trainees, our friends and squad mates. Resolving that against what we now know about the seeding of the planets ... well, it may take a little time."

"*!Nias* said his people needed help," said Zuri, finally trusting herself to say something. "They left their planet three hundred years ago. Is that right?" Yasuko nodded. "So, whatever was happening on Stratan, they were desperate enough to send people across space, to give up their lives for their people. *!Nias* said the first squad of his Marines turned 'bad'. It's possible ..." Zuri couldn't finish, pushing her chin down into the cushion to prevent the welling emotions from taking over.

"It's possible they need help," said Smith. "I know you are all running through a whole gamut of pain right now. I should know, they killed me after all, and my trainees. I watched Luther die by the sword. Their methods, for whatever reason, can't be justified. But we can't judge a whole planet of people by what those soldiers did. Can you imagine doing that on Earth, with some of the decisions and actions made at every level of command? By every army? Even back on Tiq, we walked away from Company people who may well have followed orders to turn off the oxygen in that Space Station or sent their soldiers to die to save their skins. If we were judged on that, would we be found wanting? Or Havenhome, where we fought and killed soldiers who were just following orders, because we wanted to get home."

"Might I suggest we get full information?" said Noah. "Land at the base. Yasuko gets what she needs for the ship, and we work through whatever we can glean from sensors and the base data. Take the emotions out of it until we have full information."

Finn and Zuri looked towards each other and nodded, pleased to move on.

"There's something else," said Yasuko. "The space between the Nodes. It was empty."

CHAPTER 4

Moon Base, Planet Stratan's Moon

Yasuko brought the ship around the moon, the horizon's smooth curve eventually broken by the outline of block buildings as the base came into view. The buildings, a blend of moon rock and metal, appeared intact, with doors and window portals sealed tight. Without an atmosphere, erosion was very unlikely, but if the base had been abandoned, it had certainly been left ready to be used again. The only sign that anything was amiss was the small shuttle like ship standing away from the buildings, its doors open and internal parts scattered nearby.

Yasuko eased the ship onto the rocky ground, with the landing gear adjusting to ensure the spacecraft was level despite the undulations in the surface. Nobody rushed out to greet them, and the radio remained silent. She had little doubt the place was empty. But Finn was taking no chances.

"Okay, we ready Yasuko?" said Finn, his powered armour side by side with Smith, Zuri behind, and leaving Noah sulking in the ship's control room.

You don't do your exercises, then you're not prepared.

"Yes. Sensors clear, no life signs or automatic defences powering up. Opening the hold doors." Yasuko dropped the ramp, Finn sending Smith ahead to take point as he covered behind. They were a hundred metres from what they judged to be the main airlock entrance, with five large piles of drilling sections between them and the door. Smith reached the first, his sensors fully up and SA80 rifle in hand.

"Clear," he said, Finn following while Zuri covered their rear. After she joined them, Smith moved on and they continued like that until reaching the airlock.

"Smith," said Finn, "You're up."

Smith flipped out a front panel on his powered armour, pulling out a data plaque that linked to his own. Since the encounter with S'lgarr, he'd decided he wanted his personal plaque to stay inside the suit in future. Attaching it, he reached past Zuri, who stood with her back against the wall.

"No Raffles, gentleman thief quote today?" asked Zuri.

"Nope, a member of the British Space Commandos would not belittle themselves that way," he replied.

"Space Commandos? You know, I quite like that," Zuri said, eyes checking her HUD data for any thermal images.

"You do?"

"Yeah, sounds … more like us."

"I've got a badge mocked up and everything," said Smith.

"Why am I not surprised? I bet you've even got a motto," said Finn, trying to keep the grin off his face, and failing badly.

"Working on it, though there's no Latin for 'space' or 'spaceship'. I have 'ad astra' for 'to the stars', but we're stepping on RAF toes there. I'm in." The airlock button array flashed briefly, a four-digit sequence running through the large buttons. The seal broke, and the door swung inwards.

"What about breaking and entering? You got any Latin for that?" said Finn, using his mirror sight to look round the opening doorway. "It's clear."

Finn moved through, with the airlock only just big enough for him and one other as Smith joined him. The metal bulkhead door had a small window, with Finn unable to see more than just the grey corridor beyond when his suit lights switched on. Inside, a single orange emergency light flickered.

"Zuri, spin up a drone and wait outside while Smith gets us in. Noah?"

"Here," came the less than happy reply from the Ship.

"Eyes on Zuri, she'll be alone for a minute or so."

"Will do. Zuri's drone feed enabled."

Finn closed the outer airlock as Smith attached his plaque and got to work, this time with prior knowledge of the operating system. The digit sequence repeated on the lock, and the bulkhead wheel spun automatically. Finn used the mirror sight, and with the corridor lifeless, signalled Smith to let Zuri in.

"Yasuko, taking samples for analysis. You got any initial thoughts?" said Finn, eye-clicking his HUD to activate the filter sampler. The corridor was bare, no dust and little light. To the left it ended in another bulkhead door, a standard safety feature they'd seen on other human built bases. Turning around, another stood to the right.

"Going by the data, it has a lower oxygen level than Earth, but breathable, so something still works in there. We have zero knowledge of what viral, bacterial or other contaminants could be present, Finn. Without a full analysis, you will all need to maintain the integrity of your suits."

"Okay. This place gives the impression it's abandoned, or dead."

Zuri stepped through the inner airlock, her drone buzzing above her head, followed by Smith with the door automatically closing behind. Finn signalled to move out right. The impression from their initial sweep over the base showing most of the building lay in that direction. Finn examined the doorway, the handle at its side coming with instructions, a written form of Khoisan they'd already seen on external signs. His HUD couldn't translate, with Yasuko still compiling the language structure as they worked through the base, providing more examples. Finn hauled the handle downwards, a clunk announcing the lock's disengagement, and he pulled the door open a crack, with Zuri sending the drone through.

"Common room area to the left, kitchen and dining area to the right. Two corridors leading off north and west," said Zuri. "It all looks neat and tidy, dishes on the racks and chairs all in place. No dust, no signs of movement, no heat signatures."

"Okay, in we go."

CHAPTER 5

Research Facility, Kabbo Equatorial Grass Plains, Southern Continent, Planet Stratan

The radio crackled. Against the buzz of static, the hard voice of command bellowed out, making Mansse jump up from his snooze, his sergeant's cap slipping off to land on the dirty jeep floor.

"We have *!Kora* approaching the fences on the western side. I repeat, we have *!Kora* approaching the western fences. About five kilometres out. I need security there now," said Field Commander Otegnoa. "They are after the Quia herd. Damn these cameras, too many are going wrong. It's a large group, too poor an image to say how many. Camera 325."

"On our way, Commander. ETA about twenty minutes." Mansse dragged his cap from the floor, brushing it against his uniform trousers and placing it on his balding head.

"Fire us up, Uma. We're in a hurry," he said, clapping the huge man on the shoulder. "We can't afford to lose any more of the herd."

"Yes Sarge." Uma shifted the solar panel off the jeep boot, stowing it away with practised ease before turning the electric engine on. The gentle hum rose in pitch as he hit the accelerator, the four-person jeep surging onwards through the ruts and bumps of the grass plain. The large wheels rolled over most, but the occasional deep hole threatened to tip the bouncing vehicle more than once. Mansse gripped the strap above his head, taking care not to hold on too tight, with the ache in his old shoulder injury playing up.

"Could you at least miss some of the bloody puddle holes? Ah, you know, drive round one or two, man?"

"You want to drive, Sarge? You're welcome to it. Hold on." The right wheel caught a large rock, sending the vehicle up onto its left side wheels for a second or two before crashing back down through the high grass onto the ground. "See what you made me do?"

Mansse let the strap go, his shoulder howling at him as the jeep jerked again. He pulled at the seatbelts, tightening them down across both shoulders, with Privates Yeta and Osineh doing the same in the back seats. They hit another sinkhole before the wheels finally gripped the stone surface of the service road. The jeep sped off, tyres throwing the stone chips into the air as they powered towards the western fences and camera position 325.

"This might be a feint, Mansse. Like last time," said Yeta, her hands gripping the back of the sergeant's seat. "They attacked at point 204 on the northern fence, then another group came in on the east. Split us up."

"Yeah, might be right there. But that's Otegnoa's bag, not ours. We deal with what's in front of us. And no holding back, you hear? If we don't hit them hard enough, they'll just keep coming back—they see the Quia as easy meat rather than tackling the wild herds. Lazy. We should shoot a few, then they'd leave us alone." Mansse settled back in his seat, message given. He lifted the stun rifle from the door holster, running over the charge level and upping the power to maximum. At his hip, the pistol he wasn't allowed to use unless life was threatened. After all, there weren't that many humans left.

After a few more minutes, the fences came into view. Three metres high and chain linked, and when they'd been built fifty years ago, they had been electrified using solar panels and battery backups strung around the Stratan Council Facility. Now, less than fifty percent worked, just enough for the Quia herds to learn to keep away. If they ever charged them en masse, well, they'd have to become hunters rather than farmers.

Fifteen *!Kora* swarmed over the panel nearest the dwindling water pool, with some of the mutated humans forming a human pyramid, enabling the top three to drop on Mansse's side of the fence. As they spotted the jeep heading their way, they raised their barbed spears, gripped by four fingered hands covered in a patchwork of rough, hardened skin.

Uma spun the jeep sideways, giving Mansse and Yeta a clear shot at the three *!Kora* as he slammed on the brakes ten metres from the group. The first spear flew their way, the powerful muscles of the tribeswoman driving the tip into the nearest wheel. Yeta fired, the electric surge of her weapon sizzling through the air and slamming into the woman's chest, forcing the air from her large lungs. She made no cry as she fell to the floor. Mansse released a bolt, his aim true and hitting the second *!Kora* before he could throw. The third fell as Osineh stood on her seat, the rifle bolt fizzing over Yeta's head and striking home.

A rain of rocks clattered down on the jeep, its open top design allowing the barrage to strike all four of the security personnel, Osineh coming off worse, a rock cracking against her skull. A second wave from the other side of the fence fell short as Uma pumped the accelerator, the jeep jerking away a few metres before the whole team piled out over the doors. Spreading themselves outwards in an arc, they fired through the fence, driving the remaining *!Kora* back into the scrub bush as the stun shots hit home. At the ever-increasing distance, the bolt's effects were more painful than incapacitating.

"Osineh, you okay?" asked Uma, walking over to the bruised woman, a lump rising on her temple.

"Blurred vision, but I still hit more than the sergeant," Osineh wobbled, then sat down, the world around her lurching. Uma crouched next to her, hands rummaging for his first aid kit.

"Ha – hilarious. Yeta, get these tied up and we'll take them to the gate. And watch out for them waking up. Th—" The bullet split Mansse's skull, shattering teeth as it exited. The next three shots pummelled Uma and Yeta, their bodies shaking as the whirr of heavy rounds tore through their flesh. Osineh tried to stand, the ground spinning as she scrambled towards the jeep. The heavy calibre bullet hit the ground near her feet, digging inwards and exploding when it hit a stone. She reached the side of the jeep, dragging herself along its metal doors, rocks clattering down around her. She yanked open the driver's door, dropping into the seat with the dashboard moving in and out of her vision. But an orange light flared at the periphery, and she slammed her palm onto it, the engine engaging and the jeep driving forwards as the auto-return program kicked in.

CHAPTER 6

Moon Base, Planet Stratan's Moon

Finn stared through the portal window, the small lab beyond crammed with cryotubes that buzzed and glowed, and many that didn't. Each of the tubes was roughly constructed, the welds tight but clearly not manufactured in a glitzy, modern factory. Wires and tubes protruded from all angles, the orange lights intermittently flashing to show they were at least functioning. If he hadn't known better, he was thinking more Dr Who from the 1970s, rather than anything near the 2000s. Smith seemed to agree.

"Wow, these are a little different from the Haven versions. Almost like they were built from a do-it-yourself kit after half a bottle of whisky." Smith said. Inside, he could just make out the faces within the four remaining operational ones, estimating their ages from forty to sixty years old when they'd entered stasis. Each face exhibiting the wide nose and enlarged eye sockets they'd expected. The other six systems were completely dead, and thankfully, their windows were opaque, with no back lighting.

"Come on, we'd better record this for Yasuko and Noah," said Finn, opening the door and scanning the room with his mirror sight before entering. Like the rest of the inner base buildings, it was neat, tidy, and empty.

Smith followed in, noting the computer system hooked up to the cryotubes against the right wall. All lights and whirring fans that gave him a little concern, and when opening the door, the increasing pitch doubled his worries. He sidled over, the powered armour not conducive to easy movement in the cramped room, and placed his secondary data plaque against the computer screen. He half-expected to be sucked into a Victorian world of clockwork robots and wind-up televisions, only to be faced with a sheath of complex algorithms that were not quite like any AI he had met on his travels. It was like the system had armoured itself, an outer shell of protection against time. And the more he looked, the more obvious became the extremely low power levels it needed to function.

A cryotube for an AI – keeping itself functioning for as long as it can.

Smith withdrew. Subtlety was not his strong point, deciding he needed Noah and Yasuko's analysis prior to attempting anything that could cause the cryotube systems to crash.

"Well?" asked Finn, peering into the window of the oldest looking Stratan. "Anything?"

"There's a locked down, low-powered AI in there, and it's not coming out to play. I'll need some help to wake it up," replied Smith.

"Finn, I have something here," said Zuri over the radio. "Looks like a graveyard."

"I count thirty graves," said Zuri. "Assuming each grave has a marker. I've sent the images to Yasuko to see if we can translate any dates." She peered through the glass window, the low-wall beyond containing a space akin to a Japanese Zen Garden. The rock and gravel carefully marked in swirls and lines, wrapping around the raised graves. "It has a strange beauty, calming. But placing it here feels like there was an inevitability behind it."

"Or preserving resources," said Smith. "Nearby means not using too much oxygen and stored energy."

Finn nodded; his mind strangely calm when he'd expected anger at finding Stratan alive on the base. The whole place felt…

Sad. This place feels like they gave up, and that wasn't the way with the soldiers we faced on Earth.

"Until Yasuko can connect in with the cryo system, there's little else we can do here," said Finn.

"Can you patch into the data storage banks, Smith? Find us the story behind this place. I've got a feeling we may get some insight into the reasons behind *!Nias'* journey to Earth," said Zuri, her eyes still scanning the garden and its sorrowful contents.

"I'll give it a go," he replied, patting Zuri on the shoulder on his way past. "Don't get pulled into too much emotion. You'll lose the edge; we have survived over the last six months because we are on point. We need to distance ourselves from the past and analyse the present."

Stay frosty. Otherwise, we'll make mistakes that'll bite us in the arse.

CHAPTER 7

Research Facility, Kabbo Equatorial Grass Plains, Southern Continent, Planet Stratan

Osineh grabbed the edge of the bed, her eyes flitting from side to side, her addled brain replaying Uma's death as he tended her. The explosion of the whirring bullet followed by the sudden absence in his eyes, the soft, cooling pad against her temple. The blood splatter against her uniform, the bullets slamming into the ground while scrambling for the jeep. And Uma lying on the grass behind her, arms outstretched, glassy eyes declaring his spirit walked with the gods. Osineh cried out, jerking awake, sweat staining her clothes as her eyes flickered open. Her brain couldn't cope, the movement too much and the concussion made its presence felt. Osineh threw up, throwing her head to the left of the bed, the sudden movement adding further to the nausea, and she retched again.

"Hey, hey," said a calming voice she couldn't quite place. "Take it easy. You are concussed, only minor, but no rushing about. Slow movements, ya?"

"Yes," Osineh's brain raked through the options, dragging up a name. "Tâa Alkinta, ya?"

"Yes, girl. But pay no mind, I may be the Tâa of this facility, but we must work together now. The rest of our people are setting up a defence. It seems you stumbled on an organised attack. The *! Kora* are not only raiding for the meat. They have attacked a few guard posts inside the perimeter. It appears they want inside for whatever reason and have a few old weapons to back up their numbers."

"Then I must help, yes. I should be out there."

"You're not in a fit state. Rest, take these." The older woman, her eyes deep black and skin wrinkled with time, handed over a few pills. "We may need you in the coming days, so we need to get you fit and ready. If you hadn't come back, well, we would have been even more unprepared. It's been a long time since the mutated ones have sought us out like this, certainly not since you've been with us, likely before you were born. But this place was built for war, Osineh. We may not have the people, but we have walls that kept our grandparents safe during a nuclear war. A few mutants with spears and rifles will not get through."

"But the Quia? We need the cattle, Tâa. And the other animals, we need them all. The rewilding needs a wider gene pool."

"We'll just have to start again, ya? It won't be the first time. We just need to keep the labs safe."

Field Commander Otegnoa clipped the digital binoculars back into the jeep's door, letting out a deep sigh. His grey, thinning hair contrasting against his sun-kissed face. One of the few Stratan whose ancestral line lived consistently in the warmer equatorial regions, many of his family still retained traits from their origins, able to deal with the higher UV levels and heat. Not uncommon prior to the Great War, but now rare after the swathes of radioactive soot killed millions in the huge cities that sprung up in the warmer sections of the planet. Most of the remaining Stratan population had moved away from the blurring of the hemispheres, retreating to the colder climes nearer the north and south poles. But as the world recovered, they needed to repopulate much of what was lost if they were to survive. The southern continent reseeding programme had been a success, and the larger bushes and smaller trees were propagating well. But the rewilding of the larger fauna was taking longer, hampered a little by the increasing !*Kora* population and their lack of self-control, but mainly by the Fire Ticks – always the Fire Ticks.

Another six months and Alkinta would have been ready to release the next batch of animals.

"Geoboe, you can proceed. The guard station appears empty, but use caution. The !*Kora* appear to have learnt some new tactics," he said into the mic, the headphones battered and strung together with black tape.

"Affirmative, Commander."

"Datin, take us in closer. Hundred metres away in case we're needed," said Otegnoa, eyes scanning the horizon as the plains grass swayed in the wind. He pulled out the stun rifle from its holster, resting it on top of the windscreen frame as the jeep lurched over the rough ground. When the jeep came to a stop, he slid his eye behind the rifle sight, the optics giving a narrow but well-defined view of the station. Geoboe reached the main door, his partner waiting at the side with the other team moving along the ten-metre wall, aiming for the rear.

The normally empty guard station had been Mansse's base of operations for the last week or so. But the radio system had gone down, the old drone sent to check it out reporting the main aerial had been snapped at the base.

Geoboe signalled, clattering the door open and diving inside with his buddy following. At the rear, the other team entered the building quietly, using the noise of Geoboe's entry to cover theirs. An experienced squad, but they all were now, with so few available to recruit from. A flash of energy exited the window, and a buzz of static soon followed in the commander's ears.

"Clear, Commander. But they've been here, wrecked the place and taken anything not nailed down."

A rifle report echoed across the plain, the whirr of the bullet sending a deep-seated fear through Otegnoa. The round tore through the side door, ripping into Datin's thigh and exploded. The man screamed, blood erupting from the severed artery. The commander threw himself down, the fizz of an energy bolt tracing across his scalp, setting his hair on end as the charge raced across his head. A second bolt flew through the open window, slamming into his ribs, the pulsing charge setting his nerves on fire. He grabbed at his chest, his old heart crying out as the energy surged within his body.

No, no, no. Calm, breathe.

Inflamed nerves raged as he fought to push the stress down, each breath a struggle as the pain rose to his left shoulder and down the arm. He felt the flutter, the sudden skip in his heartbeat, sending his mind reeling and on the brink of losing self-control as the panic rose. Then it passed, the muscles locked rigid, his heart bouncing back with a steady beat, sweat pouring from his scalp.

Datin died, his last painful moan strained at the edge of Otegnoa's hearing. He wanted to reach out, to touch the greyed head, to send his spirit to the gods for his deserved rest. But he could not.

Calm. Breath. Go with peace, my old friend. I am so sorry, but I hope the land is bountiful, and the milk flows.

As he descended into blackness, Otegnoa felt rough, calloused hands drag him from the seat. His last thoughts of home and Alkinta.

CHAPTER 8

Moon Base

"The AI has wrapped itself in a preservation program, like Smith said. Yasuko can unlock it piece by piece, but she's worried the cryotubes will go down if it's too fast. She's indicating it'll be safest over a six-hour period," said Noah, flexing his metal toes under the table.

"Yeah, sounds good," said Finn. "Zuri?"

"I'd say we get on with it. Can she connect from there?"

"Yes, Smith has set the receivers up, so we don't require a physical connection despite its dormancy. We need those air samples though—can you bring them in?"

"You suit up and collect them yourself. Assuming you've been doing the exercises Yasuko set," said Finn, throwing Zuri a wide grin.

"Yes—and I bet you got Yasuko to count each one. Ankle flexes starting now." Noah stood up, running to the hold and his suit, desperate to get out of the ship for a little while. On reaching the powered armour, he raced through the set-up procedure, making sure the new leg was fully functioning after the repairs. Satisfied, he instructed the suit to open, easing his legs in first. When it wrapped around him, like a familiar blanket, he eye-clicked the HUD to receive Yasuko's timeline for the grave markers.

"So, these people died from old age?" he said.

"Assuming they have the same DNA make up as when they left Earth, I'd say yes. There are no younger ones among them, and I'd have expected at least a few who may have succumbed to disease. All died within the last fifty years, with no one younger than sixty years old. From the information I have from surface data, I think the cryotubes contain some younger Stratan's, but not by much."

"Any first thoughts?" Noah asked as the hold doors opened, his stride lengthening, eager for the chance to walk on a new moon.

"I think they were abandoned or marooned up here. The shuttle requires a support vessel, or an orbital way station like on Vai. No way home," said Yasuko, her voice petering away before picking up again with a new thought. "I've initiated the wake-up program, this AI appears limited compared to those on Havenhome, and old. It has been restricted by the moon base's data capacity, so it hasn't matured either. I may need Smith to help at some point if it struggles to accept me."

"The pathogen is a virus. It's at a trace level because you disturbed it when entering the main moon base building," said Yasuko. "Noah has taken samples from all the surfaces and it's prevalent everywhere. There are other viruses, quite common ones, variants that we have seen in other human-seeded worlds as designed by the Haven. But this one is so different in structure, I think it's manufactured, human made."

"Why's it got you so spooked?" asked Finn.

"Because it's so different I don't know what it does. I only looked for it once I went through the AI's medical data on the cryotube inhabitants. It fed them a vaccine before they went under. From what I can tell, the virus mutated back on Stratan in a cycle spanning approximately twenty years or so, leading to regular massive vaccination programmes. The data goes back a long way, and before *!Nias* and his crewmates left for Earth."

"So, we need to wake these people up, and get some insight into what's going on. Is there anything you can tell from *!Nias'* body?" said Zuri.

"I checked under our agreed ethical levels after Vai. No invasive practices. The scans showed little, other than he was clear of the virus. But he left two centuries prior to this base being built. To know any more, we need to talk to these Stratan and get the background on what's happened. In the meantime, you need to keep the integrity of your suits until I know more, and I'll use their data to manufacture a vaccine. But it'll be different on the planet, quite possibly mutated many more times, negating any effective protection."

The cryotube drained, the orange liquid escaping from the lower rear as the AI gently raised the temperature of the female scientist inside. When it reached two degrees below normal levels, the protective TDP proteins wrapping the cells dissolved and the revival process kicked in, gently restoring each bodily function. After an hour, the AI declared the Stratan human as functioning, though requiring another hour's natural sleep before awakening with a fully operative brain pattern. Yasuko ran through the lines of code, adjusting elements for efficiency and upgrading the AI's functionality while it prepared the next three Stratan for revival. She shaved an hour off the wake-up procedure and negated the need for natural sleep by instigating this within the tube. For all her worries about the AI, it accepted the upgrades readily, eager to serve those it had nurtured for so long.

"No one wants to wake up surrounded by a squad of Space Commandos in full powered armour. Nearly as bad as if they were Space Marines," said a smirking Smith, adjusting the projection system and retreating, ushering the rest of the powered armour crew outside of the lab with him.

As the scientist's eyes fluttered, Zuri's image appeared opposite the med-table they'd moved her onto, Zuri wanting to wait, to give her time, but having little patience while her emotions roiled. The hologram stepped from foot to foot, the relaxation exercise calming her as usual.

"Someone's there," the hoarse, dry voice was rough with age. The clicks and harsh syllables setting Zuri immediately on edge before the translation program kicked in.

"Yes, there's water at your side. I am opposite you, a projection."

"From Kabbo Command? The Council?" she said, feeling for the water, eyes slitted despite the extremely low light in the room.

"No. We are next door, we thought we'd wake you gently. We are from … from Earth," said Zuri, wincing as she said it.

Why lie or hide it? Maybe we are a bit of hope.

"Earth?" the grey-haired woman opened her eyes further, blurred vision seeking Zuri's image. When she caught the blue tinged light, she opened them wider, rubbing at the hardened rheum, the mucus formed during sleep. "It worked? Our ships arrived?"

"Ships?" said Zuri, catching herself and storing that for later. "Yes. Though the contact was poorly made. But we are here. Listen, all this will be a shock to you. My people and I are next door, we are wearing some pretty heavy-duty equipment because we didn't know what to expect here. But inside the suits we are humans, so don't panic. If we wanted to harm anyone, we could have done it already. Take a little time, clean up. We have touched nothing, so all your stuff is wherever you left it. We'll wait in the common area."

"And the others?" the scientist said as she rose from the table, her eyes finally focussing on Zuri. "How many are still alive? The cryotubes were hand built in desperation—we couldn't go on watching each other die of old age and boredom."

"Three if the wake-up protocols work. We have improved them a little, so they should be okay if the tubes functioned correctly."

"Three? Oh." The scientist scanned the room, taking in each of the functioning cryotubes, a sense of relief visibly washing through her as she touched the nearest tube's window. "My daughter, the last born on the base."

CHAPTER 9

Research Facility, Kabbo Grass Plains

"Take it, ya?" said Alkinta, shoving the dusty rifle towards the soldier. "Safety here, double trigger—top for the energy bolt, bottom for the armour piercing round. No bloody time for practice—get me?"

The flustered soldier grabbed the rifle, eyes wide as the Tâa strode past him, shoving another rifle towards the older uniformed soldier behind him. The woman nodded, her hands expertly moving over the stock as she checked the charge level.

"I remember, Tâa. I'll show him," grabbing the younger soldier by the arm, she led him away, turning as the orders were shouted down the corridor.

"You keep the seed stock safe; I'll focus on the laboratory with Osineh. They do not get in, authorisation code *Xu*, shoot to kill. We now defend our future, ya?"

"Yes, Tâa. The rest of the detail will be with me—but just two of you for the lab?"

"It's an annexe, Iwobi. There are auto-defences that still function. Then they'll be facing me if they get through."

"Yes, Tâa. Like old times."

"No, Iwobi. New times, I fear the *!Kora* will not be going back to their old ways after this. Without more resources, the rewilding will fail." The soldier saluted, pivoting on her heel and leading the younger man away, firing clicks and harsh words at him as she explained the weapon.

"And this is for you," said Alkinta, handing over the third rifle. "I'll sit you somewhere you don't have to move too much, covering my back."

"There are no defences, are there?" said Osineh, her eyes wide but pupils beginning to lessen as the drugs took effect.

"None of any use. If they attacked with airplanes and tanks, we could last a month. But on foot with spears? Not something they planned for. We could hole up in here for ever, and we still may have to, but the egg stock in the lab is vital. We will be stuck in a never-ending cycle, living behind walls and eating fungus and fish, hoping we recover enough to perpetuate the species each time the Brain Fever hits. Come on, time to prepare."

Alkinta led Osineh out of the front entrance, the heavy metal door slamming shut behind, the lock and seals engaging as they strode on. The square edged, ex-barracks stood starkly against the grass plains surrounding it, only broken by the crumbled remains of an old town with a long-forgotten name. The whole area had been swept clear by the blast radiating a kilometre above Kabbo, the first Stratan Council city hit by a Minoas nuclear warhead. But not the last.

It survived a nuclear blast beyond imagination, I'm sure it can protect our future. We get through this, then Otegnoa needs to see sense and bring all the stock inside and put the people out.

The lab sat low and squat inside the three-metre-high fence. Its roof covered in solar panels that also occupied its southern facing edge, out of view of the fence line. Alkinta reached the lock, keying in the code, lips moving as she recounted each step. Inside, the cold hit Osineh, dragging back memories of her home on the southern continent. The snow and ice that perpetuated her existence prior to joining the project three years earlier. A sudden longing swept her, for a family left behind. But not for the cold itself, a most unnatural environment to live in, in her opinion.

They passed by the main lab, the rows of metal growth chambers all glowing in *the green* due to the skill of Alkinta's lab team, now holed away in the ex-barracks. Brilliant with the embryos, useless with the gun.

"Up on the roof there's a nook with cover facing the fence. Take station there, while I fire up the fences for as long as the generator will work."

Osineh climbed the ladder, unclipping the ceiling hatch and clambering through onto the roof. Peering out, she could see the *!Kora* running towards the gates of the compound. She lost count around the thirty mark and began to worry as the collection of mutated humans gained ground. The myriad of skin colours, hair patterns and deformities heightened by their stripped, ragged clothing, and the crystal piercings adorning their bodies, raised her unease. A nightmare of colour and *otherness* she struggled to cope with. They had no off switch according to rumours, and were always hungry, seeking their prey raw. The only certainty being the *!Kora* were not cannibals, shunning *normal* human blood but venerating their own dead through blood rites.

And possibly immune to the Brain Fever, only their harsh life keeping the numbers down.

"They are here," shouted Osineh. "Lots of them. I see no rifles."

"Keep your bloody head down. I'm coming up," said Alkinta. The ladder rattled as she climbed up, a white helmeted head emerging above the trapdoor, followed by the gentle creak of the ceramic plate embedded in a black material. In her hands, a rifle very much like Osineh's, but emblazoned with scratches and faded writing. On her back, the handle of a spear protruded.

"Ha, what you looking at? Put those eyes back in your head, girl. And watch my back, ya?"

Osineh nodded, her boss clad in the fabled Marine suit bringing a little more hope into her heart.

"Just like old times, indeed. If I fall, shut the hatch and guard my embryos. Those animals are precious." Alkinta dropped off the edge of the building, the servos at ankles, knees and thighs absorbing the landing as she fired into the throng of *!Kora*.

CHAPTER 10

Kabbo City, Southern Continent, Planet Stratan

The microship spluttered briefly, the engine catching on the clouds rising from the city below, its thrusters disturbing the layers of dust up into the thick atmosphere. It adjusted automatically, only dipping slightly as they flew over the multitude of ruined buildings. Nature had reclaimed sections, but much of Kabbo remained barren, shattered walls and roofs laid bare. It went on for kilometres, radiating outwards from a central, completely flattened section where the dust swirled at its thickest. Uhi-dorro choked, tears streaking down lined cheeks as she peered through the view screen. Her black-haired daughter taking her hand and squeezing, sat next to her with a morose set to her features.

"Do we know how long ago?" she asked, her brain addled and unable to see the obvious.

"You said contact was lost ten years before you chose stasis. By your AI's data, I'd say we are looking at ninety years ago," said Smith, eyes scanning the sensor readings for any residual radiation. There were patches, but nothing for them to worry about. Even so, the yield must have been high. He switched over to thermal imaging; inaccurate at this height, he brought the ship down further.

"Anything? Any life?"

Smith brought the craft down to hover about a kilometre from the city's edge, with only a few intact buildings in sight.

He activated the thermal sensors, showing an assortment of small animal life going about their daily lives. Smith swept the sensors in a complete circle, with little above the size of his hand showing up.

"Some small animal life, but nothing big. No human habitation unless they've gone deep. Is that the site of the Space Laser?" he asked, pointing towards the massive, twisted lump of metal rising over a shattered building half a kilometre away.

"Probably, my bearings are a little shot with the devastation, but the shape … well it was something like that."

"Yasuko, can you overlay the AI's map of Kabbo?"

"If you're looking for the Laser Site, that's it." The map emerged over the view screen, correlating the position a few seconds later. "And that's the Command Centre, or at least it was. I am picking up no large, functional conurbations along the line of the equator. A few weak radio signals, definitely current, so signs of life. I do have stronger data towards the south, I can detect at least three centres for communication and the images show intact buildings. To the north, there are much smaller settlements, but I suspect there's a larger underground development in the northwest continent. Like Sanctuary on Havenhome," said Yasuko, pausing as she checked incoming data with Noah. "There are multiple sites that indicate nuclear explosions all over the planet, but most were centred in or around the cities along the equator."

"Where the Stratan Council governed," said Uhi-dorro. "The Minoas held sway over the northwest and eastern continents, controlling the smaller countries with fear and bribes. It was there that the pathogen was released, nicknamed the Brain Fever."

"Deliberately?"

"Who knows? Certainly, they suffered as much as we did, at least that's how it appeared in the media."

"I have sent Finn to the west," said Yasuko. "There's a distress call from a small settlement, around an old army command centre. Looks like we have a first contact opportunity."

"Second," corrected Smith. "Send me the coordinates. Strap in."

◆ ◆ ◆

"Bring us in low, Noah. I want you in the air, as backup if we need you," Finn ignored the audible sigh that slipped from Noah.

Something to deal with later.

Noah brought the microship down towards the grass plain, trampled by the rampaging charge of an apparently maddened horde of semi-naked humans who assailed the compound fences in three different places. The flash of the occasional familiar energy bolt enough for Finn to recognise desperation, they were preserving their shots, only hitting those that reached the top.

Finn was impressed as Noah skilfully skimmed the microship above the grass at a running pace.

Make an astronaut of you yet.

"Go, Zuri," he ordered, watching her land on her feet and keep running as their old suits, those that last saw action in Bathsen, absorbed the impact. Finn followed; his landing less graceful, though he was pleased with the move into a forward roll after the initial stumble.

Styled it out.

"Saw that," said Noah, the radio crackling in Finn's ear. Shaking his head, he ran to the left, his designated target group at the gates with two prone guards on the other side. He raised his rifle on the run, his *weapon of choice* releasing the stun bolt that took down the blue and grey-skinned male at the rear. Finn had decided he was the one directing the five others, enough to make him the first target. However, it meant those standing in front turned and released their weapons in return, the three barbed spears flying towards Finn with unerring accuracy. No time to dodge the first, it clattered into a ceramic plate and bounced away, snapping as his powered leg came down on the shaft. The second pierced the material and kinetic gel at his shoulder, the shaft hampering his vision, flapping in front of his visor. Finn was forced to wrench it away, preventing another shot when the third clattered into his thigh, sliding off the plate and snagging in the material.

So damn hard when you're not trying to kill. Should have used the drones, but we might need them later, and they're not so hot against large numbers or in open spaces.

Finn halted, dropping to his knee as a fourth spear came his way. He fired, his stun shot rewarded with the female warrior collapsing to the ground, shaking in pain. Finn fully expected them to disperse, to see the overwhelming power of his weapon and armour and run. He was wrong.

The two clambering over the gate started down the other side, spears and clubs strapped to their backs. Finn kept his position, the two remaining warriors splitting and coming round on his flanks. They approached at speed, Finn's rifle bolt stunning the one on the left as they closed. He rolled out that way, momentarily crushing the arm of the shaking warrior on the floor as a club rushed by his helmet. He felt the spear point snagged in his thigh cut through the material and press against the inner liner.

Crap, what if it's poisoned? Or worse.

He came up firing, the stun bolt slamming into the remaining mutated warrior's solar plexus as he raised his club again. The crystals embedded in his skin sparkled, the electrical pulse surging between them. The man hit the floor, convulsing violently. Finn made a quick decision. There were two inside and they were his priority rather than the outcome of the warrior's seizure. Finn stowed his rifle and leapt, the leg servos on the suit sending him three quarters of the way up the fence. He heaved again, gauntleted hands gripping the fence pole, the arm servos wrenching him upwards to grab hold of the fence frame at the top. Ignoring the electrical wire, he jumped over, this time deliberately rolling on landing and waiting for the applause that never came.

Yeah, you missed that one Noah. Typical.

Finn came out of the roll and was powering forwards as the two warriors reached the door to the solar panel covered building. The first shoulder-charged the door, Finn hitting the other in the back, slamming the woman into the stone wall, her face and shoulder taking most of the blow. The man battering at the door spun quickly, lashing out forcefully with an old metal knife that clanged against Finn's upper arm, the ceramic plate absorbing the blow. Finn punched him in the jaw, locking his wrist servos as the power surged through his arm. The warrior was out before he hit the floor, matching the rough-skinned woman on the ground beside him, a livid bruise forming on her already blue cheek.

Choices, choices.

Finn flipped open his pouch belt, rummaging inside until his thick gauntleted fingers found a few cable ties. He quickly bound the two mutant humans, their skin hue strange with hardened lumps protruding at the joints. Red crystals were embedded in strange places, especially around the eyes and cheeks. Finn avoided looking at them, disconcerted by the way they reflected the light, almost as if they moved. Once finished, he sped off towards the gate.

Zuri raised her rifle, the stun shot slamming into the back of the main group clambering up the fence next to a solar panel covered building. The scarred warrior at the top released his grip, falling inwards towards the camp. An energy bolt lashed out, full power and familiar. It hit the tribesman in the back as he fell, ending any chance of ever getting back up. Zuri marked the source of the bolt, and she fired again, mindful to take those out on this side of the fence. A warrior spun, his sling whipping round and releasing a rock at half pace, but so accurate. With her servos whirring, Zuri propelled herself forward, head lunging underneath the rock spinning towards her visor, feeling it bounce off a ceramic plate as she rolled back up, face to face with the warrior. He lunged, the crystal encrusted club in his other hand flashing a painful memory in Zuri's mind as she raised her rifle to block the blow. The blue glow from the *weapon* marked its transformation, the sudden growth of the staff causing the wide-eyed warrior to step back. Zuri brought a metal shod end down on his foot, immediately clattering the shaft down on his head as her left arm's servos pushed on forward.

Zuri swept her eyes across the scene, seven mutant humans on her side, four facing her. Two more nearly over the fence, facing certain death if she couldn't bring them down.

Drone? Use the strobes?

Then it all changed. A flash of white hammered into the fence, and with one push off the metal fence pole the figure reached the top. Zuri's HUD focussed in on the servo's whirr as the new player in the fight threw the first warrior off the fence, then brought down a familiar rifle to crack across the skull of the second, before jumping to land at her side. The ceramic armour absorbed the landing, the servos at each joint responding when her feet hit the ground. They raised their rifle, sights on the advancing warrior. Zuri automatically swung her staff across the soldier's line-of-sight, hoping they would respond.

"No, we don't need to kill," she broadcast, the Khoisan harsh as it emitted from her speakers. Not waiting for a reply, she swung towards the approaching warriors, facing three spears and a club wielding man. Zuri exploded forward, the staff catching one of the spear carriers before they could move, the smack against their chin cracking the jaw as they collapsed. A spear whipped towards her hip, the attempt well-timed, recognising the gap she had exposed. Zuri brought the rear of the staff down, catching the spear head, forcing it downwards to scrape against her hip plate as she cursed at her own lack of foresight. Zuri pulled her left hip back, automatically bringing her right arm into the combat, surging the staff down onto the warrior's grip. No cry, but mouth wide, the woman dropped the spear as Zuri heaved herself backwards, the movement bringing the metal shod end up, smashing into the warrior's jaw.

To her left, a flash of metal hit a third warrior, the armour-clad soldier wielding a spear much like the short-shafted version Zuri favoured. Not the easiest weapon to avoid the killing blow, though the soldier's skill was impressive as they probed forward. The first two moves parried her assailant's thrusts, the third slit across their wrist and her fourth sliced thigh, forcing them to the floor. As the warrior fell, the soldier spun out towards Zuri, avoiding the club winging in towards her right arm, bringing the spear round and down low to slash the edge across the mutant's bulging ankles. Before they could move, a following blow to their head sent them out cold.

Zuri stepped in, her back to the armoured soldier as she knocked the bloodied, prone, warrior out, eyes on the last of the mutant warriors dropping from the fence. A flash of energy washed past them, the bolt sizzling against the links as the man let go. Immediately, the ceramic clad soldier raised her hands.

"No, Osineh. We have this," she shouted, Zuri's translator providing the likely gender in its tone.

Zuri waited, expecting the mutant human she faced to run. He stared at her, black eyes red-rimmed and faded – seeing right through her. The red crystals piercing his shoulders, and on down to the chest, glistened in the sunlight, distracting Zuri as she sought to understand the human in front of her. Behind those eyes wasn't hate, but a distance, absence. He stepped forward, raising a knife shaped from an old piece of worked metal. But then his jaw dropped, briefly slack, and he burst sideways, running back out towards the grass plain.

When Zuri turned back around, she got a clear view of the woman behind the visor. The formidable set to her jaw and piercing gaze letting her know who expected to be in charge, the rifle at *low hang*, and easily within reach.

"You speak an old form of Stratan Khoisan, ya? Who are you?"

"Long story," said Zuri, the embedded translator broadcasting as her visor cleared. "And a long way from home."

"Zuri? Sit rep," said Finn.

"I … well, I've found an old Stratan Soldier. We've incapacitated the main threat here."

"Less of the old, ya? I can kick your arse. And I was a Marine."

"Strike that—a feisty ex-Marine."

"Damn right I am."

"She's told me there's a security guard on the roof, name of Osineh, with an old rifle like ours and a dodgy aim due to concussion. Just stay away from this section until you're given clearance. We're moving out to the south side of the compound, there's a seed store Alkinta thinks is under attack. Their comms are down," said Zuri, her breathing heavy.

"On my way, I'm inside, heading for the gates. I'll spin out to the seed store." Finn eye-clicked the HUD, reaching behind for a mini drone and sending it up. "Noah, you got eyes on the compound?"

"Just coming around. Smith's on the way…you have five, no six enemy inside the fence and they've broken through the windows on the right side of the nearest building. They're going in, thermal shows some energy fire," replied Noah.

"Good work, Noah. On cover, set a perimeter and watch for any further attacks. Stay on it. If these are local tribes like on Earth, they'll be damn good at hiding and ambush. Want my arse covered."

"Yes Finn, on it."

Finn reached the leading corner of a stone building, no solar panels, with a pitched and tiled roof. From the far side, the muffled sounds of combat reached his suit microphone. He sidestepped along the wall, keeping his back against the stone as he reached the corner. Using the mirror sight, he took a double take. Next to Zuri stood a ceramic armour-clad woman, same height, same grace in her movement. In her hand was a short spear with a rifle on her back, and around her temples, greying hair against lined skin. He had a feeling the similarities didn't stop there.

This is going to be fun.

Finn signalled, turning the corner and approaching the shattered window. Once he reached the frame, he slipped the rifle round, the sight giving a clear view of five warriors with multiple energy wounds, piled on the floor. Next to them stood another older woman, dressed in a uniform, rifle raised as she surveyed the dead and dying. On seeing Finn's muzzle, she dropped the weapon into both hands, pressing the trigger, splintering the frame and sending Finn's *weapon of choice* spiralling out of his grip.

"Hey, Iwobi. Stand down. That's a friendly you just shot, ya?" shouted the ex-Marine from behind Finn.

"Then they should be more careful, Tâa. I have a twitchy finger right now. All clear in here, but I think we lost the two on the gate. Coming out."

CHAPTER 11

Research Facility, Kabbo Grass Plains

Smith secured the last of the *!Kora*, the cable ties pulled tight enough around wrist and ankles to prevent them running. He shifted each under the shade of the protruding eaves of the seed store, stopping for a second to scan the plains grass swaying in the gentle breeze while the red sun approached the horizon. He sighed inwardly, looking down at the huge, powered hands of his Atmospheric Battle Armour, the only one of the squad still clad in the intimidating kit.

To be, or not to be, that is the question:

Whether 'tis nobler in the mind to suffer

The slings and arrows of outrageous fortune,

Or to take arms against a sea of troubles…

Or some such rubbish, wish I'd paid more attention to Shakespeare in school. Wonder if Noah knows the rest?

Noah knelt opposite him, working with one of the security officers to wrap the last of the dead *!Kora* in a plastic sheet. Iwobi had explained they knew little of the *!Kora* traditions and way of life, except the blood rite. Before the present standoffs, when the *!Kora* had let the Stratan seed the plains unopposed, a study had begun. But once the last round of Brain Fever hit, people and resource priorities ended that project, and soon after the raids had started.

"Hey, Noah," called Smith. "You know your Shakespeare?"

"Where did that come from? Smith and Shakespeare, like fish and cheese – never together."

"I like … I used to like fish and cheese; I'll have you know. In a fish pie. Anyway, it's that famous one – you know – *to be or not to be*. Can you write it down for me?"

"If you tell me why," said Noah, standing up and glaring over at Smith.

"When did you get so headstrong?"

"When my supposed friend didn't tell me I'd died. Generally, that puts a crimp in your day. Especially from one who'd already been through it."

"How…? Did Yasuko tell you?"

"No, and thanks for the confirmation that you did know. Sitting in a regrowth chamber for hours on end gives you time to think. And when the leg didn't take, I checked over the medical records to find an anomaly or two. A gap in my timeline where Yasuko logs our biochemical chronology. Two and two makes five until you factor in my hair regrowth. I checked the ingredients of Yasuko's magic formula. Hey presto, it's a placebo, does nothing. Like my friend."

"I'm sorry, Noah. We all thought —"

"It was for the best. Yeah, I guessed that. But my mind's been a whirl, Smith. Not connecting, having emotions and absences I don't recognise in myself. And now I know why. Being a … a copy of yourself, it's not as simple as being who you were before. Yasuko was right, there's an emotional disconnection. A piece of you is lost, and I don't even remember which bit it is." Noah slumped to the ground, sitting cross-legged despite his armour, head in hands.

"Sorry, Noah. The Shakespeare thing, I'm thinking of not taking up the body Yasuko offered me. I fear I might reject it, and then what happens to it? And to me? It doesn't feel right. But nor can I be this," Smith gestured towards his bulky legs and arms, "all day long."

Noah sighed but raised his head to look directly at Smith's helmet as he spoke, "I can help. I need to help. I may have my own troubles, but you've all been there for me despite this crappy news. In return, I want to know how I died, Smith. I think that's important."

"Oh boy, you sure?"

"Yeah, and no running to Zuri and Finn first. They'll only tell you to smooth it out," Noah stood back up, hands on hips.

"How about Yasuko? She'd tell it how it is, you know, all scientific. You need scientific, trust me."

Alkinta sat opposite Finn and Zuri, the steaming tea cupped in both hands filling the air with a pungent herbal smell their filters allowed through. Beside her sat Uhi-dorro and her daughter, the younger woman fidgety around the strangeness of her surroundings.

"We will need a vaccine if we are to function on the planet effectively," said Zuri. "According to Yasuko we would succumb to the fever despite what we've already taken, you are all likely to be carriers in some way or form. If we can take blood samples and some of your current vaccine, it'll speed up the process."

"I am no expert, Zuri. My field is geology, but if a new strain appears you may still be infected," said Uhi-dorro.

"Yes, but the alternative is to be trapped inside a helmet day in and day out. We may not all take the risk, but I am certainly willing. We can send Noah back to the moon base with it, or Smith." Zuri glanced towards Finn, his nod showing agreement.

"We're willing to help you find your partner, the Field Commander," said Finn. "If these !Kora have him, then two of us should be enough, now we know what we're facing."

"Three," said Alkinta. "I am coming too." She glanced over at Iwobi, her mouth half open. "Not four. You stay here with Osineh, I need you to keep my babies secure, ya? My life's work." The old soldier's eyes briefly betrayed a hint of rebellion before she nodded.

"Okay three."

"I can contact Kaimas. Alkinta says it remains the major city in the south and the base for the government. The Stratan Council still exists to oversee the remnants of my people, so I will prepare them for your arrival," said Uhi-dorro. "And Abbe, my daughter, has a talent with electronic systems. I think she'll be able to work her magic on your comms, Alkinta. And the others will have valuable skills that may have been lost over time," the old scientist sighed, gripping her daughter's hand.

"You'll need the current vaccine too," said Iwobi. "I'll arrange that with the lab workers. For you and your fellow scientists."

"Thank you. Zuri, what will I say you offer to our people?"

"Hope," said Zuri. "We offer hope."

CHAPTER 12

The Politico Building, Slabin, Capital City Of The Minoas Confederation, Northwest Minoas

"You're certain?"

"Yes, General Hardin. Two craft with supersonic capabilities. Our radar confirmed their movements near the Kabbo Plains. Once the satellite comes into view, we'll check the ancient thing's data for atmospheric entry. But, unless the Stratan have hid these from us, they must be from off-planet."

"You are thinking, maybe, from the moon base? They certainly had chemical-based transit shuttles. We have the records of those," said the General, fiddling with the green crystal amulet around his neck, the chain leaving a raw mark after years of constant fidgeting. He caught himself, urging his fingers to squeeze at his earlobe instead.

"Hard to tell, the system on the Eastern Continent is as old as you or I, General," said the Prime Minister, her hands scratching below her uniform sleeve as her mind wandered to thoughts of the satellite.

"Yes, well. The rest were burnt out by the Stratan. Okay, we need to know. Who's on the ground?"

"Yabbin leads the Shadow Squad, General. You ordered him directly, remember?"

"Yes, of course I remember. Has he made contact?"

"No, the area's a blackout zone for radio transmissions. The !

Kora seem to know this and they favour such places. But, by the mission parameters, he should make contact in a few days, with or without the Field Commander."

"He'd better have him. I owe that man some serious pain, and that woman of his too. When Yabbin does call in, I want him on those ships. You hear? I want full knowledge of their capabilities at the very least, and if he can manage it, one for our military to copy."

"Yes, General. Understood. All actions agreeable?"

"Yes, I don't give a crap if the Stratan know we're there. Do them good to know we haven't gone away. Yabbin has an open order."

"Good to hear, General. Like old times." Prime Minister Mwandin clicked her heels together, right hand hitting above her heart in salute as she left. She slipped the ancient tablet from her pocket, the scratched screen still able to respond to her presses, and checked the times for the satellite to enter range.

"Yes," said the General, the low hum in his ear rising again due to the adrenaline kicking in. He felt his head thrum, responding to the biochemical surge, and the first tinge of a headache formed at the back of his head. "Just so."

Yabbin scratched at his wide, hooked nose with the ancient energy pistol, then lashed out, swiping the muzzle across the Field Commander's cheek, the nicked trigger guard slashing the wrinkled skin. In return, old training kicking in, Otegnoa stared at the floor, silent.

"I want your codes, old man." He lifted the pistol to his nose, sniffing at the blood. "Tainted, like all Stratan. I have no patience, Otegnoa. And yes, I know who you are. I am on limited time, and unless I get the codes to your lab and barracks, you will face my full wrath," Yabbin shoved the Stratan leader to the floor with his boot, the rope on wrists and ankles preventing him from getting up. Yabbin kicked dust his way, then strode off towards the campfire where most of his squad were eating, half an eye on the interrogation.

"Captain," said Corporal Mehin, his black armour absorbing the light from the fire, "are we reporting in? The Prime Minister needs to know we have the Field Commander."

"Not yet," said Yabbin, taking a seat on the rock at the Corporal's side and lowering his voice. "They'll want an evac, Mehin. The mission will end, the Stratan will disappear under my father's pet torturer for some imagined slight from twenty years ago, and we will be no closer to getting the samples we need." The Minoas Captain grabbed the bowl from next to the fire, ignoring the contents as he ate. Better not to know out here on the Stratan plains.

"Go against orders? That wise? Your family status will only go so far with the Politico, even with your father, the General. And you may take us down with you. I am loyal, Yabbin." Mehin dropped his voice even lower, "But these others are new blood, from the hatchery. We don't know them."

Yabbin sat back, placing the spoon quietly into the metal bowl. He eyed Mehin, taking in the man's balding head and wide, grey moustache. He'd been his right hand for the last twenty-three years, training the core of the Minoas Shadow recruits together for most of that.

If he has doubts, shouldn't I? But things cannot carry on as they are.

"This is our chance to get hold of the animal samples, Mehin. We have already copied their replanting programme, and in places it has succeeded. Reports claim they have developed a strain of Quia resistant to the Fire Ticks. Immune maybe. If that's true, then it can be used for the other large animals too. We can come out of the dark, seed our land again with life. Possibly grow our own food, instead of this bloody fungus." Yabbin threw the remains of his bowl in the flames, the scrub wood hissing as the wet mass hit the ashes.

"I know your dream, Yabbin. But it is not shared by the hierarchy. Your father's Politico shares his … his concerns about the future. The Brain Fever, the Fire Ticks, radiation, the Stratan —these all add to their fear."

"If we don't do something soon, we will die out, Mehin. The hatchery," Yabbin spat on the floor, "can't sustain us. Our gene pool is weak, shrinking, despite the vaccine. And our people increasingly paranoid about leaving the cities, but we can't sustain even our low numbers with fungus. Too many variables, Mehin. You've seen the reports, the Stratan have the same struggles yet, though slow, they increase in number."

"Until the next bout of Brain Fever, or the Fire Tick antibiotics fails." Mehin threw the remains of his food in the fire, watching the pieces bubble with his large eyes.

"Life is full of risk. But at least it isn't boring."

CHAPTER 13

Research Facility, Kabbo Grass Plains

"I have no problem with going back," said Noah, keeping his gaze just over Finn's shoulder, eyeing Smith's lurking powered armour behind his Lance Corporal.

"Really? You seemed—"

"Sorry. Yes, a bit down. It's the leg, I'll get Yasuko to look at it. I assume I am clear for field duty, though? This isn't just a way to get me out of the way?"

"No, you're cleared," said Finn. "Take the microship back with the samples, get the vaccine sorted and then call in. Zuri may want you to arrange the Data Drop with Uhi-dorro too."

"You're not gonna need me, either," said Smith. "Not with the three of you chasing a few spear-carrying mutants. Besides, I am not the subtlest looking squad member, not so many robots around here hiding in the grass. If Yasuko has acquired enough ore, I can get the other ship refuelled and prepped. Maybe return with the vaccine and act as cover if need be."

And be there if the crap hits the fan if I can get Yasuko to talk to Noah.

"Yes," said Zuri, her eyes narrowing as she peered at Smith. It wasn't like him to miss out on the action. "Sounds good. We drop the *!Kora* near the fence breach and then you join Yasuko. We'll follow them with a drone."

Smith cut the last cable tie, his hulking armour looming over the shaking, bruised *!Kora* warrior. Around him, lay the wounded and the dead from the fight at the compound. Nineteen warriors had survived the combat, and without the squad's intervention it could have been much worse for both sides. Smith took a step back, Zuri and Finn flanking him with their rifles raised.

"You can go. Don't come back. The Quia and the buildings are not for you. Stay away, next time we will kill more," said Smith, his speakers booming the translated Khoisan towards the *!Kora*. Alkinta had adjusted a word here or there for him to update the meaning.

Mind you, they have no idea if the !Kora understand it, anyway.

Smith turned and strode into the hovering microship. Zuri followed, with Finn backing off, his rifle not wavering from the *! Kora.* He stepped backwards into the ship, the physical door closing and merging with the hull. The *!Kora* stared on, not moving as the hum of the engines rose.

The microship eased up from the ground, its thrusters weaving patterns in the green plains grass. The *!Kora* stared, then hummed in unison, their tone adjusting and matching the engine's vibrations. Around their eyes, cheeks and chests, the red crystals vibrated, matching the oscillations of their deep-throated sound. When Smith eased the ship forward, the warriors rose. Their utterances stopped, and they turned, as if in a daze, to those that lay dead around them. In pairs they hefted the dead upon shoulders and walked towards the broken fence.

Zuri and Finn dropped from the microship, flattening against the grass covered ground as Smith flew over. Zuri's HUD displayed the drone's images, hovering fifty metres away from the *!Kora* tribespeople who gathered their dead. Switching to the drone's thermal imaging, she picked out Alkinta's faint signature on the far side of the fence. The woman's older armour had lost most of its thermal retention capabilities, yet the light camouflage functioned as it should.

Still kicking myself I didn't get Noah to ask about the light-wrap before he left.

Zuri eye-clicked record, tapping Finn on the shoulder when the *!Kora* moved out. She took a crouched *at ease* position, her rifle across her elbow, scanning ahead, one eye on the drone feed as the raiding party passed.

"They've passed me," said Alkinta, her suit patched into their comms.

"On the way," said Finn, taking the lead while Zuri covered behind.

They approached the area where the *!Kora* had been cut loose; the grass flattened with their footprints. Finn checked the differing prints, the warriors using tanned animal skin as foot coverings. The ground beneath the grass would take an occasional print, recent rain meaning the soil had some give.

Should be okay to track, but I'm betting these !Kora usually tread lightly and leave little in the way of a trail. Carrying their dead should negate that.

They approached Alkinta's position near the start of the scrub bush beyond the fence, her light-wrap camouflage switching off when they neared. Greeting them with a nod, she indicated the direction the warriors left in.

"I have a drone following at a distance, high and to the rear. Will they know what it is?" asked Zuri.

"I do not know," said the Stratan woman. "We use larger ones to track the cattle when they move west, collecting data on their eating patterns. And when we first released the wild herds, we had a few watching migration patterns. It's possible, yes."

"Okay, I'll keep it well back. But you think they're heading north?" said Zuri.

"There's a sea cove, around an old nuclear plant. We know

they used to congregate there before the last Fever hit, when we had more people to cover the area. It's a radio blackout zone, there's a mineral formation in the bay producing disruption for about a kilometre. They postulated it was causing ionisation, and that's why the *!Kora* have so many issues with their skin. It possibly has something to do with their physical mutations too, they seem to persist despite the length of time since the war. But every time they ran them off, they returned." Alkinta took a position at the rear, enabling Zuri to be Finn's cover whenever he checked the trail. She matched them stride for stride.

They weaved their way through the scrub bush. The flora lacked variation, with only a thorny, small leaved plant of two metres in height, interspersed by another sporting small flowers cascading downwards off limp branches. The grasses below had more variety, with green and yellow variants forming clumps between the lessening plains grass they left behind. Finn eyed the trail from time to time, aware that the drone had the group in its vision but wanting a handle on how the warriors moved, and picking up any tell-tales of specific people where he could.

They wound between the bushes, the direction clearly northern, but Finn had his usual nagging doubts when tracking. He paused after a few minutes, replaying the drone images back and forth.

"Zuri, there were nineteen, right?"

"Yes. Have they dropped a few I didn't see?"

"No, but that's a big group. I don't want to send up a second drone, we may need it fully charged later. How does thermal look?"

"At this distance, not much use."

"Okay. Focus on the *!Kora.* But stay aware. Alkinta, don't assume we have them in sight. These tribespeople know the bushland, however strange they may look."

"I assume nothing. Especially when working with the young

and inexperienced," the old woman snorted, Finn taking it as a laugh.

"Young? I'll take that," said Zuri as they continued on.

Kuishi kwingi kuona mengi. To live much is to see a lot. And she's still feisty. Hope I'm like that in my old age.

Soon after, the *!Kora* split, four of the blue and red patterned warriors running off ahead of the main group. Zuri relayed it to Finn, who listened while scanning ahead. Nothing much they could do, they needed to follow whatever the advanced party was up to. He signalled them onward, sighing as he engaged the second drone to fly up and above their rear. Finn set it on a ten second cycle between thermal and normal vision with a wide camera angle.

"Maybe not so inexperienced, ya?" said Alkinta.

CHAPTER 14

Moon Base

"Why me?"

"Because you'll do it all scientific like. You'll use big words and explain things matter-of-fact. Noah likes big words, and he wants it straight," said Smith, Yasuko standing in the ship's hold, staring open-mouthed at him, arms crossed.

"You're his friend. He'll take it better from you."

"And you're not? He cares about you as much as us, probably more so. It needs to be done. He's worked it out, so hiding anything else will just make it worse. Besides, you know me. I can't do it straight; one poorly timed mushroom joke and it'll be a complete mess."

"You wouldn't? Would you?"

"Can't help myself. It's a character flaw." Smith closed the microship door, the nanobots swarming over the hull, prepping it for refuelling. "I cover stuff up with distraction and poor jokes. It's a human thing. You go quiet and introspective, I get louder. Look up 'imposter syndrome' from that data you downloaded from Bathsen to help Noah. I wouldn't say I have it, but the doubts creep in on me. Started in Afghanistan when I was in line for a promotion – one day cock sure, the next doubting my judgements. Being dead isn't helping my confidence."

"Doubts? I understand the body issue now. It is not one the Haven would have suffered, but when I put it alongside your ethics, well I should have seen it. But you seem so sure of yourself." Yasuko moved alongside Smith as they approached the airlock.

"Yeah? Then why do I let Zuri and Finn lead. I'm the Corporal," said Smith, turning to face Yasuko.

"Ah. Yes. But dead. That's why they think you do it."

"Maybe it is, maybe it isn't. Either way, please stay quiet about it. They have enough to deal with, and to be honest, I prefer it this way. I'll sit in with you and Noah when you talk, but don't be surprised if my fingers go in my ears when you discuss *fruiting*."

"Fingers in your microphones. You don't have ears." Yasuko stepped through the airlock door, returning her best smile towards Smith as she turned. "Yet."

"Now who's the comedian. We need to do this as soon as possible. He's stewing over it right now, and he's promised to help design my new body if we tell him."

"He already has. I talked over your plans with him before he went down to Stratan. I think you've been played. I mined enough ore to release some for the build, Noah's looking it over right now."

Noah looked green, the colour from his lips draining and eyes sinking while Yasuko talked. When she got to *mycelia* and *fruiting*, Smith appeared to briefly shutdown, the blue glow from his helmet fading out as his armour sat still. When he powered back up, Noah quickly left the room, grateful for the suction power of the Explorer Ship's bathroom.

"That went well," said Yasuko. "He appeared engaged throughout."

"You know where he is right now? Yeah?" said Smith.

"He said he needed the bathroom. Ah, you think he's checking for spores?"

"No, I think he's throwing up from the thought of the fungus lacing his body. Not mushroom in there for much else."

"You said you wouldn't."

"No, I said *you* needed to do it so *I* wouldn't say it to him. He's coming back." Smith stood up, pacing behind the couch in the control room when Noah returned. He stopped to look at the pasty young man he'd come to like, even admire. His ringlets were wet with sweat, but his eyes were alive again, colour returning to his lips.

Tougher than all of us, we just don't see it sometimes.

Noah raised his hand as Smith turned to speak, stopping Smith in his tracks.

"It's done. I'll think on it, though I might need a few of those midnight sessions to get through it, but I'll be okay. And, if it helps, you were right not to tell me back then. Not sure I'd have coped." Noah nodded to Yasuko, mouthing a *thanks*. "Come on, Smith. Let's get you turned up to eleven."

"Now that's what I'm talking about. See, Noah, you're still a fun g—"

"Smith!" shouted Yasuko.

CHAPTER 15

Kabbo Grass Plains

Zuri's drone continued to send a feed showing the *!Kora* were still heading North. They'd been walking about an hour now, with Alkinta estimating another hour before they hit radio blackout. About four kilometres in all according to the HUD analysis of her stride length and direction. Alkinta talked them through the rewilding on the way, the thickening vegetation a reflection of their early work on seeding the southern equatorial areas, using the combination of warmer climes and the trade winds to get dispersal rates as high as possible. The grasses were easy, the bare scrubland post the nuclear winter ripe for the high yielding seeds, especially with light grazing in the early days. This had encouraged a few of the ground-nesting birds, increasing seed dispersal further. The early projects had planted tree seedlings in the dips and hollows around the coast, and Alkinta's exuberance spilled over when she recounted the last satellite sweep of the area, five years back and prior to the ancient machine finally burning up. It had shown encouraging growth, matching the success of the southern forests overseen by another project team. The mixed woodland should be robust, and she was hoping for signs of recovering wildlife over and above the release projects they'd been running.

Finn reached a dense patch of scrub bush, the blossom thick with insects. He raised his fist, Zuri dropping low with Alkinta copying, kneeling *at ease*. He examined the ground around the bushes, Zuri watching the area through his drone's feed.

"Multiple trails," said Finn. "All leading off in different directions, new over old too. They've done this before. When was the last significant rain, Alkinta?"

"About a week ago, more is forecast in the next few days. It's spring, our growing season, yes."

"Then these older tracks are within that time, and the new ones overlaid are our four friends. They've picked a good spot, trails weaving in and out of the heavy scrub." Finn eye-clicked Zuri's drone feed, the picture pixelating but clear enough. He correlated the movements of the main party, picturing the most likely path in his mind and switching the feed to thermal, sweeping the drone round. A strong response came from the east, a few hundred metres away. If he wanted more detail, he'd have to send the drone in closer, which would likely alert the warriors to its presence. Weighing up the odds, he left the drone to auto-track the larger group.

"Thermal, two hundred metres east. Let's take a quick look-see. Don't want anyone behind us." Finn moved ahead, assuming Alkinta would fall in line. She didn't.

"My husband is this way, not that way. We waste time, ya?" she said.

Finn didn't stop, speaking while he maintained focussed on the site of the thermal signature, "I am not leaving someone at our back. If I'm wrong, you can moan the rest of the way. It'll be like having Smith back with us."

Zuri slotted in behind Finn, eyes scanning as he checked the trail in the direction he was heading. The rear drone image showed the woman only delayed a second, one hand on hip, before joining them. She smiled to herself.

Stubborn versus stubborn. My money's on Alkinta in the long-term.

Finn dropped low for the last twenty metres as he approached the tangled bush, the small yellow blossom cascading downwards towards the floor, a combination of winged and multi-legged insects pouring over the bounty. His HUD, confused by the insect horde, showed a large, ill-defined blur of heat beyond the curtain of flowers. He sent Alkinta to the north side, Zuri to the south while he scanned his drone images. With nothing to their rear, he prodded the muzzle of his gun inwards.

◆ ◆ ◆

"It's her?" asked Yabbin.

"Yes but …

"You have the shot, Mehin?"

"Yes, but I'm not taking it," Mehin lifted his eye from the heavy sniper rifle, waiting for the tirade from Yabbin. It didn't come, just a stoney silence that was all the worse.

"Mehin, I am disappointed. I thought …"

"I am with you, Yabbin. There's a drone up and those are not Reserve Security with her. She has two Marines in support, though their armour is strange – not standard issue. I shoot, I expose myself and the operation." Mehin whispered, despite having a good two hundred metres between him and the three targets. He shuddered briefly in the breeze, his light camouflage flickering, showing its age.

"They should not be here so quickly; they have little available transport to move personnel up here."

"Maybe they put more store by it than we thought, our intelligence is mainly guesswork, Yabbin, based on a few intercepted radio messages."

"Too late to go back. If you disable her, they will have to deal with it. It'll slow them down, give us an advantage. Send the visor image through, we are clear enough of the blackout area."

Yabbin examined the images on his HUD, the screen shorting occasionally where the data packet reacted to the ionisation seeping from the cove. The three figures were clear though, and he had no doubt about their professionalism. He watched as they moved east, turning away from the *!Kora*, and out along one of their false trails they'd used to fool him when he first arrived, prior to the blood bribes garnering a little cooperation. They stopped at a large, thick Ado Bush, flanking it.

Those weapons are new.

Finn eased the flower blossoms aside, insects leaping onto the top muzzle as he moved on in. The thermal image cleared, the huge, curved horned buffalo in front of him blowing clouds of steam from its nostrils as it looked up, startled. At its side, the calf quivered, jumping behind its mother. Finn took in the animal's eyes, the tremble in its muscles.

Oh crap.

The beast charged, its powerful rear muscles surging it forward, the head lowering and bringing the horns into play. Finn leapt to the right, hitting the curtain of branches and blossoms that slowed him down. The horns cracked into his hip, the plate smashing against the kinetic gel, and ramming into the bone, sending him spiralling out of the flowers. Zuri spun, bringing her rifle up as the half tonne animal arrested its charge, turning to trample the perceived danger. Zuri fired, the stun bolt searing into the nearest foreleg, causing the beast to stumble, and allowing Finn to roll out the way before black hooves crushed anything vital. A second shot rained in, this one catching the massive, curved horns, the bolt a killing blow anywhere else. It wrenched the animal's head round, heat burning the keratin covering and searing the bone beneath. Finn forgotten, the enormous animal twisted away, running towards Zuri in its pained madness. Zuri hit her wrist control, the extra power exaggerating her jump, handspringing one handed off the floor despite her rifle in the other hand. She pivoted on landing, expecting the crashing coming from the scrub bush to be directed at her. Instead, the calf came bellowing out, running after its mother as the giant buffalo came to a halt behind Zuri.

Another bolt crashed into the floor, Alkinta firing into the dirt below the buffalo's hooves. It snorted, kicking forward, crashing through the next bush with the calf in tow.

Zuri ran over to Finn, the man rising from the floor, tenderly holding his left hip.

"Damage?" she asked.

"Pride, dignity and my hip in that order." Finn eased his leg up, the hip complaining but clearly not broken. "Ouch."

Zuri spun, looking towards Alkinta. "That was a Cape Buffalo, my mother used to strip the meat down after the hunt. She had old photographs of her doing it, proud of what she used to do to help the village as a child. How did it get here?"

"It's a Quia, they've always been here. There are smaller animals with a similar appearance – cattle. Those we are breeding near the southern forests for now. They need to build resilience to more of the Fire Tick species prior to releasing them up here."

"Finn?" asked Zuri.

"Yeah, not an expert. But it looked like those things that I've seen on TV, the ones that can kill lions."

"Simba? Yes, four legs, golden. Fierce, a symbol of Stratan. Though they lived only in the equatorial band, down to the forest edges," said Alkinta. "The war killed the last of them off, like the Quia. The Fire Ticks first, then the human politicians did for the rest." Alkinta mimed an explosion, just as the crack of a bullet slamming between her shoulder blades hit Finn and Zuri's external mics. They threw themselves to the floor, Alkinta collapsing in front of them.

CHAPTER 16

Research Facility, Kabbo Grass Plains

"Target down," said Mehin, the crackle of the mic indicating an increase in the interference. "Moving out." He dropped from the higher branches of the scrub bush, insects skittering off his armour and visor as he clambered through the thorns and fading blossom. His old gauntlets scraped along the thicker branches as he hung then dropped to the floor, quickly checking his HUD, sweeping the space under the bush. His buddy appeared on the thermal image, the hatchling newbie at least on guard in the right place. Yabbin had persuaded the Prime Minister to send them with the untried squaddies picked from new recruits. He'd assumed they were less likely to question any strange orders, and Mwandin had been pleased, the General noting how Yabbin was taking her recruits a little more seriously. The three months of training had solidified the squad, but Mehin knew Alkinta could snap them in two, even at her age. The last time they'd faced off, only he and Yabbin had survived the raid, only for the Stratan Council to gift the bloody vaccine a few weeks later.

Politics, yeah. We're all going to be in the ground with no sons and daughters to follow our path if they keep this up.

"Hey, Omarin. We clear?" he said.

"No movement our way yet," came the reply.

"The drone?" asked Mehin, emerging from the drooping branches and scanning the sky.

"It's ..." Omarin shifted, his light-wrap camouflage shimmering with a second's delay as he looked behind. The strobe flash seared through his visor, sending his brain into shutdown as the seizure hit. Mehin ducked, one eye's vision blurred from catching the edge of the flash. With visor darkened he ducked down, the expectant gunshot not appearing. He flashed through the HUD, spinning his head round to check for thermal signatures. Empty. As he turned back, Zuri's stock slammed into his helmet, followed by the stun bolt to his back. A world of pain shot through Mehin's spine, shorting his camouflage system while his mind spiralled into the darkness.

"I don't think any of those words can be used in polite company," said Finn, pulling Alkinta up against the low pile of rocks. "My translator just says: 'bout of swearing' on repeat."

Finn checked her back, examining the slug that had impacted exactly in the centre of her spinal plate. He picked up the heavy round from the floor, the mushroomed metal still warm according to his HUD.

Not meant to kill.

"It's blown the suit CPU. No HUD, no servos. They knew exactly where to aim. It has to be Minoas Shadow Marines. The *! Kora* have some weapons from the odd cache they find, but rarely use them. They didn't have any at the compound, just spears, slings and rocks. And that was a bloody good shot. Ow."

"I have them both cable tied," said Zuri, cutting in over the radio, a heaviness to her breath as she spoke. "Both out, I've disabled their radios, and the drone shows we're clear for now."

"You able to walk? Let's look at what Zuri has caught." said Finn, holding out his hand. The old woman took it, a stiffness to her movements as she rose with the servos offline. Alkinta straightened her back cautiously, Finn catching the wince as each vertebrae argued its point. Reaching full vertical, she walked on, the judder of each step lessening as she adjusted her movements accordingly.

But a hindrance. Exactly what they were after.

Finn checked his drone, the little machine dutifully following instructions as it followed the *!Kora.* The interference was building, near constant, and he called it in, not wanting to lose it when contact fully cut out. Down to tracking only, and the tribal warriors had already proven their desire and ability to hide their trail. Finn sighed, wishing he had the full Delta Squad right now. Especially Noah – he'd know a way around the blackout.

On the ground, the two black-clad soldiers lay face down, one with a long sniper rifle at his side and a familiar looking double-barrelled rifle that a crouching Zuri was currently examining.

"Your tech hasn't moved on since you sent *!Nias* and his crew," she said, lifting the long-barrelled rifle away from the prone soldier.

"Not for war, no. We've been trying to survive a nuclear winter and the Brain Fever. Combat has been low on the list. Most of my equipment is recycled, though serving Marines have some upgrades," said Alkinta. "Can you remove their helmets, I am a little incapacitated, ya?"

Zuri nodded, reaching over and undoing the clasp that mirrored her own. The helmet slid off, a livid swelling on the man's temple testament to the force of her blow.

Alkinta swore. "Mehin. And if he's here, so is Yabbin. If he's still alive. Shadow Squad, their elite group. At least it was, before we all got old."

"You've fought him?" asked Zuri, looking towards the ex Stratan Marine.

"Back in the day, just once. Though he has a file a mile long. They came for the last vaccine batch, what, twenty-odd years ago. Dropped in on the facility in Kaimas—didn't use parachutes, not Yabbin. They used fly suits, jumping from one of the old passenger jet craft at high altitude. Tough as they come. If he's here, then Yabbin has Otegnoa, and my husband may well be dead."

"Why?"

"Otegnoa delivered the vaccine to the Minoas a month later. Freely given. But Yabbin's mother reacted badly to it, less than 1% do, but when you are already on your knees, it all hurts. She ended up in a coma. Sent his father even more paranoid, and the new beginning for diplomatic relations we hoped for, ended there and then. Yabbin is General Hardrin's only son, though a better man by all accounts."

"So, this is about revenge?" said Zuri.

"Probably. The whole Minoas people are paranoid, scared or both. Who knows how long they can hold a grudge?"

CHAPTER 17

Moon Base

Smith's powered armour bent at knee and hip, and he eased backwards to sit on the reinforced chair the squad *copies* had left in the hold. A hybrid human, lost for words at the machine facing him.

It stood exactly at his old height, the position of its torso reflecting the angle he habitually took when standing *at ease*. Its shoulders mimicked his, as did the turn of the head and the crooked smile that annoyed Finn so much. Yet it was clearly metal, the sheen of the outer skin shimmering in the glow of the hold lights, eyes heralding a gentle blue glow from within the pupil, the head bald and smooth.

Almost human.

Yasuko shrouded the machine in a copy of Smith's hologram, the features coming alive with his mannerisms as she reworked an old recording. She synced the robot to it, and a virtual Smith came alive in front of his eyes.

"So, if you wish, we can project this way within the ship. When outside, it'll remain as you saw until your plaque learns to project accurately. That'll take a few weeks, maybe a month, if you want it too. You won't appear human, light changes will give it away, but more of 'you' will be evident – body language, facial expression, etc," Yasuko said, switching off the virtual image.

"Power levels?"

"Equivalent to the combat suits that Finn and Zuri are

wearing now. Say 1.5g max, but we've followed your design so you can wear the ceramic suits and Battle Armour. You wanted lifelike, so Yasuko has reformed a thin, meta-metal for the outer skin. It's the equivalent of the Kevlar in terms of penetration, but double layered. However, impacts will damage internal systems, and you will be far more complex than the Powered Armour. Data banks, sensor arrays, gyroscope, system access, internal nanobot repair and, of course, an internal power source. All that on top of the complexity of metal bones and metamaterial muscles and tendons to get the movement as natural as we can. They are all vulnerable, and you will have to factor that into your behaviour. Yasuko has scoured the SeedShip data banks for most of this."

"Combat capability?"

"There's no way we could build in too much, we're still learning. There are a few internal systems for you to check out, and I've uploaded the judo katas you showed me and the Haven Spear Dance. But your plaque has all the data you need, and if you choose to, you can make another copy of yourself and construct your own *weapon of choice*."

Smith stood up, his hulking power armour sidestepping as best it could around the robot. He reached out with a gauntlet, pressing against the blue metallic skin, his sensors registering the vibration of power within. Of a new life.

Oh boy.

Smith unclipped his helmet, reaching inside and removing the plaque, stretching out towards Noah with the blue metal that contained his *self*. Noah slipped the square from his hand, placing it to the side of the lower vertebrae, the metal skin absorbing the plaque as the medical nanobots welcomed it inside. A twitch of the blue head followed, then a tremble in the wrist and a jerk of the ankle. The robot's head lifted, looking towards Yasuko and Noah, eyes glowing.

"Smith is at the wheel. Hold on, it's going to be a bumpy

ride." The robot head bent downwards, its chin on the blue metal chest. "Hey, I'm naked! Get out of here you two!"

"Decision time," said Finn. "We follow them in and leave all comms behind, with no chance of calling in backup. Or we go back half a kilometre and call in Smith and Noah."

Alkinta, taking care with her back, slipped each leg into the black armour, keeping her own skin suit. "We go on, time is short."

"I agree, Finn. We could send a drone. It'll leave us short, but it can transmit a radio beacon with a recorded message. Halfway house, and we've already fired one of the strobes – we could use that one. Not such a big loss."

"Will it reach the ships?"

"It should do, especially with Yasuko's sensors. I'm not an expert. But if not, they'll come looking soon enough. We should have set a time limit, but everything happened in such a rush."

"Yeah, missed that. We were chasing a tribe with sticks and spears then, not professional Marines."

"Asiyekosa hayupo. We all make mistakes," said Zuri, Alkinta stopping at the words.

"Those words sound strangely familiar, Zuri. Like I should know them, but don't."

"Like I said, my mother worked the buffalo. My origins are from a part of Earth called Africa, specifically the East. Your ancestors were from that region. Though your language is more ancient than mine, Yasuko says its origins lie in Khoisan."

Alkinta nodded, rising to slip on the arms as Zuri helped her seal the rear, a different and more awkward design than her own. The fit was tight, but her movements fluid enough and when she slotted the helmet on, the servos powered up to support her body. The relief in her back was instant, and she worked through a few turns and spins to confirm her return to combat readiness.

"And them?" she asked, lifting the visor, and pointing to Mehin and his buddy.

"We'll leave a message via the drone. And if Yabbin finds them, at least they'll be one set of armour down and no weapons."

"You should be more ruthless," said Alkinta, eyeing Mehin in particular. "The old ways would have seen them dead. The !Kora know no better, but these soldiers will just return to haunt us again. At least incapacitate them, break a bone or two. It's what you do when you are threatened."

Finn looked towards the woman, then to Zuri, shaking his head. "Not our way."

At least it isn't when we have a choice.

Alkinta returned a glare laced with fire, slamming her visor down. With no radio-link, she had shut herself off from them both.

Finn moved out, fretting over the ex-Marine that followed them, trying to work out where her last statement had come from. He needed to know he could rely on her, and the stress she was under may have forced the comments. But something nagged about it, recalling the ferocity of the sword wielding Stratan Marine back on Earth.

Yabbin's head spun, he wasn't used to things going wrong. The last time had involved Alkinta, and here they were again. Though Mehin had been true to his usual level of accuracy and skill, it was those damned new Marines that had shredded the planned kidnap. Yabbin caught himself, his mind sorting through all the soldiers and resources he was constantly denied. Look at what these Stratan had to work with.

How can they expect me to succeed against such odds?

But he had succeeded. The Field Commander lay trussed in the cave mouth back at Hakunda Cove, the ruined nuclear plant looming at the top of the cliff above it, the remainder of his squad on guard. The primary target, and he should have called for extraction as soon as he'd captured him. But what a waste, Otegnoa was much more useful as bait, drawing Alkinta away from the barrack's defences and secure walls. Capture her, get the codes, use her retinal scan and they were in. Every chance they could start again, make a real difference instead of constantly reinforcing the status quo. What happens when the next bout of Brain Fever hits? Will their scientists be able to adapt or design a new vaccine? Or will they be back to crawling to the Stratan Council, or once again sending out a raiding party?

Every analysis he'd been privy to, and the few he'd paid bribes to gain access, had shown the same analysis as the population aged. They were teetering on the edge of becoming extinct, the end of the Minoas line, with only a few artificially inseminated children being born to the Politico and the rich. Living in the dark, cramped behind walls of paranoia, and eating such a poor diet, all increased the impact of the Brain Fever. It's cycle of mass reduction in male fertility, a physical and mental strain on the surviving population. Even bribes hadn't gained him access to the suicide rates, but everyone had lost someone close. On top of that, the decaying technology prevented much more than a token effort at an IVF programme to overcome it.

Everything is so short-sighted. No risk, no gain. Another attempt to stay in power. I prove we can make a difference, then maybe they will wake up. Get our lands fertile again, and our people from behind their walls. Lower the impact of the virus and the Fire Ticks by reducing its chance to spread. Why can they not see what I do?

Yabbin brought the binoculars back to his eyes, scanning the three trails the *!Kora* were most likely to use as they approached the blackout area. The last message and images from Mehin's sight had sent him scurrying back to the edge of the zone, hoping the drone wouldn't function and preventing the Marines from knowing his position as he assessed his next action. He crawled back from the hillcrest, the last before the land dipped towards the cove. Behind him, Kebb-in was covering his back, the woman was a good soldier, proven. But black ops material? He doubted it.

"Hey, Kebb-in." Yabbin pointed to her lower leg, where two flaccid bodied black-legged ticks crawled up her shin plate. The size of a pea, the damned things grew as big as a walnut when fully fed, passing on their bacteria to the host. Kebb-in, admittedly calm under pressure, flinched, using the knife she drew from her side to scrape off the hated arachnids, crushing them against a rock.

"Get Rena and Candin, leave the others to guard our guest. And make sure they are on it – focussed. They will soon be in a serious combat situation. Ready the boat before you return, too. If this goes to crap, I want them on the sea with the Field Commander, yes? Half a kilometre out they can call for extraction if this goes wrong."

And at least father can have his revenge.

Raising his binoculars, Yabbin watched the four scouts approach the cove via the south-eastern trail, spreading out as they reached the edge of the dip down towards the bay. Each *!Kora* greeted the sea in the same way, turning to face the lazy waves that lapped against the glittering, crystal encrusted beach, with their arms spread outwards. In the centre of the encircling cliffs, a large crystalline structure stood in the purple sea. Its red fluted columns pushing upwards from the seabed, then sprouting outwards, each column tightly packed to the next. It stood three metres above the waves, solid and strong until the bad weather hit, the waves crashing rock and stone against it. The *!Kora* had constructed crystal and rock pictures during some nights they'd spent at the cove, depicting the structure in so many stages of growth or under the battering of a storm. They were beautiful, though to Yabbin they always seemed to move, like his eyes couldn't fully focus on the images.

CHAPTER 18

Approaching Kabbo Grass Plains

Smith dropped the microship through the atmosphere, the entry smooth, as if he was still directly connected into the ship's control system. However, this time his suit-clad hands worked the controls, enjoying the sensation of physically touching the few he was allowed to by the ship's minor AI. The haptic feedback from his skin thrilled him, he felt more alive, free.

Smith is at the wheel, and it's not such a bumpy ride.

He locked in the location Yasuko provided, the projected position for Zuri and Finn in the scrubland heading towards a sea cove. In his own mind, he needed them to see his new form, to give the positive affirmation he required to fully accept it. He knew they would. Friends and squad mates were like that, but he was desperate to see it, feel it. And after Yasuko detected the level of ionisation in the area, well he had the perfect excuse – to make sure they weren't staying beyond the ceramic suit's limits. That, and providing the vaccine she'd manufactured with Noah's support.

Even better if they were having trouble with the *!Kora*, he could swoop in and be the hero just in the nick of time.

Maybe I need a hero nick name, something with blue in the title. Like Blue Android? Or Cyborg Blue.

Finn gently eased the servos to drop to his knee, eyes scanning disturbed ground as footprints criss-crossed the rough grass at his feet. He used the HUD to focus in, comparing the age and pattern of the prints against those he'd copied earlier. He felt strangely alive, more at home in the wild than anything they'd faced recently. Memories of Scotland, and of the chase to rescue Smith flittered in and out of his mind. Despite the pain and anger of that day and night, he'd found himself again. Not an inner peace; the night and day mares still haunted him, smells and sounds spiralling him back into the dark realms he'd locked away. But life since awakening after the escape from Earth had been a rollercoaster, and he hadn't wanted to get off until Vai, and the horror of Nutu Allpa. Places that took their toll on his soul. Now, with feet firmly on a living planet, it felt natural. Maybe he wasn't cut out for the weirdness of space, just the rest of the strange life he was now living.

So what's going to cock that up?

"Zuri," the radio hissed, static overwhelming his ears until he eye-clicked the system off. He set the CPU on alert should anything remotely like words get through. He signalled her over, Alkinta naturally following with stiff movements, feet pounding into the ground and fingers trembling on the rifle's firing mechanism. He signalled the radio was out, and to follow hand signals only.

Zuri looked to Alkinta, the woman's visor still opaque, and signalled for her to raise it. A shake of the head followed, though she cleared it enough to show she was listening. Sweat beaded her brow, eyes were sunken and red-rimmed, but she was focussed, nodding while Zuri went through the basic signals. Zuri gave her a last glance, and looked to Finn, clasping his shoulder to turn him round. She scoured the surrounding scrub bush for any danger, flicking her eyes towards Alkinta with a shake of her head. Message getting through, Finn nodded a reply.

Finn, fretting, placed Zuri on the rear, eyes on Alkinta, reducing their combat effectiveness. He signalled them on, choosing a path leading northeast as the HUD cross-analysis agreed with his instincts. He crouched low, heading towards the last ten metres of flowering scrub, his visor flicking through thermal to check for anything underneath the drooping branches. As he reached the last, sporadic bush the HUD flickered, a haze seeping into the images but not enough yet to block them out. In the corner of his vision, an orange warning dot appeared, a radiation alert starting an exposure countdown. Finn signalled them to cover, stepping slowly under the drooping flowers of the bush. Satisfied, he returned to the rising, rough grassland that stretched a hundred metres in front of him. Interspersed among the dark green grass, glints of light shimmered red.

A killing ground. Anyone with a decent rifle and aim will be at the top of that rise. If they have the light camouflage, they will assume we don't know their position until they fire.

The HUD told him nothing, and with the drone stowed, they were down to basics. Finn smiled, he couldn't help it, despite the decision he had to make. Rather than passing the bush, he signalled Zuri in, and making sure he couldn't be seen from the edge, signalled her to flank east, and indicated he'd head west. As normal, he hated splitting the team, but after the encounter with the Shadow sniper he was left with little choice. They were up against professional soldiers, and tactically they couldn't risk being outflanked or picked off from distance. He signalled Alkinta to wait, and to engage camouflage while counting two lots of thirty before advancing. She was a Marine, he had to trust she got what he was doing.

Finn backed into the thicker patch of scrub, and keeping low, ran from bush to bush knowing Zuri was doing the same. Alkinta switched on her camouflage and ducked down onto the ground, counting and watching the brow of the bay ahead.

Zuri sped swiftly past the first red flowered bush, ignoring the clouds of buzzing insects, keeping as much cover between her and the rise as possible. On reaching the second bush, she spared a glance to the north, magnifying the HUD and assessing the most likely spots for a sniper. Too many to choose from, she sucked in a breath, and carried on directly eastwards, keeping half an eye to the crest. Without the drones they'd come to rely on, and with the light-wrap tech in play, this was more than just dangerous. Sweat dripped down the back of her neck, trickling on down her spine, and it wasn't warm.

Zuri reached the outer edge of the scrub, opposite to where the cliffs curved back out to sea. The most likely place an experienced enemy would cover to ensure they weren't flanked. Zuri's only other option was to go out even wider, likely exposing her back. She declined, stooping low and crawling under the last bush to emerge the other side, her sight up and the *weapon of choice* syncing with her HUD. They had little time with the new plaques, the *weapons* almost relying on them rather than the other way round. They didn't provide the same clarity in the sight, the same accuracy as they adjusted for Zuri's personal style. But they were damn good, nevertheless, and their personal tech had improved massively since they first encountered the Stratan. Zuri's HUD scanned through the electromagnetic spectrum, piecing together an anomaly ahead of her, something that didn't quite match its surroundings.

Makali ya jicho yashinda wembe. The sharpness of the eye is greater than the razor, enemy mine. I see you, and you don't know it.

The count hit sixty, and Zuri prepped her aim, waiting for Finn, knowing he was a slow counter. Ten seconds later an energy bolt flashed from the west, hitting something on the far side of the cove. Zuri focussed on the image her HUD had targeted, waiting for a reaction. As the movement came, a probable turn of a camouflaged head, she fired. The energy bolt surged across the grass and slammed into the soldier's chest. Zuri rose to one knee, re-sighting but losing the figure as it fell behind the crest. And she ran.

Finn watched the soldier fall behind the rocks; the energy bolt having seared the man's shoulder as Finn cursed the *weapon's* reduced accuracy. He waited three seconds, then moved to his left, using the cracked and weathered rock strata as partial cover until he stopped to check their position again. No change, he charged in low, HUD checking as he upped the pace. A bolt flared from the central crest, aimed towards the middle, to where they'd left Alkinta. The screamed response was a mix of anger and pain, loud enough to penetrate his helmet despite the mics being next to useless.

Distracted, Finn glanced to the left, assuming he'd see Alkinta under assault, or writhing in pain. Instead, she charged forwards, her rifle hot as bolt after bolt slammed into the crest where another rock strata rose. Nothing came back in response, Alkinta's wave of energy forcing their heads down, while the scream rose in fury.

Well, that seems familiar.

Finn continued on, securing his own position before dealing with anything else. As he flanked around the rock pile, a muzzle flash streaked his HUD, the explosion of the high calibre bullet echoing off the rock. Finn dived, too slow, and the bullet slammed into his shoulder, cracking a ceramic plate on impact, the whirr of the secondary explosive rising as it drilled on. The second eruption bit into the plate, the enhanced kinetic gel beneath absorbing the impact but the plate shards drove back into Finn. He stifled the cry, knowing full-well he'd have been dead and buried in his old British combat armour, rolling outwards to drop below the rock strata he'd just climbed. The explosive bullets were slow to reload, but Finn recognised a professional soldier when the second shot, an energy bolt, flashed over him as he hit the rocky floor.

I've no grenades with the stun barrel.

Finn pictured his SA80, the *weapon's* morphing slower than he was used to but quick enough. Replaying his HUD, and using the system to check for distance, he rose and released, the grenade dropping at the bottom edge of the rocks as another bolt flew his way. It glanced off his other shoulder, leaving black residue but little damage, and he threw himself to the ground. The explosion lifted rock and soldier, the cry signal enough for Finn to rise and follow in, arriving as the soldier rolled to face him, visor cracked, dead eyes looking his way.

Alkinta roared, the fire in her brain demanding action as she charged forward, the repeated blasts from her ancient rifle draining the energy store. With a last semblance of thought, she switched her gauntleted finger to the powerful explosive rounds, twitching but not firing just yet as she powered in. With the unfamiliar suit set high, her legs pumped the ground, only her old training keeping the weapon steady while she ran. A bolt clipped her knee, Alkinta dragging the weapon up, releasing a round in the general direction it came from. Without knowing the HUD controls, she was relying on her own vision, currently blurred with sweat and absences, wavering in and out. Her left side exposed, a bolt slammed into her hip, quickly followed by another, sending her spiralling to the floor, momentum wrenching her around.

Alkinta let out another roar, fumbling for the rifle that had flown from her grasp, her vision now inflamed, heat in her brain engulfing senses. As she rose, a kick to her ribs lifted her off the floor, and the slamming of a rifle stock sent her mind spinning into the void, where the fire still burned.

Yabbin stood over the familiar black suit, Mehin's if he remembered rightly, his rifle poised for another blow. He stopped, calming his heart, pushing the adrenaline rush away.

Instinct sent him to the floor as the whomp echoed from his right, a half-second later the explosion rolled over him, dirt and rocks mixed with the broken pieces of a double-barrelled rifle. Yabbin turned, the torn and twisted body of Rena lay strewn over a boulder, her armour cracked with green gel mixing amid the blood. His HUD caught the movement of the Marine to his left, the rifle in his hand strangely formed, but the smoke from the underbarrel enough to indicate the grenade's source. The soldier had him in his sights.

Rising swiftly, he grabbed the black-clad body, pulling it in close and dragging it back towards the rock. The silent response gave him hope, and he dropped behind the crest, breathing heavily while his body shook. It had been an even longer time since he'd experienced knowing he was going to lose. His rifle lay where he'd hit the ground.

CHAPTER 19

Hakunda Cove, North Coast Of The Southern Continent

Keeping low, and slowing as she reached the rocks, Zuri carefully slid the rifle round the left side of rough stone, the mirror sight showing a jumble of large grey rocks below the crest, all large enough to hide behind. Not wanting to risk the time needed to form an image in her HUD, she moved past the rock, wary, eyes searching for any tell-tales of the light-wrap camouflage. As she moved down the dip, Zuri caught sight of the cove for the first time, the old power plant perched on top of the low sea cliff on Finn's side. Despite the damage to the structure, the ruined building drew memories of those she'd seen on the coast of Scotland, all functional blocks of concrete and steel. Below it, the skeletons of old pipes pierced the cliff before entering the bay waters. Zuri caught her breath, a red crystal flower glowed in the centre of the bay, in line with the old pipes, contrasting its strange, ethereal beauty against the purple waters. It must have stood ten metres above the lapping waves, fluted columns packed tightly together, sprouting from a central core. Its oddness drew her inwards, eyes scanning the regular hexagonal pillars glimmering with a multitude of red shades.

The camouflaged hand shot out from beneath her, the gauntlet grasping her leg and forcing her off balance as she stepped across what she assumed to be a raised section of the rock strata. Zuri clattered forwards, trying to roll away, but the iron grip pulled her downwards, her shoulder hitting the other side of the dip. Before she could react, a weight landed on her back, fists pummelling into her helmet. Zuri activated the wrist switch, the power surge kicking into her hip and knee servos, and she twisted round, forcing the weight off her back. The enemy was now behind her, so she pitched the other way, throwing her hips to force a roll hampered by the rock. It was enough to give two metres distance and eyes on the rising figure, its camouflage flickering, the right shoulder ash streaked. Zuri ignored her rifle she'd thrown forward as she fell, choosing to keep watch on the soldier as she reached inside her forearm, extracting the attached metal rod. The Marine didn't wait, diving forward, attempting to knock her off balance just as a ferocious human roar echoed over the crest. Zuri rode the charge, rolling backwards and twisting, riding the armoured shoulder that slammed into her chest. The black plated soldier hit the rock first, followed by the slam of its helmet, trapping Zuri's right arm underneath with the metal rod. A punch rained down on her visor, and Zuri raised her left arm, blocking the arc for the next assault as her right leg heaved against the rock, twisting both of them above the ground, releasing her arm. Zuri backwards rolled again, exposing herself to one heavy hit that glanced off the back of her helmet. As soon as she was face down, she scrambled to her feet, exploding forwards to gain distance from the enemy. Another roar punctuated the air, followed by the whomp and ensuing explosion of a familiar grenade, mixed with enraged shouts echoing across the cove.

Facing her, the soldier reached down for her *weapon*, the rifle swinging round, the gauntleted finger pressing the firing button. Zuri tried to dive out of the way. The bolt slammed into her left thigh, the electrical charge shooting across the metal inlaid ceramic plates, the fizz hitting her nerves and shooting up her spine.

No no no no.

Zuri hit the floor, her left side numb. She slid down a rock shelf, a second bolt heating the stone edge she slipped over, fracturing the rock. Zuri reached for her side, unclipping the holster and drawing her sidearm, dragging herself upwards as the muzzles of her own *weapon* protruded over the rock ledge above her. She fired, the burst hitting the three barrels, forcing the rifle to jerk backwards, causing her second bolt to miss. Zuri felt the numbness spread, her spine and right hip began to tingle. She fumbled in her pouch, her HUD on alert, and her gun once again appeared over the edge of the rock strata. She eye-clicked and the drone shot forward, the radio interference instantly disconnecting it from Zuri's HUD.

Please. Me and mine …

Zuri descended into the fuzz of detachment, her body succumbing to the stun bolt, her eyes briefly flickering until her mind yielded, sinking into the depths of unconsciousness.

"I don't know you!" shouted Yabbin, slipping out his sidearm and pulling Alkinta in closer, her helmet removed. "But I know this one. This wasn't how I remember her, soldier. She lost it and that's not like her. She has Mehin's armour on, but I'm going to make a bet with you. I bet she's picked up a Fire Tick, and right now she's at the first stage of infection."

Finn moved closer, running from the scrub bush he'd used as cover to reach the rise at the head of the cove, fifty metres down from the shouting soldier. He stayed quiet, not engaging, with the reformed rifle in his hand. He glanced over the crest, the area below him still grassland before the rock ledges protruded from the enemy grasping Alkinta, his back against a boulder.

"Ah, there you are." Yabbin threw the weapon to the ground, its power unable to penetrate Stratan Armour, a show of surrender. "I'd quite like to live, Marine. So, there's my weapon."

Finn strode forward, silent, rifle aimed towards the man he assumed was Yabbin. As he approached, he watched the man's eyes widen behind his visor.

Yeah, I'm an alien. Surprise.

"Let her go," said Finn. "Arms out, together."

The translator working through the speaker, Yabbin watched in fascination as Finn's lips moved differently behind the visor. He noted the narrow nose, the smaller eyes and the heavier set to the man himself. He took a breath, and Yabbin complied – if this alien soldier had chosen to, he would already be dead. Finn slipped the pre threaded cable tie over both wrists, pulling it tight, eyeing Yabbin as he attempted to position his wrist to allow for some give. Yabbin shrugged, and Finn finished binding them tight.

"She has a Fire Tick. If you don't know what that is, you need to learn quickly. Otherwise, she's going to be seriously ill, likely die at her age. I can help."

"In return for?"

"Well, setting me free would be good."

Finn raised an eyebrow, and the Minoas captain smirked in return. Yabbin came to a quick conclusion, already understanding what type of man he faced. And seeing a chance.

"I have her husband down in the cove. Right now, my squad are bundling him into a boat and about to leave for extraction. You need to stop that from happening and talk to the Field Commander. They see me, then they'll stand down." Yabbin watched Finn's reaction, seeing the disbelief. "Listen, Alkinta was the target, not Otegnoa. She's no use to me dead, and well, as the plan's gone to crap anyway, I need to make the best of it. But you're short of time."

Finn moved to the edge of the rocks, scanning the bay below and catching sight of the crystal formation for the first time. He realigned the HUD, the digital enhancement focussing in on the cliff edges.

"Our cave is underneath the west cliff, there's a couple of tents around it and a RIB – got it?"

Finn didn't respond, bringing up his rifle and using the more powerful sight to focus in on the bay. "A RIB?" he said, Yabbin agreeing. Finn fired; the whirring explosive bullet was close to its maximum accurate distance. But the *weapon* adjusted, and the round bore its way through the outer shell of the boat before exploding. Finn fired a second, the two soldiers dragging it to the water's edge diving out of the way.

"Nice shot," said a deflated Yabbin.

"Yeah, thanks. Stay here, get your next story clear in your mind while I check on something. Make this one more believable." Finn slid a paired cable tie over Yabbin's legs, pulling it tight. Yabbin watched him leave, sighing as he leaned back against the rock.

Aliens on Stratan. Could the Council have succeeded? Are they from Earth? Three hundred years in the making. A people with a long-term view, unlike my own.

Finn strode towards the western side of the bay, his HUD alert to the presence of a prone, black-clad figure shaking on the rocks. He upped his speed, the armour powering him forwards, and he darkened his visor, instructing the HUD of what might occur next. The drone rose, responding to his movements, and the strobe fired. Finn ignored it, removing Zuri's rifle from the Marine's pulsing grasp. He spotted the edge of the rock ledge, a black smudge highlighting where an energy bolt had struck. On reaching the edge, Zuri's leg came into view. Finn jumped down, quickly scanning for any sign of injury. With none visible, but Zuri's eyes closed, he knelt next to her, physically linking his HUD into hers, running through the life signs with a sense of relief. He peered over the ledge, the soldier no longer immersed in a seizure, had lapsed into unconsciousness. Finn returned to Zuri and rifled through her pouches, taking out the cable ties and prepping them.

Getting through these today. Just like old times, with a little less death.

After incapacitating the Marine, Finn lifted Zuri, carrying her back towards Alkinta and Yabbin. He placed her down, noting Yabbin hadn't moved except to remove a bag from his belt.

"Lucky for you, she's alive," said Finn. "Otherwise, whatever story you might have would be a short one."

"But you might lose Alkinta if you don't act soon. Emergency First Aid kit. There's a removal tool in there, and two shots – one an antibiotic the other for the area around the bite." Yabbin proffered the kit. Finn searched through, removing the familiar large tick removal tool wrapped with two prefilled hypodermic kits. Sighing he unclipped Alkinta's armour, hoping and praying the woman didn't wake up halfway through, the vivid imagery of the ensuing carnage going through his mind. Luckily, he only needed to strip back the top half, the bulge under her skin suit near the neckline a clear sign of what might lie underneath. Finn peeled it back, exposing the huge black-legged tick, its bulbous orange sack pulsing. Finn slid the tool around its head, the insect immediately trying to push itself deeper into Alkinta's neck. He twisted, the foul thing coming off in one piece, reducing the chance of further infection. His boot put paid to any of its future plans as he ground it into the rock.

"The blue one for the bite," said Yabbin. "And the green for the antibiotic." Finn ran through his first aid knowledge in his head, the training refreshers had bored him silly, but he could recall enough, and he injected Alkinta.

Re-clipping the armour, he laid her back down on the rock, eyeing Yabbin.

"How long until your squad get up here? I'd like to avoid

killing them if I can."

"Ten minutes, though I think they'll stay and guard the Field Commander, as per their orders. Can I ask, Mehin, the man whose suit Alkinta is wearing – is he …?"

"Alive when we left him, and the other one with him. Though, if there's Fire Ticks in the area, then the quicker we get sorted here, the sooner we can make sure they stay that way." Finn waited for Yabbin to answer, the man clearly caught between multiple loyalties and whatever plan he was running. Whatever else was happening, Finn could sense there was far more going on than just a simple kidnapping for revenge. "There's another on the west side of the cliffs trussed up too. Like I said, we don't kill if we don't have to."

The data packet dropped into Finn's HUD, the small text system they'd been forced to use when battling S'lgarr. Eye-clicking it, he breathed a little easier with Smith alerting him to his impending arrival. Finn rapidly eye-clicked a message back, sending the best location he could for the two Minoas Shadow Squad members left stranded in the scrub bush.

"Okay, Yabbin is it?" the captain nodded. "We do this my way. And if you think I'm alien looking, well you're in for a surprise."

CHAPTER 20

Kabbo Grass Plains, South Of Hakunda Cove

Cyborg Blue strides through the thick undergrowth, wary, eyes and sensors scanning everywhere for his arch nemesis, Finn or Killjoy to those who know his true identity. For months they have fought across the stars, and now, on this alien world, they approach their final battle. Cyborg Blue readies his deadliest weapon, the Put Down.

Smith's sensors picked up the subtle heat signatures emanating from underneath the flowering scrub bush, despite the curtain of insects hazing the system. He strode on, parting the layers of flowers with his armoured hand, checking for any extra heat signatures or likely dangers. The two Marines were tied together, a rope linked through as they sat back-to-back against the tree trunk, a feast for the local life looking for blood to reproduce. Smith knelt between them, throwing his broadest smile at the pair as his servos creaked at knee and ankle. One, helmetless and in his skin suit, Alkinta's armour laying at his feet, peered straight at him, watery and red-rimmed eyes widening as he peered through Smith's visor.

"Oops, did I leave the visor clear? Well, I guess the secret is out the bag. I'm an alien, right? Don't give me any trouble or I'll do *alien* things to you. Got it?"

The man nodded, though the set to his face was red and angry, barely under control. Sweat poured from his scalp, a little froth at the mouth. Smith scanned the man, the wave of heat off him palpable even to his newly calibrating sensors.

"You're ill," said Smith. "Anything I should know?"

"Fire Tick," said the soldier tied the other side of the tree. "He needs it removing. The meds are in the first aid kit in his pouch. He'll fight you all the way, it sets the anger button to full-on."

Smith nodded, retrieving the kit and analysing how it worked while taking out his razor-sharp knife from its thigh sheath. Once satisfied, he lashed out, the carotid slap hitting the helmetless soldier on the side of the neck. The strike so swift, Mehin was out cold before he could flinch.

Okay, so I couldn't resist. Not quite a judo move, but hey, I'm no one-trick pony. Not got long. Thirty seconds, maybe a minute.

Smith slit the cable ties, eyes and hands working in unison as he searched the skinsuit for any tell-tales.

There

He slit in under the arm pit, the bulbous orange body of the tick quivering when it was exposed, expanding as it sucked from Mehin's body. Smith knew a little about ticks, on earth they could cause Lyme Disease, and he'd seen one or two squad mates get really sick with the bacterial infection. Most talked of muscle aches, feeling almost flu-like. What they didn't talk about was the danger to the hypothalamus if left untreated. Infections could lead to issues with low mood, depression and brain fog. He was sure there were worse symptoms, even death. The problem with soldiers was the need to appear strong in front of your mates, after all, who's scared of a tick and a bit of flu?

Smith twisted the tool, the plump tick coming loose whole from the soldier's body despite its attempts to dig deeper in. Raking through his memory, Smith was sure this beast was much larger than any he'd ever seen. Maybe ten times the size, possibly more. Even in robotic form, he shuddered while squashing the insect with a rock. He delivered the medicine, guided by the soldier at this side before Mehin stirred. Smith swiftly tied the man's arms and legs, lifting him up and carrying him back to the microship. On returning for the other soldier, he lifted them to their feet, slicing the lower cable tie and removing the helmet.

Underneath was a young man, probably in his early twenties, a receding hairline exaggerating the length of his face that sported the typical Stratan wide nose and large eyes. Smith threw him a grin, his deep blue metal lips sliding to the sides to expose perfect teeth.

"Going to give me any trouble? I love trouble," Smith said, the shake of the head enough of a reply.

"Now, I know you won't tell me any military secrets, or let slip information that compromises your government. But these ticks. Now that you can talk to me about, right? And the Brain Fever too. I just saved your buddy back there, that should be enough for you to know what I'm all about. Hate needless death, experienced too much of it in my time."

CHAPTER 21

Hakunda Cove, North Coast Of
The Southern Continent

Finn watched the cave, his sight enhancing the image, picking out two highly stressed Shadow Marines bickering over their next decision. He peered over to Yabbin, the captain was a real enigma, and Finn felt unsure where all this was going. Right now, he wanted to take down those two Marines bloodlessly, but it was too far for the stun rifle, and the energy bolt's strength uncertain right now. Acclimatising to the *weapon,* and it to him, he assumed would take time. Last time, the learning phase had been on the fly, under constant stress of combat, and when it failed, he and the squad had been close to being the next casualties of the alien … the Stratan, incursion.

Zuri stirred; the stimulant he'd administered needed another ten minutes according to Yasuko's past instructions. And he wasn't sure how fit she would be, brain fog after a nervous system shutdown was a potential problem.

The data packet dropped into his HUD, the short text a basic coordinate with the message 'here'. Finn eye-clicked a quick reply. Now with two squad members, maybe they could finish this and leave most of the Minoas Marines alive.

Though Smith in full Battle Armour may well be enough for them to surrender on the spot.

He glanced to the south, expecting to see the bulk of the power armour appear over the horizon, only to be greeted by the white sheen of the ceramic plate they all wore. As it closed in, he caught sight of the blue-skinned man underneath, the features so familiar yet different from the Smith he knew. Finn wasn't sure how he felt about it, but Smith was Smith, in whatever guise he wore.

Another data packet appeared: *Explain later*, and Finn nodded in reply. Duty first. Bringing up the combat text menu they'd prepped for Nutu Allpa, he explained the next steps, and the random fly in the ointment of the *!Kora* who had not intervened – yet.

Zuri watched the cave mouth. Her *weapon*, now morphed into the SA80 of old, featured the ARILLS sight, giving her an enhanced image improved further as her connection with the *weapon* grew.

And hopefully it'll compensate for the shake in my hands and the fog in my brain.

The thermal imaging of the dark cave mouth showed the two soldiers who were their primary concern. One was clearly packing up; his backpack being stuffed as she watched. The other on guard, a good line-of-sight back towards the cove and its beach, not expecting a sea approach. Behind them both, a hunched figure sat against the wall, the heat signature bringing peace of mind, showing the Field Commander was still alive. Zuri adjusted her position, settling in as she waited for Finn and Smith.

Within a few minutes, she noted Smith emerge at the top of the cliff face, easing a rope gently down the vertical rock face until three metres above the crystal beach. He signalled across; the data packets unable to reach this far with the ionisation, the crystal growth standing in the purple sea between them. He descended, Zuri remaining watchful, her role to cover his swift descent, with one eye on the time in her HUD. After reaching the drop-down point, Smith locked in, feet resting on the rock face. Zuri glanced across at the cave mouth, the guards halfway through swapping roles. The *!Kora* remained an enigma, their stone structures built right at the head of the small cove. They had not stirred, and as night showed signs of arriving, they were focussed on building a pyre.

Finn emerged, his actions mimicking Smith's as he descended the cliff face nearer the sea, to the north of the cave and with only a thin strip of beach to drop onto. As he reached the bottom, he signalled a halt, locking into place until they hit their time mark. Missions without communication were tough, but what wasn't these days?

Umoja ni nguvu, utengano ni udhaifu. Unity is strength, division is weakness. Work together and we survive, me and mine.

Smith and Finn dropped in unison, the crunch of their landing on the crystal enough warning for the guard to tense up, calling the other over. Zuri's cue. Should they pose a threat to the Field Commander, then she'd start firing. Both soldiers took a cave wall each, peering round, and their own mirror sights coming into action. Their reaction giving her little doubt they now knew they were under attack. Zuri fired, the three-round burst pummelling into the guard on Finn's side. The soldier's shoulder plate cracked under the extra power of her weapon, and he spun as the bolts drove him back. Zuri knew Finn would drive in, turning her attention to Smith's side. The soldier had already bobbed down, the rock pile clearly placed as a cover point. The exposed leg from her angle though was enough, and her second burst clattered into rock and ceramic plate. The soldier slid his leg inwards, the movement delaying his response as Smith appeared over the rocks, his stun bolt surging into the man's helmet. On the other side, Finn's weapon burst into life, a stun shot hitting the prone soldier in the chest, with his return energy bolt clipping Finn's left shoulder, forcing him to duck, waiting for the paralysis to take effect.

Nice and clean.

She glanced over at Yabbin, his curious face watching in return from behind the helmet visor, his speakers switched off, but a muffled voice could still be heard.

"It would have been easier to kill them," he said. "With that weapon you could have made it quicker and safer. Your armour is no better than ours."

Zuri didn't respond, the man was fishing, and she had no intention of giving anything away. And it was up to him to view their actions however he wished, as a strength or a weakness. She didn't care, Zuri knew how far she had gone and would go again to defend her own.

And he made no attempt to stop us, either way.

CHAPTER 22

Moon Base

Yasuko checked over the mining bots. Satisfied they were still working efficiently; she instructed the inventory system to provide a rundown of the current status. If they'd chosen the outer planet, she doubted they would have started by now, so being halfway through was a real boon. At this rate, the Explorer ship would be fully resourced and running at maximum capacity by the end of the next day. Now the logistics were sorted, she could turn her focus to the long list of issues that were arising from the planet, ignoring the brooding human sat in the hold. A sulking Noah, bouncing a ball off the wall, rather than running over her initial concerns about the ionisation where Finn, and the rest of the squad, were right now.

Damn right, as Smith would say.

Yasuko gave up, compiling her list in priority order, knowing full-well that Noah was at the top whichever way she tried to work it.

"Okay. I can't keep away, I know what you said, but all 'giving you space' is doing is thickening the black cloud over your head," she said, appearing on the chair next to his, briefly pleased with her use of the idiom.

"Go away. Please."

"No. I tried that once, and I didn't like it. I can't focus on what needs doing while you are unhappy, depressed. I know it'll take time, and talking now won't immediately solve anything. But we need to start somewhere. You told Smith one thing, and then you gave me a different answer."

"Smith has his own problems."

"As do I – I have a minor identity crisis going on, which you might have noticed."

Noah missed the ball, his hand frozen in mid-air. He turned to face Yasuko, eyes welling. Yasuko desperately wanted to take him in her arms, make contact. Her entire 'life' as an AI had been built on distance from emotions, from the closeness social connection required. The Haven Scientists had been increasingly distant as they copied themselves across the centuries. And now, after conforming to her programming for so many years, she wanted nothing more than to hold a human in her arms.

What do these people do to me?

Yasuko formed the nanobot body, the trainer, and eased her hologram within. The shimmer of metallic feathers forming across her shoulders, her new sign of self-doubt in who she was. She took Noah in her arms, the sobs racking his body echoing off her metalled body. Yasuko's mind flickered, residual memories intertwining as she recalled the last few months amongst the emotional baggage that was her crew. Would she want to be without them now? Her friends? An answer was clear in her mind, but at odds with the growing awareness of her connection with Th'lgarr. A creature whose snippets of memories, coupled with his words, swirled within her. She needed to know.

Soon. A creature that drank life, whatever way you measure it. Am I that thing? How else could I know what it knew, see what it saw, have those words within me that affected S'lgarr so much?

Yasuko felt Noah's body calm, the sobs quieten. Sensors let her know his need for sleep, and her experiences of previous episodes of deep sadness suggested it should follow with some detailed work, when his mind would release tightly held emotions, allowing him to open up.

We have a few conundrums to resolve. Not least the manufactured virus that's affecting the Stratan, and that ionisation from the !Kora cove. Things we can get our teeth into. Another idiom!

CHAPTER 23

— I sing ...
— I sing but ...
— I sing but they ...
— I sing but they do ...
— I sing but they do not ...

— Listen
— Hear
— Respond

— Leave

CHAPTER 24

The Politico Building, Slabin, Capital City Of The Minoas Confederation, Northwest Minoas

"Anything?" General Hardrin squeezed the bridge of his nose, giving some relief from the developing migraine. He sat up in bed, hoping to give his brain further respite from the constant hum echoing around his skull. "From Yabbin?"

"No, General. It has only been a few hours. I woke you because one of those ships has landed close to Yabbin's position. If he's still inside the blackout zone, which communications indicate he is, then he won't be aware. If it's a strike ship, he may be in trouble," said Mwandin, eyes staring at the wall above the General's head, uncomfortable, and avoiding looking at the ill man sweating under the covers. She'd have much preferred this meeting where it should be, formal and in the conference room. But the General's ever-increasing paranoia denied her that, especially when it was in the middle of the night. Soon, she suspected, he would be reduced to conversing with only her. Maybe then she could get some much-needed changes into the decaying system.

Maybe. If there are any of us old timers left who can still think independently.

"What have we got available? Anything that can arrive in time to help?"

"The support vessel Khoe-San could drop a Marine detachment off the cove within thirty minutes. It would be dark then, ideal. Though Yabbin will be displeased after years of cultivating the *!Kora* for so long. He has been adamant that we should not interfere, their understanding of the world very simple, and gaining their trust full of complexities due to their rituals and blood rites."

"Do I care?" said the General, swinging his feet to the floor and rising. "I want that man in my hands, you understand. That is the main priority. That spaceship is the second. And Yabbin's precious mutants are at the bottom of that list. In fact, so low I never wrote them on it."

"Yes sir. At what strike level?"

"Fully open. If the ship is Stratan, they'll know anyway. And though Otegnoa no longer has the Council's ear, they'll be aware something's up by now and taking action. Time is precious. So why are you still staring at the bloody wall?"

Prime Minister Mwandin nodded, spinning on her heel and heading for the door. She reached for the handle, waiting for the General's usual last word.

"I want an extraction team as near to the Khoe-San as possible, Mwandin. As soon as Otegnoa's arse is on that vessel I want them on the way for pick up. No more delays, it is time," said the General, Mwandin nodding while she left. The General dropped to the bed, flipping open the silver locket on his chest. Powdered green crystal lay within. He knocked it out into the teacup at his side, refilling it with a solid stone from his bedside table drawer. The lump of rough, olive-green crystal, sat within the polished steel necklace with its top exposed. The General closed the clasp, the locket immediately beginning to vibrate, and the hum pitch reverberating in his head changing in line with it. The General let out a heavy sigh, sliding back into bed.

Otegnoa, I will so much enjoy the next time we meet.

CHAPTER 25

Hakunda Cove, North Coast Of
The Southern Continent

The Field Commander took a long, deep breath, large eyes bewildered by the blue-skinned alien within the upgraded armour, similar to that Alkinta wore for so many years. The alien had taken down one guard, rapidly tying the soldier up after the second fell to the other stranger. As Otegnoa scanned across, his sigh stopped, this one clearly an alien too. But not blue-skinned, nor wide of nose and large of eye. He'd seen the AI created versions of Earth humans, their ancestors, and one stooped in front of him, incapacitating the other soldier.

Did they make it? Three hundred years, and forty light years distant. Yet here they are, in the flesh. Was there hope?

The blue-skinned alien looked over; its face clearly metallic but features matching those of the Earth human. Its electronic eyes focussed on him, a flicker of movement indicative of it eye-clicking its HUD, much as the later models of the Stratan armour had been capable of. The alien walked over to him, the sharp knife slicing through his bonds and a hand held out to bring him to his feet.

Otegnoa flinched, the movement caught by the alien resulting in only a wry smile.

"I don't bite," said Smith. "I don't eat, for that matter."

The Field Commander reached up, accepting the gauntleted hand, allowing himself to be pulled up, legs and knees painfully arguing with him as age and the effects of his returning circulation hit him simultaneously.

Old age versus aliens, which is the biggest problem. Neither, where's Yabbin?

"I'm Smith, and that's Finn. He's the strong and not so silent type. We have come to rescue you."

"Smith," said Finn. "Chill. The man's just been through a kidnapping and met an alien. Two aliens."

"Aliens?" said Otegnoa. "From Earth?"

"Good guess," said Smith. "Yes, from Earth. But it's a long story. Let's just say we got here quicker than your Marines got to us. But it didn't go so well, less rescuing and more shooting."

"But you are here to help?"

"Probably," said Finn. "Though it'll depend on how and why. Make our losses at home less of a waste if we do. But we need to learn a little trust first, and evidence. We are definitely in the mood for evidence. You seem to have blown up your own world, and from what I know from Alkinta, potential nuclear devastation wasn't the reason why you were looking for Earth."

"Alkinta is here? With you? Is she okay?" said the Field Commander, eyes scanning Finn for any sign of trouble.

"A Fire Tick bite kinda changed how she acted, went a little crazy at their captain. She's had medicine from Yabbin's kit, but you need to check out it's the right stuff. With the mess she was in, I had to trust he was being truthful," said Finn. "My other squad member is with her, and the other Minoas now."

"A blue and green injection kit? They use the same colours as us, keeps it simple. For all the enmity going on, we all help each other with those bastard ticks."

"Then it should be okay," said Smith. "But we've got an awful lot of Minoas to babysit, Finn. Going to be a pain in the arse."

◆ ◆ ◆

Zuri checked on the Minoas' bonds, the high-quality cable ties still in place on feet and ankles, none of the soldiers able to manoeuvre so they could slip out – yet. If they managed it, then their dilemmas would grow in the light of the *!Kora* pyre that illuminated the head of the cove below them. Finn had wanted to check the rites out, but Zuri argued for restraint. The *! Kora* had not interfered so far, and she wanted to keep it that way. Besides, according to the information from Smith, Yasuko wanted them out of the area within the hour because of the ionising radiation.

On Finn's return, with two more Shadow Marines and the Field Commander in tow, Yabbin's mood changed significantly. The chat had ceased, the captain constantly looking anywhere but at Otegnoa. She knew Finn had picked it up, that man read body language so well when calm, and right now he was fully focussed.

Nyumba nzuri si mlango, fungua uingie ndani. A good house is not its door, open it and go inside. What is Yabbin hiding?

The Field Commander knelt next to Alkinta, the grey-haired woman's back leaning against the rock ledge. The sweating had stopped, though with her cheeks still red and eyes puffy, she was still struggling.

"It looks a bad one," Otegnoa said. "How long was the tick attached? How big was it?"

"About an hour," said Finn. "Maybe a little more. It was about this size." Finn picked up a stone, the size of a small walnut. The old man shook his head, eyes a little distant for a second.

"I need her in hospital as soon as possible. And the Minoas, as well. These are bigger than the ones we've seen recently, and we can't take the risk with the bacterial infection. At some point, I'm going to need to find a sample of the damn things. Will it never end?"

Finn turned to Smith, eye-clicking a message across, and receiving an answer quickly via data packet. The microship could fit the Minoas and Alkinta, but with the whole squad it'd be such a tight squeeze they were opening themselves up to potential trouble. The nagging concerns at the back of Finn's mind weren't helpful either, sowing doubt, and Smith had agreed with his assessment of Yabbin and the Field Commander. One glance to Zuri, and his mind was made up.

"You okay to watch these, Smith?"

"Yep," he replied, shifting the rifle into both hands and sending a huge grin the Shadow Marine's way.

Finn grabbed Yabbin's cable tied hands, lifting the man up easily as his servos kicked in. He led him over the crest of the darkening hill, the light rapidly dropping as the sun approached the horizon.

"This going to hurt?" asked Yabbin.

Finn gave no reply, pushing the man down to the ground and eye-clicking Zuri a quick message.

"You want Mehin treated, right?" Yabbin avoided Finn's gaze, eyes to the floor. Finn carried on, "Yes, you were worried about him before. You heard the Field Commander."

"I'm not giving anything but name and rank."

"You already let me know a few things, Captain. Beyond that. What's going on here?" Yabbin stirred the rock dust at his feet, head down as Zuri walked Otegnoa over the crest.

"Would you sit, Commander? Opposite Yabbin, and explain what's really happening," said Finn, Zuri behind him, arms crossed, rifle slung across her back. "I'm just a grunt, but I see what I see. You have two minutes before I decide no one can be trusted, pack my squad up and leave you and yours behind. Get me?"

Otegnoa glanced behind him, receiving a fierce Zuri smile in return. His mind quickly turning to Alkinta, another specialist in intimidation. He felt his heart give.

Will she forgive me?

 Otegnoa peered over at Yabbin, the Minoas captain looking up and giving him a nod of agreement. He sighed.

"Yabbin and I … we had a plan," he began, eyes downcast. "We have an area of mutual interest. I want the rewilding to succeed, to free our people from the cold and grow in number again. To achieve that we need food, space and time. The reseeding has worked, and Yabbin made contact a few years back, wanting to start it in the northern areas. Speed it up, rather than depend on any wind dispersal. It had to be, you know, under wraps. The Council would have said no after the vaccine debacle, and the Minoas likewise. Too much mistrust —"

"And downright paranoia," interjected Yabbin. "On both sides, but mainly mine."

"So, I've been syphoning off seeds for a few years, dumping them where I can or Yabbin has persuaded the *!Kora* to make a few raids in return for some of the Quai. For their religious rites. Up to now it's been bloodless."

"But not now?" said Zuri, thinking over Osineh's description of the attack on the fences.

"No. There's no way Alkinta would give over any of the Quai, or the cattle. She has lost too many Marines in skirmishes in the past. After Yabbin's raid for the vaccine she retired and took up a security role at the compound. Within two years she was overseeing resource management, in three we were married," Otegnoa stopped talking, the pain in his chest tightening as he finally let himself realise the risks he had taken.

"The Quai on the range are mainly sterile, a side effect of the process to make them immune to the Fire Tick bacteria," said Yabbin. "And the bulls have zero sex drive. Up to now, Alkinta's scientists have been unable to get them to produce enough hormonal signals and urges to even get an IVF programme to work successfully. We need the Quai and the cattle to ensure the rewilding works, to get the ecosystem in balance, and with their immunity, ensure the Fire Tick population doesn't kill it off before it gets going. They are an inhibitor to both the larger animals, and human repopulation."

"And you believe in this enough that you'd kill? Or allow your own people to die?" asked Zuri, arms stiff, fingers gripping her own biceps.

"There are lots of layers to this," said Yabbin. "But you said two minutes, and time is up. We both have a stake in what you decide next."

"Aye, you do," said Finn, looking towards Zuri as she eye-clicked a message over. Finn shook his head, not disagreeing, just wondering how the hell he got himself in these positions. He headed over the crest, showing Yabbin his rifle as he did so. "Wait there."

"Well?" said Zuri, her back to the prisoners.

"All fits. But I have zero trust of people that betray their own, whatever their motives."

"What do we do? Both are beginning to sweat up again."

"You go with Smith, take the Field Commander and the rest. Leave Yabbin with me, so they can't plan anything. Get them to a hospital, and the Minoas … well whatever their authorities want to do with them. Not our problem. According to that story, they know little to nothing about Yabbin's plan, so they were here to kidnap and kill without remorse. Then return to a designated evac point out of the blackout zone and pick us up."

"Shall I radio Noah and Yasuko too, see if he's made contact with the Stratan Council about the SeedShip data package?"

"Yep. You taken your vaccine?" asked Finn, Zuri nodded. "Good, me too." Zuri slipped her arm briefly around Finn's waist, pulling them both closer together before turning to find Smith.

Finn walked back over the crest, pondering his next step as he returned to a silent pair of traitors with a cause he could understand, but a method that gnawed at his sense of duty and loyalty.

What drives people like this?

CHAPTER 26

Kabbo Grass Plains, South Of Hakunda Cove

Zuri bundled the last Shadow Marine into the corner, threading the wire coil through each of their legs and arms. Smith ordered the few nanobots left aboard to absorb the metal ends into the wall. The show caused raised eyebrows and muted mutters, and Zuri's smile swiftly quietened even those. She slipped into the chair next to Smith, turning it round to face her prisoners as Otegnoa tended to the Fire Tick victims. The Field Commander had already set the destination and Smith lifted the microship from the ground.

"They'll have more awareness of what works for these bacteria, Smith. It's far better they go to their own hospital. By the time I've analysed it all, we could lose them. Their life signs are dropping too," said Yasuko.

"Commander," said Smith. "I need you to radio ahead, let them know we're coming." Smith brought up the medical sensor reading on the screen, instructing the limited AI to translate with the program he fed it. "Not looking good. And if Alkinta's reaction is anything to go by?"

"Yes," he said, nodding towards Zuri as she cable tied Mehin, then Alkinta. "I understand." He took the headset Smith proffered, adjusting the frequency.

Noah examined Yasuko's images. Blood samples and vaccines

were far from his speciality, but Yasuko needed to talk them through. Since taking on a human crew, and their general lack of scientific knowledge, the old Haven way of working was no longer viable. Beforehand, she simply furnished results and outcomes, with Haven scientists deciding causes and next steps. A data provider in the past, now she was her crew's analyst, and she argued that having a sounding board supported the process, the human brain having the flexibility and insight she currently lacked.

"You're saying this is human made, a synthetic virus with inserted genetic code that has mutated."

"Yes, or at least that's how it presents. Remember, this is a branch of genetics that the Haven were developing at a pace. They were using humans as conduits to adapt the environment for themselves, as it was culturally unacceptable that they were the carriers. Unclean if you will. So, my data banks have a vast store of processes and synthetic viral research, especially in relation to human biology."

"But why? It's madness to think this was deliberate. Who would?"

"My initial analysis shows the virus was a bacteriophage, aimed at killing the Fire Tick bacteria that infects the hypothalamus. But it was poor science, ill-conceived and probably poorly tested. Maybe a panic response. They used the wrong type of phage, leading to the virus mutating the bacterial strains and adding some of its own DNA. One of the major effects of the original bacteria is a massive reduction in male fertility, coupled with huge behavioural changes, depression, massive mood swings and violent behaviour as a consequence. Paranoia too."

"And the regular mutations?"

"It's what viruses do, survival of the fittest. Plus, added to the mix, will be some adaptations over time in the original bacteria the ticks transfer. They produce a vaccine; it stops the spread and then it flares again in a newly mutated form. I'd like to see the data on the frequency of large outbreaks. Though, with the massive reduction in population due to the nuclear war, any data set comparison will be difficult."

"Can we help? We don't know how much of this they already understand, and that small matter of a nuclear war in between is likely to have reduced their capacity to do anything about it."

"I can help. It's going to take some time, with proper testing. We aren't aware of their ethical standards, and we've only really considered the Stratan Council in this. There are other governments on the planet, too. They may or may not want our help. But this – this I know," said Yasuko. "It's what I was programmed for, the development of microorganisms in relation to human/Haven biospheres. But I'll need you, Noah. To navigate the human side of things -what causes the fear and panic, where their ethics lie, what I can test and do. If they know this was created by people, how will they feel about my involvement?"

"Especially if they find out you were part of the original SeedShip programme," said Noah. "My turn to be there for you. Uhi-dorro left a radio message a few minutes back, about us contacting the Stratan Council. If Zuri agrees, do we make a start?"

"I would like to, but she's the captain," said Yasuko, her feathers glistening in the ceiling's glow as she deliberately ruffled them. "And I'll put my feathers away for now. Human for the time being."

CHAPTER 27

Hakunda Cove, North Coast Of The Southern Continent

The ARILLS sight was not giving him any good news, the RIB bouncing over the gentle waves was heading directly for the cove from the small, frigate sized ship off the coast. He counted the black armoured Marines, four in all, and armed as Yabbin's crew had been. In the increasing absence of sunlight, they could well slip into the scrub and be out of sight before they landed. But he had Yabbin to take with him, and the Minoas Captain was not on his most trusted list. Better to stay and not reveal the microship's return point? Or, if he can make it out fast enough, radio them about the issue.

Damn.

The RIB passed by the red crystal, its form beautiful as the last vestiges of sunlight hit the structure, sending shards of cascading red light across the bay. The *!Kora* roared in union, the sound echoing off the cove walls, and answered by the rattle of gunfire as the RIB lit up under the glow of crystal refracted light. The ARILLS sight flared, the ionisation peaking and ruining the thermal and night vision tracking as the sight searched for the best image.

"If I recognise those sounds right, that's one of our boats with a Marine Sergeant showing the usual restraint of the Shadow Squads when faced with an unknown. Shoot first, shoot again, then shoot the survivors. Once complete, check who they are and what they were doing. An effective strategy that goes against everything I taught them." Yabbin banged his helmet against the rock behind him. "How many in the RIB?"

Finn thought for a second, the man's voice had a genuine combination of regret and frustration to it. But that didn't mean he couldn't fake it. He was special ops, and he knew just how much they put them through to cope with being captured. He ignored the captain, trying not to show any tension in his shoulders.

"So that's where we stand? Okay, if there's eight, we have a full-on assault. Four, and they've dropped half the squad off at a cliff face and they'll be trying to flank whatever they think they're after. Probably me. It'll be timed, so the climbing group is now at the top and covering their approach to the beach." Yabbin let out a sigh, heavy and entwined with emotion.

Finn turned round, flipping the man's visor down after checking the comms system, so similar to his own, was off. He reached down, lifting the man to his feet, and slicing the leg ties with his knife, hands then urging the captain forward, towards the scrub.

"Move," he said.

Yabbin turned, determined to give the Earth human his full glare when he caught sight of the movement on the eastern peninsula. Without his full HUD he couldn't be sure, but thirty years of combat training honed instincts. He threw himself to the floor, hitting the wrist control, and hoping the angry alien took the hint.

Finn had been waiting for something, it had been too easy so far. Growling, he reached down towards the place Yabbin lay when his mind caught on, a little late.

Damn.

The shot rang out, the whirring round glancing off his already damaged ceramic plate at his left shoulder, bruising the bone underneath, and carrying on through to explode against a rock behind him. Finn ducked down, rolling behind the rock ledge. He brought his rifle around, the ARILLS better here away from the main point of ionisation, and it was learning. The haze faded out, and it flicked through the spectrum, forming a more rounded picture. Finn picked out the blurred area where the sniper lay, and the three figures running along the rocks towards their position. He launched the grenade, subsequently bringing the SA80 down to fire a focussed burst towards the onrushing Marines, forcing them to ground. The explosion gave him hope, and Finn morphed his *weapon* to its usual form. If he'd learnt anything today, it was the stun weapon acted quickest on those in Stratan combat armour. Especially at close range. He quickly fingered his pouch, extracting a circular power disc and slapping it on the blue plaque where his thumb sat.

Wish I had one for this bloody shoulder.

Finn wanted desperately to check on Yabbin, but needed his HUD focussed on the approaching Marines. His weapon's sighting system not the same quality as the ARILLS, with the new data plaque still learning. He picked out the lead soldier, the black armour flickering as he crawled towards Finn. No doubt signalling to the two behind what he was doing. Finn fired, the explosive bullet slamming into the man's helmet, the enhanced round boring its way through the first layer before exploding, shattering the entire thing and penetrating the skull beneath.

Two down. Just the six to go.

He sensed the other two Marines flinch at the sound of their leader's death. Their armour flickered, his HUD giving him a rough direction and position. But Finn was short on time, unless the *!Kora* had put up more resistance than he expected. The second explosive round erupted from his rifle, the whirr of its approach enough to encourage the soldier into a desperate roll.

The shadow at the corner of his eye flickered briefly, the Minoas captain slamming into his side, sending Finn rolling over the edge of the rocks. Instinctively, Finn grabbed the man, grappling as he hit the first ledge, pulling his arms inwards to prevent any further strikes as they rolled and hit a second and third tier. Finn's armour absorbed everything except the shock running through his shoulder, with the initial wave of pain simultaneously sharpening his mind and kicking in an adrenaline surge. As they landed on the fourth ledge, Finn roared, on his back and facing the captain visor to visor. Finn lashed out, crashing the rifle into the soldier's helmet. Yabbin remained unmoved, absorbing the hit and pinning Finn's elbow down, his bound hands driving down on the joint with a power surge from his armour.

"Stop," shouted the captain, the muffled sound still audible beyond the visor as close as they were. "Stop." He rolled off, avoiding the swing from Finn, and on reaching his feet, raised his tied hands, palm outwards. Finn rose, his rifle pointed single handed towards him. "Stop."

Finn's finger tremored over the firing button, a sharpened mind battling the urge to kill his enemy. For now, the mind won. Yabbin had given up the advantage, could most likely have taken him down. Holding himself back, he watched as Yabbin thumbed his visor up, eyes scanning towards the crest while he spoke.

"A Shadow Marine got around the back, one of the team from below. Possibly two, hard to tell with no HUD. We need to move," said Yabbin, turning to face down towards the beach fifty metres distant. The pyre was raging, and the layer of bodies strewn nearby distressed him greatly. He knew none by name, they never spoke. But after years spent among them, a stir of pain rose, emotions he thought absent in his life. An affinity with a people who had found their place in the world, however … alien … it felt. But they were now trapped between two sets of armed professionals, ones he'd trained. Go down to the cove, and they were likely facing two or three soldiers. Up, probably three or four, and they'd have the higher ground. Eyeing the Earth human, knowing he'd be thinking through the same issues, Yabbin proffered his hands. Finn's shake of the head an exasperating but unsurprising response.

"You want to help? Play prisoner," said Finn, pointing down towards the cove. "If it's the Commander they want, then they may not shoot you to get to me."

"Oh, they will. I trained them, and the Prime Minister sends in the orders on the word of the General. Any sniff of doubt and I'll be target practice, as will you."

Finn grimaced, the pain in his shoulder lessening, but a numbness seeped in. Not a sign he liked. He needed to act now.

Be decisive. Having a prisoner is a burden.

"Stay here," he indicated the lower ledge. "If you want to help." Finn shot him, turning to pound down the slope as the stun bolt took effect. He didn't have long.

CHAPTER 28

Approaching Kaimas, Capital City Of The Stratan Council, Southern Continent.

Smith kept a check on the radar, setting the microship to calculate the air lanes as it analysed the data. He checked over the responses when they filed through, and satisfied the small AI was up to the job, let the ship run on autopilot for a while. The air traffic was low, reduced to a few high-flying jet aircraft, with propeller driven planes and helicopters operating as the land became progressively colder. In his mind, he had pinned the continent down to be much like Northern America, though devoid of the forests. Grass plains giving way to scrub bushes, then temperate, low-lying trees, regimentally planted in rows. The trees were clearly still young in places, and the small patches of green woodland soon ended when the microship reached low-lying hills. These were dotted with new settlements, away from the ruined remains of much larger towns and small cities that had suffered the same fate as Kabbo. Here and there, they passed over more intact conurbations, but as the light faded away, no lights spluttered to break the darkness. By the time the microship gave him a ten-minute warning of their impending landing at Kaimas, the frequency and size of the settlements had slightly increased. The visible road network was partially lit, and he noted the snow ploughs in constant operation to keep them open.

He let Zuri know how close they were, knowing she would be mulling over the choice to leave Finn behind. Personally, he would have trussed the Minoas Captain up and tied him to the roof. But he understood Finn's approach. The ship was massively cramped, the overcrowding putting Zuri on constant edge, fretting over the captives as well as Alkinta's health. Finn wanted to separate the two traitors, ensuring there was no possibility of concocting something to endanger the squad and their charges.

Cyborg Blue would take no crap from anyone. Kick some butt, crack some heads, and back home in time for tea and toast. Give me my minigun that goes all the way to eleven – this ethical stuff sure gets in the way sometimes.

The radio-link opened, "This is Kaimas Military Garrison calling Field Commander Otegnoa." Smith looked over to the Field Commander, the man struggling to keep his emotions in check with Alkinta so ill and the impending repercussions around his actions. Smith tapped his headphones, indicating to the Commander there was a call. Otegnoa stepped over his wife, swapping places with Zuri and taking the headphones.

"This is Field Commander Otegnoa, aboard the Earth spaceship. Come back," he said, the tone devoid of tension as his military training took over.

"We understand you have a Minoas Shadow Squad aboard. Divert to Kaimas Garrison, sir. We have an emergency medical unit on route, expected to arrive by the time you land. Sending beacon signal."

"Acknowledged. This spaceship has two Earth humans aboard, they will be leaving as soon as the prisoners and my wife disembark. Do not interfere. I repeat, do not interfere. They are returning to bring Captain Yabbin of the Minoas back to Kaimas."

"Acknowledged."

Smith looked over at the ageing man, his wrinkles deeper and eyes blacker than he remembered. A military man about to face an unwelcome fate for his betrayal, and the potential loss of his wife. Smith felt a flicker of concern, understanding touched his systems. Among all the potential reasons for his choices, Smith recognised a torn and troubled man.

Nothing Cyborg Blue can do to heal a soul.

"Coming in, Zuri," Smith said, checking the lay of the small city as its residual light and heat shone on the viewscreen, the snow piled high along the roads and paths between the mix of buildings. The falling snow swirled gently around the lights, minimal traffic cutting through the thin covering on the roads. If he squinted a little, he could be flying over Edinburgh in the winter. A pang of homesickness mixed his emotions up even more. One more Node jump and they'd be back on Earth, but was it still home to a metal man?

The ship's landing gear extended, with the AI shouting multiple warnings about target locks and laser painting on the hull. Smith acknowledged them all, making sure Zuri had sight of them.

"Nice to be welcomed," said Zuri. "They hit us with all that and we'll be fertiliser. Give me a line." Zuri ran through all the data, smiling to herself as she did so.

"This is Zuri Zuberi, of the British Space Commandos. Nice greeting, Stratan. You send a ship forty light years to find us, then when we arrive, you treat us like the enemy."

"Two," said the Field Commander behind her. "We sent two ships."

"Zuri and Smith have reached Kaimas," said Noah, his microship hovering next to Alkinta's compound. "She's agreed to us making further contact, though she warned us they are nervous."

"Yes. I don't think she liked their greeting. I have alerted Uhi-dorro that you have arrived, she is on the way out with her daughter and the other scientists. She states you have clearance to head for Kaimas and meet with the Stratan Council soon after," said Yasuko through Noah's helmet radio.

"Not sure this is really my thing, Yasuko."

"We are all engaged in actions that are new to us, uncomfortable if you will. But you have faced every challenge so far and succeeded."

"I can name one occasion when I didn't, and my electronic leg suggests another when it came close," said Noah, quickly flexing his toes, remembering his exercises. "At least I have Uhi-dorro to help with introductions. She has no family to return to, just her daughter. The Stratan lost so much in that war. It's hard to believe they recovered as they have."

"Humans are resourceful and survivors by nature," said Yasuko. *"Especially after Xxar and his Scientocracy genetically enhanced your characteristics."*

"All humans?" asked Noah.

"..."

CHAPTER 29

- I sing …
- I sing but …
- I sing but they …
- I sing but they do …
- I sing but they do not …

- Hear
- Respond
- Function

- Breed

CHAPTER 30

Hakunda Cove

Finn used his HUD to scan the areas to the west and east of the pyre burning on the crystal beach. The heat from the flames rendering his thermal sensors useless, and negating the benefits of the night vision, he enhanced the screen using the natural illumination. The dancing shafts of light refracting off the crushed crystalline beach scratched at his ragged nerves, the beauty of it in stark contrast to the bloodied remains strewn around the *!Kora's* ceremonial circle. Finn bit at his lip, trying to contain his anger at such a senseless killing. How could spears and rocks be a threat to armed soldiers in full armour? What had they achieved, except perhaps a little less hassle when they landed?

Murder, to be precise.

Finn swallowed some pain-relieving tablets, not much use now, but he was hoping to be alive long enough for them to kick in. Finally, he caught sight of the third Shadow Marine, striding back across the beach from Yabbin's cave. He threw the grenade, the explosive spiralling through the air to land between the two Marines guarding the RIB with a thud. They both reacted with impressive speed, diving for cover as Finn let loose, the stun shot taking the first guard as he hit the floor. The second missed, the soldier twisting to fire a bolt in Finn's general direction. It hit his rock cover, Finn ignoring it and releasing a third bolt to slam into the soldier's helmet.

The last soldier's round smashed into the rock by his hand,

the whirr of the explosive bullet grinding into the stone before it exploded, Finn throwing himself back as stone chips pinged off his armour.

Crap, these are good. Three above, probably making their way down right now and this one. Odds are not good.

Finn briefly scanned the direction he'd come from, the night vision adjusting now he was looking away from the pyre. They were on the move, the camouflage flickering in and out as they mixed sudden movements with covering each other. If he moved now, they'd have him. If he didn't, they'd be on him soon enough. His only advantage, possibly, was they didn't know where Yabbin was. Hopefully, the stunned man's camouflage would keep that secret a little longer.

Finn grabbed the flashbang, a brief image of Zuri wavering through his mind as he acted. The explosive landed ten metres in front of the approaching soldiers, thudding gently into the crystalline pathway. As the soldiers dashed forward, the timer clicked over. The intense flash and sound erupting, with Finn congratulating himself on a well-timed throw while making a run for the RIB as his next point of cover. The flash of an energy bolt surged behind him, the soldier on the beach letting fly. But then a second, third and fourth slammed into his back, throwing him into the side of the boat to bounce back and hit the ground, the hues of red light bouncing off his armoured plate as his mind shut down, closing him off from the pain.

The microship lit the grassy ground between the flowering scrub bush, Smith easing the engines down when it settled into its landing spot.

"No sign of Finn," said Zuri, tapping the viewscreen. "Something's up, he should be here waiting."

"Yep," Smith took his rifle from the rack on the wall, taking an extra power disc and slapping it on. "Time for Cyborg Blue to rescue his trusty sidekick."

"Eh?"

"Did I say that out loud?"

"You did. Cyborg Blue?" said Zuri. "Really?"

Smith slid the door open, his sensors kicking in and confirming the microship's readings. He stepped out, covering as Zuri joined him.

"Go ahead, superhero. You're on point," said Zuri, the smile at odds with the nerves railing her stomach. She attached her own additional power disc, expecting trouble. When was it ever anything else?

Finn should be here. What has Yabbin been up to?

Smith moved out, his electronic brain comparing data from his thermal and night vision sensors. Given enough time, he may even stretch the entire array to include the sound and motion capabilities he'd utilised as Finn's helmet. He just needed time to adjust and *evolve* the new body. Responding to Zuri's tension, he upped the pace, confident his sensors were up to the job.

◆ ◆ ◆

Everything hurts. Everything.

Finn's head spun, the world coming in and out of focus before realising his eyes were still closed and the flickering, orange light, shone through his eyelids. Attempting to open them, he found they were gummed up, the intense heat from the pyre drying them out with his visor up. Using the edge of his helmet, one eyelid cracked halfway open, an empty pouch finally coming into view a couple of metres from his head, laying on the floor next to his holstered sidearm. Reaching around with his arm, cable ties bit deep enough to shout through the pain in his back, informing him it was not going to happen.

And everything hurt.

Finn felt rough hands on his face, the four fingers digging into his eyelids and breaking the gummed seal. As the full light hit his eyes, Yabbin's blurred features slipped into view, a grim smile on his lips.

"Hurt?" he asked. "It's hell when you get shot in the back, you know. Especially when you're not expecting it." Yabbin tapped his visor and continued, "The visors adjust, we have magnesium grenades too." He dropped down to his knees, Finn's rifle in his hand, muzzle pointing to the floor. "Nice stun attachment, I'll have to get one myself." He reached behind Finn, slicing the cable ties with a wrist knife. "One chance, hope you can move. The two you stunned are still out and I can't take all four without a distraction. You need to roll and take up your handgun, aiming behind. Whatever you do, don't expose your back. Your armour's way tougher than mine, otherwise you'd be dead three times over. But it's useless now. On my mark."

Finn's eyes widened, his addled brain working through what Yabbin was telling him. His back disagreeing with the rolling idea.

"Mark," Finn moved, his back stiff and speed slow with the powered suit shutdown.

"Hey, he's loose!" Yabbin shouted, stepping sideways and away, the Marines responding rapidly to Finn's movement and the shout. Yabbin raised Finn's rifle, the stun bolts hitting the first two Marines who were grabbing their own weapons, the second pair standing up as the reality of Yabbin's betrayal hit home. Finn's sidearm fired, the lower-powered bolt glancing off their armour but serving as a distraction in the confusion. An energy bolt surged into the ground next to him, missing by a metre as Yabbin drained the additional power cell with two more stun rounds.

As the soldiers shook, Yabbin ran towards them, his wrist knife out and glinting red in the strange light emanating from the crystal beach.

"No," Finn croaked, his body shaking, pain setting his nerves on fire.

"We can't risk it," said Yabbin, raising his knife to plunge into the Marine's neck. An energy bolt slammed into his shoulder, the pulse surging through his body, and the knife dropped from numbed fingers. Yabbin followed it to the ground, a second stun bolt in such a short time too much for his body and mind to cope with, blacking out.

"No way," shouted Smith, "that Cyborg Blue is going to allow murder when he's around." Smith walked into the light thrown by the still burning pyre, armour glowing orange and red. Zuri sped past him, checking the two previously knocked out Marines before cable tying them.

"We need shares in those," Smith said. "Or just shoot a few instead to save on the plastic. Not good for the environment you know." He walked over to Yabbin, nudging him with his toe. "Especially this one."

"He did just save me," croaked Finn.

"Did he?" said Zuri, walking over and checking on Finn's eyes. "I think he may have been preventing anyone from finding out he was a traitor. If you'd died first, well he was in the clear. If you didn't, then he took them down, and no one was the wiser." Zuri moved from examining his head to check his back, fingers probing the bare, bruised and singed skin beneath.

"Oh crap," she said, suddenly rising and stepping back, eyes dancing in the refracted light. She scanned the floor, searching. There was movement everywhere, the shafts of red lights flickering in and out as the crystals appeared to shift and move in ripples. "Fire Ticks, Finn. You have three attached to your back. You need to move, now. Head for the edge of the sea.

They're everywhere, the beach is seething with them."

Finn moved, despite the pain, his wretched body quivering at the thought of the things burrowing into his skin. He stumbled towards the sea, the crunch of crystal and tick echoing beneath his boot.

Zuri, visor now down and sealed, searched the Minoas for their first aid kits, Smith making sure each soldier's armour was fully sealed as she worked. He saved Yabbin for last, then dragged him towards the sea, wanting him close by.

Finn sat down among the lapping waves, eyes on the floor as he watched twenty of the ticks turn round and head back to the beach when they encountered the water. Mentally, he was urging Zuri to hurry. His brain not allowing any other thoughts other than the ticks sucking his blood, their bodies expanding and exchanging it for the bacteria that had sent Alkinta over the edge. He shuddered, darkness pressing at the edge of his mind. The smell of the pyre, the heat of the flames assailed his senses, and he felt the old fear rise from the pit inside his head. It had been a while since the darkness had pressed in when awake, but the smell of napalm and burnt flesh filled his nostrils.

Must not think on it.

Zuri returned with two med kits, extracting the tool and getting to work. Finn held himself still, forcing muscles to hold against the shivers running down his spine. He couldn't feel anything, his back had been through far too much to sense the tool against his skin. Zuri talked to him the whole time, asking what had happened since they had left, letting Finn recount in as much detail as he needed to distract himself. Finished, she let him explain the medicine shots, using the one designed for the bites as best she could with the Fire Ticks latching on within the same patch at the base of his spine.

While Zuri worked, Smith checked and tied each of the Minoas Squad, the ticks swarming over their armour, sensing the carbon dioxide the filters exuded. Unable to find the warmth and a lack of bare skin to attach to, each Fire Tick lost interest, crawling down to the crystal beach and scuttling for cover. Smith searched through what he knew about those from Earth, enough to tell him they would look for grass patches to wait for their next meal. He marked a warning about the cove on his data map, and with sensors fully up, moved over to the inner circle of *!Kora* riddled with the bullet holes from the second Shadow Squad.

Smith stopped at the edge, scanning the pyre and noting the bodies burning on a collapsing platform within it. Yabbin had mentioned blood rites, and Smith recorded what he saw for Yasuko and Noah to interpret. He moved on, turning over the body of a male *!Kora*, the blotchy skin peppered with bullet holes near his heart. Across his chest and up over his face, the man had embedded red crystals, skin cracked and dry around them. Smith reached down, his sensors indicating one crystal was moving, and he pulled at it, the skin bulging, and out skittered five smaller ticks. Smith stepped back, dropping the crystal to land among the rest on the beach. His mind ordered his stomach to heave, the bodily response strange and confusing electronic systems briefly before being closed down. The other crystals across the chest began to rise and fall, the motion sickening and the thoughts of what lay underneath forcing Smith to move back further. Sensors homed in on the ticks, and as he scanned the ring, they noted the same movements among more of the *!Kora*. Smith, holding a non-existent breath, turned over another of the corpses, choosing one his sensors showed as inactive. This corpse had lost all its crystals, the holes larger, and one tick's head slid out, easing out a blood-filled sack that wobbled behind it as it reached the surface skin.

Cyborg Blue decides to take a rain check, possibly reporting to his squad leader and absolving responsibility as fast as possible.

Smith returned to the sea edge, Finn now standing, though a little unsteadily, as Zuri packed away the first aid kits. Yabbin still lay at the edge of the sea, apparently unconscious, gently sprayed by the lapping waves.

"Err, you're going to love what I just saw," he said.

CHAPTER 31

Hakunda Cove

"We need to go, now," said Zuri, hands on hips and eyes flashing red, reflecting the pervasive light from the beach. "You have been here too long with the ionisation, and you've had ticks attached."

"Not for long, you said they'd hardly fed," replied Finn, massaging his thighs, desperate to repeat it on his back, hoping the pressure would block out the pain. Then his shoulder kicked in, and he gave up.

"Even so, no risks. We have no idea how any bacteria will affect us. We go now."

"Five minutes. Get a sit rep on this place," said Finn. "We need to know what's going on."

Zuri sighed, she'd expected him to ask for ten and take fifteen. It'd do. She glanced up at Smith, the blue-skinned face flinching as he guessed what came next. She raised an eyebrow, and he nodded back. They'd been together as a team so long now; it was becoming second nature.

Clocks ticking. By the numbers.

"Smith, can you and Zuri take the buildings," said Finn. "Scan and record, we get Yasuko to help with analysis later. But get a sense of how it feels, she won't pick up on whether this was a cover or front for Yabbin and his crew. You know the drill, same as in Afghanistan: does it feel false? We did more by instinct back then."

"Aye," said Smith. "On it." Ignoring the corpses, they sped off, focussing on the houses clustered by the eastern edge of the beach, built out of the path of prevailing winds. They covered the fifty metres rapidly, eyes on the doors and any side windows they could see, each rammed with a clear crystal. They passed racks of strung up nets, and behind a second row of sturdy shelves containing drying fish. Zuri noted the line and tackle laying at the side, with multiple footprints and discarded twine around the work stools. Buckets stood, the water fresh and clean, and warm firepits smoked with scorch marked cookware swaying gently on the breeze.

Smith reached the first door woven from the scrub bush branches, it was light and hinged with twine from stripped bark. Zuri stood at the side, her back against the wall as he opened it. His sensors scanned the space. Clear of the funeral pyre, thermal showed little of concern and on going in, he engaged night vision. The room was clear of life, but felt lived in. Everything cared for, well-used but extremely basic. Just two rooms, yet clean, and a place for everything.

A home.

"Clear," he said, moving out and repeating the procedure on two more dwellings before calling it, heading back along a well-worn trail to the pyre where Finn stood. Zuri knew his body language, despite the injuries. At his feet lay the corpses of four children of various ages, eyes vacant.

Wapingapo fahali wawili, ziumiazo ni nyasi. When two bulls fight, it is the grass that suffers. These !Kora were in the way of the Minoas, and now they are not.

Zuri slipped her arm gently around the Lance Corporal, bringing him close enough for a little comfort, hoping Smith had read the signs. His silence showed he had.

"We must go now," she said.

Finn nodded slowly, eyes scanning the circle of dead. "The

kids have no crystals, just the adults. Smith, can you put some of the ticks in here?" Finn handed him the empty canteen.

"I hate to say it," said Zuri, eyes sliding over the children and onto the adult corpses, "but we may need to take some of the *!Kora* with us. For analysis."

Finn nodded, "But sealed. No chances, we survive first. Is there anything on the microship that'll do the job, Smith?"

"Yeah, but I'm not keen. These things make my metal skin crawl. Smith most certainly isn't at the wheel."

CHAPTER 32

The Politico Building, Slabin, Capital City Of The Minoas Confederation, Northwest Minoas

Mwandin let out a heavy sigh on entering the conference room, knowing full-well the meeting would not go well. But then again, did they ever when Yabbin was involved?

"The Khoe-San reports the landing party have not responded to any semaphore signals for thirty minutes, General," she said, choosing to stand while the General ate. "Out of standard procedural timelines."

The General continued to chew at the plain food, looking up at his Prime Minister with hooded eyes. He swallowed. "I know the procedure, Mwandin. I bloody wrote it. And Yabbin?"

"Nothing sir. The ship's captain reports the Shadow Squad engaged in gunfire and energy bolts on the way in, but no reciprocation. Only later was there any response, on the cliff edges and again in the cove below. He recorded what they could see with the help of the *!Kora's* fire." Mwandin pushed the memory stick into the wall hung viewscreen controls, engaging the recording.

They both watched the silent recording, the *!Kora* falling to the wave of energy and bullets as the Minoas Marine approached the beach, the picture hazed and pixelated by the ionising radiation but clear enough. As the mission proceeded, and night fell, radiation fogged much of anything else, only the sight of vague figures and brief combat could be discerned.

"I'll see if the tech team can clean the picture up," said the Prime Minister. "If I am okay to divert the resources."

"Granted," The General dropped his knife and fork, pushing away the half-eaten plate of processed fungi. He pressed his fingers into the bridge of his nose, squeezing hard to push the waves of nausea away. "Suggestions?"

"I am bereft, General. If the Field Commander remains at the cove, then you could choose to lay waste if you feel it is worth the political risk. But the satellite showed the spaceship leaving and heading off in the direction of Kaimas before returning later."

"So, he's already gone, or was never there if Yabbin failed. I swear that boy has his own agenda."

"Boy? Maybe to you, General. But he is the Captain of the Shadow Marines and acted against your orders. Again." Mwandin pursed her lips, waiting for the barb to poke at the General's paranoia. She didn't have to wait for long.

"Are you questioning my decisions, Mwandin? Now, of all times?"

"It was on the list of requirements when you took me on. If you want me to always agree, then I will do so by your order. Otherwise, I am here to advise and act on your wishes, as well as liaise with the Politico," Mwandin bristled, partly the nerves kicking in, but partly tired of always having to play the game with the old man. The tech team were running out of the Peridot he relied on, the quality of the gemstone still available poor for meta-development and adaptation. If the bacteria overwhelmed him before they found more, well, they'd need another leader.

Or we won't if his paranoia grows to where his need for revenge overcomes any common sense.

The General stood, hands astride his plate at the table, fingers quivering as they pressed into the marble top. His eyes roamed over Mwandin, evaluating her as he automatically did whenever anger rose, looking for the weak points, assessing her as an enemy.

Mwandin refused to flinch, eyes on the old man, ignoring the searching analysis as best she could. The sweat at her armpits professed a lack of success.

How powerful a presence must he have been before succumbing to the bacteria? No wonder he held our people together when others failed.

"We wait," he said finally. "We wait and see if we get any response from the Council. And I want your spies on this, Mwandin. They are our eyes and ears right now. I need information on the Field Commander, and the fallout from the operation. Clear?"

"Crystal clear," said Mwandin, spinning on her heel and letting a sigh slip from her lips.

CHAPTER 33

— I...
— I need ...
— I need to ...
— I need to know

— More

— Change
— Adapt
— Breed

— Listen

— Leave

CHAPTER 34

Kaimas Military Garrison, Kaimas, Capital City Of The Stratan Council, Southern Continent

Noah sat still, running through a checklist in his mind, the microship's engines easing off, landing complete. Lifting his chest, and squeezing in his stomach, he stood up, trying to hold back the wave of nausea and vertigo.

From the lecture room to the barrack room. And now First Contact. Hate this.

Noah removed the armoured suit's helmet, Finn always drumming home the importance of eye contact and body language when dealing with unknown people. Placing it under his arm, he practised his smile while approaching the door, the resupplied nanobots creating the exit for him. Noah stepped out, the party waiting outside a mix of military and suited politicians. And then it clicked.

They look as nervous as me! Rabbits in the headlights.

Noah raised his hand, palm out, and deciding against Smith's usual greeting, he stepped forward.

"Hello from Earth," he said. "I'm Noah, pleased to meet you."

Damn that went well.

A woman stepped forward; her woven robes beautifully cut in shades of grey slid aside as she raised her hand, mimicking his. The wrinkles at the corner of her eyes betrayed an age her eyes didn't show, and Noah suddenly felt under examination.

But not threatened.

"How do you greet each other, on Earth?" she asked, a smile touching her lips.

"We either salute if we are military, or shake hands if we are not. Some cultures bow, but not mine, unless it is in polite response to another."

The female politician held out her hand, "Then I welcome you to Stratan, Noah. I am Lead Councillor Abioyi. We are pleased to have you and your compatriots here, though times have changed since we sent out our ships. And not for the better. I must ask whether you have any Stratan with you? The Marines?"

Noah sucked in his lips; the question he'd dreaded coming. "No. I'm afraid their arrival on Earth was … inappropriate? We had no SeedShip, and they were aggressive when they woke from your cryotubes. However, they activated our Haven Explorer ship, and we have been travelling the anomalies these past few months trying to find a way home. But," Noah sucked in a breath before continuing, "we can offer help. Yasuko, our AI if you will, has a data store from another SeedShip we discovered that we are happy to share. And she is an expert in genetics, especially related to viral and bacterial development." Noah looked to the floor as he finished, hoping it was enough of a carrot. He glanced up, the politician's sharp eyes glistening, the smile a little broader.

"Then you are welcome, Noah. Doubly so. We are in desperate need."

Yasuko reaffirmed the stock levels, pleased with the progress and assessing her possibilities. Right now, she was at eighty percent capacity. She could leave the mining operation to work independently, feed the communication lines through the moon base systems to keep a track and possibly upgrade or replace the AI with her own algorithm. The ship had not been built for battle or the relentless hard flying they were putting it under, and the constant need for mining reflected a resource hungry system the Haven had accepted as efficient enough for the role it played. It was designed as a flying laboratory, to visit, land and analyse each planet at a time. Not to battle hostile aliens or batter its way through an atmosphere like on Bathsen.

Time to contemplate a redesign, maybe. Use some of those metamaterials for a different purpose. Starting with the shields and hull.

Yasuko allocated one data bank to analyse the possibilities, and with an afterthought, added the option of armament for the ship. Not that she'd be letting the crew know until she was sure it would be of use, and Noah had worked through the plans.

Once that was up and running, she split off a part of her to integrate into the moon base systems. The independent program built the links she needed between the mining vehicles and the nanobots including rebuilding the base communication array into a more efficient system.

"Yasuko," called Noah. "Knock, knock."

"Hah, hah. Just don't follow it with one of Smith's awful jokes. How is it going?" she said, a little on edge with what they had proposed. Her drive to help her crew, and the people they encountered, causing a thrill of excitement she barely recognised.

Is this how humans feel when the adrenaline hits? When they cannot hold back?

"They are more than receptive to the idea of us helping. I'm not sure they understand what you are," he replied.

"And I am, Noah? I think I have barely scratched the surface after intervening with S'lgarr."

"Granted. Anyway, they want as much help as we can provide. On first look, they have older, pre-war data sets, and more scant recent analysis that will help with the initial research into the mutations. I think if we go for a joint effort, a working team of specialists, then things would be much smoother."

Yasuko paused, her mind reeling as she contemplated Noah's words. The second rush of new emotion swept over her, one laced with fear and apprehension. She found it difficult to speak, paralysed of thought.

"Yasuko? You there?"

"Yes. Yes, Noah I am here. A group of scientists from Stratan? What … what would my role be?"

"Damn… there are times I forget myself, Yasuko. Not thinking before I speak. If you can demonstrate your knowledge, then you'd be leading the team. Chief Scientist if you will. Their major focus has been on the Quai programme, overcoming the Fire Tick bacteria in their animals. Crossover human research has gone on, focussed on prepping for the next adaptation to the vaccine should the bacterial strain mutate, or Brain Fever evolve once again. But not on eradicating it."

"Chief Scientist? Me? Are you sure?"

"You lead they follow. If there's any chance of ending the cycle, they are in. And the Stratan Marines will have accomplished their mission, too. Seems we will have come full circle."

"So, they will follow *my* instructions. Do as *I* say?" Yasuko felt the tension in her words. Over the last few months, she had learnt to be valued, not only accepted, but a part of the crew. Cared for, and dare she say it, loved. And she reciprocated, despite emotion being a relatively new concept in her own systems. Yasuko regarded her actions on Nutu Allpa as a demonstration of how far past the Haven Convention shackles she had come.

But to be in charge of others?

"Yasuko?" queried Noah. "You've gone quiet again. Is something wrong?"

"No," she said. "I think something is very *right*."

PART TWO

CHAPTER 35

Explorer Ship, Kaimas Military Garrison, Kaimas

The sweat-stained pillow slid to the floor, hitting the polished concrete with a wet thump. Finn's head still shook from side to side, his mind lost, unaware. Fever creased his brow, sweat pouring from his neck and below the eyes with heat raging in his brain. No darkness within, just a constant fire that burned with anger and hate, railing at the loss of something unknown, stressing his brain in a biochemical maelstrom. His eyelids sprung wide open, staring straight ahead, arms reaching out, pushing away the shadow of *threat* overwhelming his senses.

Yasuko urged the nano-arms forward, metal limbs wrapping a spring belt across Finn's upper torso, locking him down before administering the medicine into his neck. Zuri watched alongside Yasuko, eyes searching Finn for the improvement she'd been assured was happening.

"I know it looks worse, but the Stratan antibiotic is working and the adaptation I've made should speed up the process. It should kill off the bacteria in his hypothalamus, and we should see rapid improvement over the next three days. Analysis shows it has spread no further within the brain, or to the spinal fluid, at levels the antibiotic can't deal with." Yasuko sighed, turning to Zuri, wanting to take her hand. "He'll recover. But these bacteria spread through the body so quickly. I saw something like it on Earth. The ticks there, though, were so much smaller and the bacteria transfer much less."

"Is this the result of Haven meddling? Adapting humans to

ensure the biosphere is ready for them?" asked Zuri, her gaze remaining on Finn while his head rocked again.

"I will look deeper, but my first thought would be no. I need to check the *samples* you brought in with you, break down the data and work from the current position. And get a better understanding of the human population's medical data as well, to cross-reference everything."

"You do know that there's water buffalo on this planet, and cattle. They look very much like they do on Earth, Yasuko. Scarily so. There were times out there when I could have been in a colder version of Africa," said Zuri as she turned to leave, her brow furrowed and arms crossed, with hands dug into her arm pits.

"Really? I don't understand that ..." Yasuko paused, her mind rushing through surface data about the human-seeding programme. "There's nothing in my system on that, but I could do with knowing more. Each Explorer Ship was assigned to a different planet, and the seeding tailored to planetary circumstances."

"You focus on Finn, and then the Brain Fever research. Smith and I will gather what information we can from local sources. Finn first, yes?" Zuri glanced back, receiving an affirmative look from Yasuko that she desperately needed. "And I'm okay to go helmetless? We're going to be here some time, I feel."

"Yes. There's always some risk that you will pick up something, but the boosters should provide a level of immunity. Keep the medical monitors attached, and if you experience any signs of feeling ill, come and see me immediately. Even for a head cold. The same goes for all of you."

Zuri walked out of the med-lab; her usual grace marred by the stress running through her body. The emotional imbalance caused by arriving on Stratan, marred further by Finn's reaction to the Fire Tick bacteria, and in a stranger way, by the senseless deaths of the *!Kora*. Nothing they had encountered posed a targeted threat towards them, more the circumstances of what they got caught up in, which, considering their inability to walk away, was not a surprise. But Zuri's survival instincts were making their presence known, she felt ill at ease and wary. There was a sense of the unknown prodding at her defences.

Akili ni mali. Knowledge is wealth. And I need to start somewhere.

Zuri walked down the hold ramp, turning left to be met by the rapidly forming laboratory building the Stratan Council were building next to Yasuko's ship. Noah stood at the edge of proceedings, hands on hips, a large smile spread across his face while he directed the newly arrived equipment to storage areas. He turned, eyes sparkling, and waved at Zuri before speaking to one of the builders and subsequently walking over.

"How is he?" Noah asked.

"Hot, fevered. But Yasuko says he's fighting it off. It'll need a few more days, possibly three to be sure, but the signs are positive. How's the prep going?"

"Quickly. I think they are taking our arrival as a sign of hope. Got my fingers crossed we can live up to it. And they know their stuff. The lab equipment they've brought rivals some of Yasuko's and their data retrieval programme has to be applauded. With all that radiation and EMP flying around from the nuclear war, you'd have thought more would have been lost."

"Millions – maybe billions – died, Noah. With all that knowledge, how can that have happened? And the larger animals and plants too, just incinerated or irradiated. And for the survivors, decades in the cold and the dark by the sound of Minoas. Madness." Zuri kicked the floor, finally recognising the cause of her unease.

"I – I don't know what to say, Zuri. I ..."

"Sorry, Noah. But think about it. *!Nias* and his crew risked the void of space, the possibilities of dying in a cryotube, or worse, and 300 hundred years on ice, only for the people he was trying to protect to blow themselves bloody up. We are here because of that, and lost our friends, and more. For what?" Noah flinched, the venom in Zuri's eyes unseen since the day she'd challenged the Companies on Vai.

"We don't walk away, Zuri. We help, it's what we do. You said that – what is the point of having the ability to help if we choose not to? Should we not stand for what is right, even when it hurts?"

"*Adui wa mtu, ni mtu*, Noah. The enemy of man is man, and Stratan is a painful example of that. Carry on, help them, on my order as captain. Get the lab set up, help Yasuko with the politics and nuances of humanity. Be Noah and make a difference. But don't forget how it got like this in the first place." Zuri spun on her heel, shaking as she walked, desperately needing a focus. She set off in search of Smith.

CHAPTER 36

Kaimas Military Garrison, Kaimas

Cyborg Blue stares into the eyes of his enemy, trying to penetrate down into the depths of his soul. What has this man done? How low did he go? Will anybody think less of him if he tweaks his crooked nose and pokes him in the large eyes?

Probably.

"Are you going to stare at me all day? Or can I get some downtime? It's been a busy few weeks, and it's tiring being a traitor to your own country," Yabbin said, trying to keep the sneer from his voice, and failing badly. The blue man was unnerving, setting him on the defensive without a single question being asked. Yabbin glanced up towards the Stratan Marine standing against the wall and then the supposed Council member sat at the blue man's side. He didn't know her name, but the piercing eyes and crappy demeanour shouted military intelligence, where the clothing did not.

"Captain Yabbin, you stand accused of assaulting a peaceful facility and murdering members of its security team. Do you have anything to say on this?" said Shante, the given name of the woman at Smith's side. "This Earth … human then bore witness to you attempting to murder your own squad members. Again, anything to add?"

"I'm not talking until I get someone from the Council in this room, and preferably with Otegnoa present. None of this will make sense otherwise." Yabbin crossed his arms, dropping his head and shutting down from the interrogation. By reputation, the Stratan were not into torture, but reputations can be broken. Especially when his own people would likely do the same, should he be returned to Minoas.

It's going to hurt, but I knew that beforehand.

Smith stared at the man, his electronic mind filtering through the events and recorded images involving Yabbin's squad. He held little doubt the Shadow Marine was guilty of it all, but Yabbin had already given Finn the only reason that fitted. He hated what the captain had done, but everything he'd heard since arriving in Kaimas affirmed the difficulties in Minoas. Smith prodded his white teeth implants with the false tongue he didn't really need, working through the possibilities.

And Cyborg Blue takes a measure of the soul he finds behind those eyes and finds it wanting.

Shante shuffled the papers and photographs in front of her into a neat pile, glancing up at Yabbin before scraping her chair back and rising. Smith copied, aware that he was only allowed in the room to corroborate events. Politics. He followed her out of the room, to find Zuri pacing the concrete corridor outside, much to the annoyance of the soldier guarding it. Zuri looked to Smith like she was spoiling for a fight, and mentally crossed his fingers that the guard kept quiet.

Shante bid goodbye to Smith, surprisingly warm to him despite his appearance, and nodding towards Zuri, headed off to report to the Council.

"Well?" asked Zuri.

Smith flinched internally at the tight tone; it was worse than he expected. "Nothing. But I wouldn't talk in his shoes either. His gamble failed, and now he's stuck between two countries baying for his blood. He gets to be locked away in the dark, hoping to be forgotten. But Otegnoa won't get that luxury, and when Alkinta recovers, he'll have even more to worry about. She reminds me of you." Smith flashed her a smile.

"Thanks. I'll take that as a compliment." Zuri sagged, the tension easing off just a little. "They won't be letting us in on that interrogation, I'm surprised you were in on this one."

"I have recorded evidence of his acts; I was just a physical manifestation of his guilt. He got it. Come on, let's find somewhere quiet and set a plan of action for the next few days, and you can tell me how Finn is." Smith reached out his hand, taking his old friend's arm as he led her out of the corridor and on towards the open garden near the main building.

Zuri let a little more tension fade at the touch, despite the sadness she felt at his cold, metallic skin. A result of the Stratan incursion that had brought such pain yet raised the squad to where they could make a real difference in the lives of others.

More conflict.

"Okay Corporal," she said, sitting on the only dry bench in the garden, parked inside an island of cleared snow. "Noah and Yasuko are caught up in the lab's construction and their research into the Brain Fever. We, on the other hand, need to find a focus. We need to know about the Council's relationship with Minoas, and why Yabbin and Otegnoa were driven to betray their own sides, and for Otegnoa, people he loved. And why we have water buffalo forty light years from Earth. Which one do you want to take?"

"Ah thanks, Zuri. Just what I wanted, an investigation. Cyborg Blue will take the animals, you get the humans – far too complicated a species for me."

CHAPTER 37

Kaimas Military Garrison, Kaimas

"Okay, ask away," said Lead Councillor Abioyi.

"I'd like access to someone who can run through the history of Stratan for me. I want to gain some insight, connect the dots between what we know from the Haven seeding and what happened here, afterwards," said Zuri, allowing a small smile to show her gratitude, despite the weight of Abioyi's regard.

"Yes, I can arrange that. Perhaps, I can help initially, set you on the right track maybe," said Abioyi, bringing out a tablet from a drawer in the grey-metal desk she sat at. "I take it you recognise one of these? I can let you have one with some access limits, I'm sure you understand why. But let's start with a bigger picture."

Abioyi ran through the recorded history, starting with the original oral stories handed down from generation to generation, forming a major religion that soon splintered into multiple interpretations and factions. Most of this related to a 'beginning', when humanity simply started, appearing from nowhere, the animals coming into existence alongside them. As knowledge grew, and curiosity led to the discovery of deeper mathematics and the evolution of science, their progress very much aligned with Earth's development, though at a faster rate with their 'dark ages' occurring in more recent times as humanity fractured.

Deeper investigation of humanity's origins clearly pointed to the old stories having a ring of truth, there was so little evidence of humans evolving on Stratan. And as science explored further, it became clear that neither had much of the larger fauna they encountered. About five hundred years ago, two hundred years prior to *!Nias* leaving for Earth, caches of ancient bones were discovered. None of these matched the animals they knew and could not possibly have been their ancestors. Their evolutionary pathway would never converge with that of the current animals that they tended or roamed the planet. This sudden emergence of new species stumped everyone until they pieced together the oral evidence handed down from person to person over the millennia, and the theory of colonisation developed.

"But why no animals? Or at least larger ones?"

"There are multiple theories around that. Some form of catastrophic event, perhaps. Many of the discovered remains were found together, a mix of species, but in their thousands. Very few signs of violence, including teeth and claws, have been found. To all intents and purposes, they simply died. Maybe a meteorite strike? Or an atmospheric disruption. The smaller species mainly survived the event, whatever it was."

"I recognise the larger animals I've seen here, from Earth. No other planet we have visited had our animals, just an evolved human population. Adapted to the conditions as your people have," said Zuri, shifting in her chair. "Will I have access to a catalogue of animals on the tablet?"

"Yes, though some species have not been reintroduced since the nuclear winter. The conditions are not there yet, the diversity of plant life is too low. But we have many of their embryos in cold storage, ready for when we can. You know of the Fire Tick programme; we will need to alter the animals' resilience to the bacteria, especially – according to our scientists – as it constantly mutates into new forms. We just don't understand how it does it so fast, or for that matter, why. Most successful bacteria, and viruses mutate to a point where the host survives, otherwise it soon runs out of hosts to infect. This isn't happening." Abioyi looked to the tablet, her eyes distant, lost.

Zuri reached a hand out on impulse, unable to stop herself despite the distance she felt from the Stratan. Midway, she expected the Lead Councillor to pull away, but instead the woman placed her own hand on top as Zuri's rested on her arm.

"The ticks became an issue as our population grew, spreading across the planet. The more animals we bred for food, the greater our towns and cities became, the more Fire Ticks appeared, and their variants evolved. It became a blight, the bacteria infecting the animals in greater and greater numbers. The more the infections appeared in humanity, coupled with the mental and physical issues it caused, the greater our need became. Birth defects began to appear, and there were theories that the bacteria had inserted itself into some of our viruses and on into our genome." Abioyi raised her hand, to Zuri's surprise it sported four fingers and a thumb. "The Marines we sent were all related to each other, it made the tuning of the cryotubes simpler, even on the second ship. I understand from the records they all had four digits?" Zuri nodded.

"So you found the SeedShip, and after it self-destructed, you used what you found to head for Earth?"

"Not quite. We applied what we found as best we could after breaking in. The Minoas used the fragments of genetic and viral knowledge to construct a bacteriophage. The antibiotics had stopped working completely, the bacteria strains becoming resistant to those we had. Previous experiments with bacteriophages had seen partial success – these viruses kill bacteria – so with the extra knowledge they put everything into its development. Initial trials were a triumph, so they released it into their population. But something went horribly wrong, somehow a temperate phage had got involved, either by the bacteria's response or potentially a deliberate act. The virus took on some of the bacteria's DNA rather than killing it, and boom, the virus spread from person to person, affecting similar strains of the bacteria already latent in the human population, including those humans who previously had proven resistant. The infection spread rapidly, the symptoms of heightened anger, mood swings, male sexual impotency and sterility had massive implications that humanity could not deal with. Paranoia rose, the Minoas being blamed for what happened, riots, mini revolutions, wars. The worst of humanity all magnified. That's when we sent the first ship, more as a sign of hope than anything else."

"I can't claim to know anything about viruses and bacteria, Councillor. But you are talking about a double hit. The initial Fire Tick bacteria and a new virus that heightened its potency and ensured it affected those with higher resistance? With the same symptoms?" Abioyi nodded, her hands now steepled in front of her, her chin resting on the tips. Zuri continued, "And you topped that off with a nuclear war? Why did the Minoas do that?"

"The Minoas? No. We started the war. The first nuclear strike was ours."

CHAPTER 38

Explorer Ship, Kaimas Military Garrison, Kaimas

(Four Days Later)

Yasuko set her systems to run through the data sets again, changing the structure of her search to focus on the new blood sample analysis beginning to come in from the Stratan Lab. The scientists and lab technicians had arrived two days earlier, their efficiency and speed of setting up a sampling process had impressed Yasuko, and their attitude towards her had been a surprise. Once she had shown the initial medical analysis on Finn, and the revisions to the antibiotic and dosing regime, they relaxed and engaged with the programme. Noah's insistence that they all plan together, with him in the team, heightened the mutual respect and Yasuko had to admit, improved her plans for data gathering. Her experience was based on primitive societal structures, and with the benefit of local knowledge and population density, they could refine the plans. But the time scales were large, even with her powerful computing power, and the historical factors of past mistakes running through the whole community.

The Fire Tick bacteria, and subsequent virus, had affected the culture of the Stratan population. Zuri had talked about the ebb and flow of humanity that reacted to the explosion of infections over hundreds of cycles and thousands of years. Each bout of infection led to multiple deaths and an element of societal breakdown. Populations would move away from the warmer parts of the planet where the Ticks were most prevalent, and cities would expand in the colder regions. Then a new tick variant would rise in prominence, seeking food sources within these places, taking advantage of their close proximity, and people would move out into smaller family groups or population centres. When the infection rates reduced, and those resistant bred, there would be a resultant expansion of humanity back into the warmer areas and, at a simple level, the cycle would repeat itself. After humanity discovered antibiotics, the potency of the bacteria suddenly surged, the cycles of infection and societal breakdown coming closer and closer together.

Yasuko could see the historical patterns, and despite the information being based on external data and knowledge, developed an overall picture of a biosphere almost balancing itself out over thousands of years. And humans, as they always seem to do, appeared to have tipped that balance. But this time, the scales hadn't reset, despite the logical attempts made, shown by the scientific data, to eradicate the bacteria and the Fire Ticks or develop long-term treatments. To Yasuko, data was key to finding out why, and she had a secret weapon. Noah's malleable mind, an ability to see behind logic that she couldn't – and his humanity.

"I know we must base everything on data, and that the key baseline is already available from the years of sampling the population while you attempted to develop effective antibiotics. But we need to widen that further, taking current samples from the healthy population, and those known to be infected, those who were effectively treated, even those that weren't. Everything you would normally do but as up-to-date as we can make it," said Noah, Lead Councillor Abioyi watching him carefully from across the conference table. At his side, Xantathi, the scientist placed in charge of the Stratan research team by the Councillor herself, nodding away as he fiddled with his thick grey beard.

"Xantathi? You agree? This is a huge undertaking; our people are spread across a vast area. That is, if you wish to sample everywhere? And how will you get the computing power to run the analysis?" said Abioyi, her gaze falling on the increasingly nervous scientist.

"Errr ... well. It is what Yasuko wants," he replied, blue eyes focussed on the table and only briefly meeting the Lead Councillor's as he finished. "And she says that she has the capacity for this."

"Okay. What's your opinion, Xantathi? Really? We have been here a hundred times before, chasing the dream of eradicating the Fire Tick scourge, and the Brain Fever. Is this worth the time and investment, or do we just accept the impossibility of it?" said Abioyi, her eyes flicking back and forth between the old scientist and the young Earth human.

Xantathi squirmed in his seat, struggling with the depth of the Councillor's gaze and the enormity of the question. He looked towards Noah in hope he'd say something profound to get him out of giving an actual opinion.

"Lead Councillor," said Noah, loving and hating the attention he was getting in equal measure, "the plan was agreed by your team in consultation with Yasuko." Xantathi nodded vigorously at Noah's side. "I think our presence has given them a voice, and Yasuko's knowledge and processing power hope. But they lack —"

"Leadership," interjected Abioyi, "and confidence. And belief they will be listened to. It seems you have found a role here, Noah. But our meetings will include Xantathi or his deputy, understand? I can't appear to be listening just to you. Especially, if I'm right, when this isn't your field of study?"

"That's correct. But it is Yasuko's, and if need be, we can bring her in on the meetings. If my opinion is worth anything, your scientific team is excellent."

"But not brave, Noah. They don't enjoy giving a definitive view."

CHAPTER 39

Explorer Ship, Kaimas Military Garrison, Kaimas

Cyborg Blue eyes the target intently, knowing the power he contains to ruin any moment with a bad attitude and a poor joke. Killjoy, his arch nemesis.

"I don't know what you're thinking in there, but your eyes go vacant when your mind wanders. Might be a defect in your programming," said Finn.

"Better than the 'no one's at home look' you've had for the past four days. How you doing?" asked Smith, arms spread across the back of Zuri's sofa.

"I've been better," Finn replied, easing back in the opposite sofa. "Had some seriously weird thoughts and dreams. I think delirium would just about describe it, and if full-on Brain Fever is worse than that, I pity anyone that's bitten. And waking up to realising you really are blue, and it wasn't part of the dream, well that's screwing with my mind."

"Yeah, about that. Everyone is running around trying to find some type of cure. But no one is talking about what we *saw*. You know, the *!Kora* and the Fire Ticks. Yasuko has been busy with other stuff, but I think we need to divert her a little, to consider what it might mean. And maybe we could do some field studies in that area, find out more."

"The *!Kora* don't speak if I remember right and are not interested in communicating. You got something in mind?"

"Something, yeah. But not sure the Stratan will like it. Not sure I do, either."

◆ ◆ ◆

"No."

"Hear us out," said Finn.

"He's a murderer, and a traitor. I suspect the Minoas would like him back just for those reasons alone. Otegnoa has corroborated everything he has said. They were working together and sacrificing my people for their cause," said Shante, her eyes rapidly moving between Smith and Finn, with Zuri easing back in her chair next to them. The plain, white walled room they sat in had a long mirror on one side and a metal table.

"He's all those things," said Smith, "but you need answers. Yasuko's initial analysis of the *!Kora* shows they were definitely feeding the Fire Ticks. Maybe even breeding them, moving them from host to host as they go through their life cycle. This isn't just important, it's vital to the work your scientists are doing."

Shante shook her head, "No. He needs to go on trial, and then see nothing but four walls for the rest of his miserable life. You take him out from here, and he'll try to escape. You know this."

"Yeah, but we have a plan for that. Ever see *Escape from New York*?" said Zuri, a smile finally reaching her lips.

◆ ◆ ◆

"No."

"Not a choice," said Smith.

"I have rights," said Yabbin.

"Yeah, under Stratan law. Don't know if you noticed, but we're not exactly from Stratan. And right now, this is a war zone. Us versus the ticks," said Smith.

"Us?"

"Yes," said Zuri, her eyes flicking across to the stern-faced Shante in the corner of the room. "Think about it. Anything the Stratan do to kill off the bacteria needs to be shared. If they don't, your Minoas Fire Ticks will still seek a meal, and nature always finds a way to cross barriers. The bacteria will only come back, possibly even stronger."

"No. Unless ..." said Yabbin, his eyes wandered over to Finn, the lost look in them stirring a memory in Finn's mind.

"Mehin is sick, the antibiotics are not working well. Alkinta is equally ill. Yasuko thinks the bacterial strain they were infected with is a new one, resistant to the current antibiotic. He's stable, that much I can say, and I assure you the Stratan and Yasuko are doing their best."

"Yasuko?" said Yabbin, his face dropping as he thought through Finn's words.

"Call her our Chief Scientist. You have my word they are trying to help. And it isn't dependent on you coming, that's not our way."

"And you?" said Yabbin, looking at Shante. "Your body language says you hate every word they are saying. Gives me more of a reason to go." He looked back towards Finn when he got no response. "What's the catch? There's always a catch, especially when you don't have a reason to trust me."

"Ever see *Escape from New York*?" said Finn.

CHAPTER 40

Approaching The North Coast Of
The Southern Continent

Cyborg Blue fiddles with the detonator, throwing it up in the air, pretending to catch it and … oops. There she blows, one less traitor in our midst.

"Why's he smiling like that?" asked Yabbin, easing the blue metal collar a little from around his neck, sitting strapped into one of the microship's seats, and eyeing Smith.

"He does that when he's thinking of something devious, or stupid. Take your pick, never sure which," said Finn. "Quite possibly running through what your head will look like if that explosive blows. I'd treat him nice."

"Very nice," said Zuri, watching the screens as they flew over the hills to the east of the cove where the *!Kora* had died under a hail of Minoas gunfire. "He's moody too, can get quite upset over the tiniest slight, feels a little blue at times."

"Oh, funny. I didn't need my super enhanced vision to see that one coming."

"Whatever you do, don't mention his bald spot," said Finn.

"Hey. No hair, I can't *be* bald."

"You just did that to make sure no one would notice," said Zuri.

"Now that's original. Take you all night to think of that one?"

"Do you mind not winding him up while he's holding my

detonator?" said Yabbin.

Zuri and Finn looked to each other, and then over at Smith's sly grin he was desperately trying to hide from Yabbin. They turned away, suppressing their laughter.

Zuri returned to the screen, the small hills giving way to an area of crushed crystal dunes glinting in the sunshine, the refracted colours spread across the entire spectrum. Its beauty took her breath away, and she could see Finn being drawn to the image.

"It's stunning," said Zuri. "Is all of Stratan like this?"

"No, just where the tides sweep in between our land masses. Those crystals are mainly from deep water, though where exactly has been a little lost in time since the war. From what I understand, the Stratan northern coasts and beaches haven't always been this way, nor our southern ones. Possibly a few hundred years. The solid formations are where you'll find the *! Kora*, often near the old, pre-war power plants. I think they grow in the warmer waters. And there's always ionising radiation."

Finn knelt closer to the tracks, the mix of sand, mud and crystal shards finally providing their first complete footprint. He traced the line of the impression, angling away from the dunes that stood in front of the flat beach, back towards the foothills where they'd left the light-wrapped microship. Up to now, he'd believed Yabbin was stringing them along, playing for time, or just ignorant of where the !Kora tribe may be. But this was evidence they were here, and scanning outwards, he caught more *tells* of their passing. Zuri stood beside him, the optical only binoculars to hand as she scanned behind before starting up the ten-metre-high dune.

"Do they not post guards?" asked Smith, Yabbin nearby, watching Finn at work.

"They have no enemies or predators to worry about, so no. I only worked with three tribes, but it was the same with each. They come across as a simple fishing people if you ignore the radiation burns and deformities. And the crystal impregnation. Oh, and the blood rites," replied Yabbin.

"And growing ticks in their bodies," said Smith. "Nothing remotely weird at all."

"That was new to me," said Yabbin, standing back as Finn stood up from examining the tracks. "Considering what I was doing, it would seem disingenuous of me to encourage it."

"Does it?" said Zuri, walking back down from the glittering dune. "Maybe it was part of your plan. Perhaps we'll never know."

Yabbin eyed her warily, already marking the woman as his most dangerous opponent. He didn't expect forgiveness, his actions too raw and bloody for that. But this woman was a warrior that did not bend, and constantly on edge. Right now, he was a thorn in her side, and he suspected one she'd pull out sooner rather than later if he proved less than useful.

Maybe it's time just to take things at face value, rather than worry about what lies underneath like a typical Minoas.

"There's a partial ruin about two hundred metres to the west," said Zuri. "Overgrown and shattered, with an outline similar to an industrial building. Guess that's the plant, lots of scrub bushes around that area, so good cover. About fifty metres past there's fifteen rough built houses, like those back at the cove. I can see a few people, children too, working along the beach. Village life. There's a space for a pyre, but it's been burnt recently, a few smoking ashes. If it wasn't for the red crystal flower fifty metres offshore, I'd say it looks pretty normal."

Finn nodded, reaching for the monocular he still favoured, and signalling for Yabbin and the rest to follow as he walked up the dune. At the top, they all lay on the crystal sand and scanned the beach, Finn passing the monocular over to Yabbin after a few passes.

"Well? Any advice? We need samples, and you know these people better than anyone," said Finn, watching Yabbin as he focussed in on the old plant.

"Your armour," he said. "It doesn't have light reflection, which is a pity. You could just make a grab and run if we identify the trails right or use the old power plant as cover."

"No, we don't," said Finn, hoping Noah would find the time, as he'd instructed, away from the sampling work to explore the light wrapping difficulties while on Stratan. It would make a huge difference. "But we do need to work at speed."

"Yes, you will. Somehow, they know when something happens. Like, when the fishing boats are returning or when someone brings back an animal for their rites. They know. The village stirs, individual *!Kora* suddenly stop what they're doing and prepare," said Yabbin. "But they didn't know what we were doing, unless it affected another *!Kora*," said Yabbin.

"If we go for a snatch and run, are we risking the Fire Ticks leaving the *!Kora* like at the cove?" said Zuri, more towards Smith than anyone, the only one to witness the ticks emerge from the dead.

"Not sure," Smith replied. "But it's much less likely than if we used the stun shots. Those affect the body's system, that disruption might change things for the ticks. Yasuko thinks the reason they left the dead was because the blood wasn't pumping. They need live hosts to feed properly."

"Okay, we go for the power plant, using the scrub as cover. Identify two targets. Take them down with stun shots – can't risk them making contact with the others. Bag and tie them and make a run for it. Zuri, you carry one, and me the other with Smith on cover. You cause me any issues Yabbin, and Blue Bottle here will blow your explosive head like a pimple, with just a thought. Understand?"

"Hey. It's Cyborg Blue. But yeah – with just a thought," Smith pointed to his head, then mimed the sound of an explosion, giving Yabbin a big smile as he did so.

"Yes, I get it. I will not cause you trouble," Yabbin glanced over towards Zuri, the soul-piercing gaze in reply enough to ensure he meant it.

Finn pulled the flower-laden branches aside, the insects underneath battering at his helmet vents, sensing the CO2 and the meal beneath. He brushed them aside, checking his visor's thermal view to be greeted by the snow and pixelation associated with the ionising radiation. Giving up, he brought up the enhanced light image, with a view of the beach past the edge of the crumbling concrete wall to his left.

Knowing Zuri should be in position by now, about ten metres to his right using a standalone ruin as cover, he checked his timer. One minute to go. Once that clicked over, they would identify approaching targets along the beach, hoping for a pair but accepting individuals. After 30 minutes with no success, they would go for a larger group, stunning them all and taking two.

Not having radios is a pain in the arse in this cover on a snatch job.

Smith was behind them, babysitting Yabbin with eyes on them both, his sensors as useless as theirs. But he had the reaction speed to deal with two roles, so best to maximise his advantages. Blue or not.

Finn gazed briefly at the sea, the red crystal flower emerging from the water about fifty metres directly north of his position. The sky had darkened, rain more than likely on the way, so it refracted little light at the moment. But somehow it made the formation stand out more, the steel-grey sky outlining the fifteen metre flutes of hexagonal red crystal as they rose above the flat, purple-blue sea. As strange as it sounded considering their journey since leaving Earth, it appeared as the most alien object he'd seen – so different to its surroundings. If you took it away, he could have been staring out from Edinburgh's Portobello Beach. It was the oddness in such a familiar and ordinary scene.

Finn snapped back, a group of six male *!Kora* were heading east along the beach, shoeless on the shards of crystal that made up much of the sand. He focussed the visor in, noting the prevalence of blue-black blotched skin underneath loose, woven clothing that these *!Kora* wore. It made searching for the impregnated crystals harder, but the gentle wind flapped across them, and he picked out red flashes on necks and shoulders. As they walked, he noted their movements, reading them as he would his soldiers. Everything seemed natural, the *! Kora* comfortable with each other, making eye contact much like other people did when conversing, though with no lip movements. Finn shook his head, trying to clear out the worries Yabbin had placed there, how they simply *knew* when something was happening. These *!Kora* were communal, having some form of social contract with each other. So not so distant from the rest of humanity and justifying his decision not to go with a full assault on the village. Underneath all the trappings were humans, families, children.

Maybe they use facial signals, or grunts and noises like apes. Either way, snatch and run – not an assault when it's not needed.

He let them pass, assuming Zuri would do the same, following his instructions. Settling into his position, he waited, manoeuvring the branches aside, so they left a gap. A few minutes later, a group of children walked towards them, three under eight, with a female *!Kora* herding them along with woven baskets in hand. Instructing his visor to enhance the image, he picked out the fronds of seaweed poking up from one basket. Scanning upwards, Finn caught her smile, feigning annoyance with the children making heavy weather of walking in a single direction. Finn watched the woman carefully, remembering the !Kora who attacked Alkinta's compound and the crystals they wore in their cheeks. They were there, six on each side, but smaller than those he'd encountered at the cove. Finn quickly glanced over the children, their rapid movements making focussing harder, but enough to see they were devoid of any crystal adornments. He breathed a sigh of relief.

What they were about to do dragged up memories of Havenhome, when faced with the choice between getting home and the Haven soldiers in their way, they fought for themselves. And he was no stranger to difficult missions involving civilians. Whether rescuing his own people, or raiding insurgent bases within civilian populations, they all, at some point, involved tackling innocents. This time they were taking people from their own village, desperate for more information, despite not knowing if the Fire Tick breeding was deliberate, or just ritualistic. He had few qualms about the mission being for the greater good. If what the !Kora were doing was causing harm to others, it was justified. And having experienced the bacterial infection at a minor level, he understood the dangers. It didn't mean they had to kill, however, and there were children and families involved.

And we want to go home, and Yasuko won't leave until she has a solution. I've seen that look before. So the sooner the better.

Thirty minutes ticked over, with thirsty flies and other Stratan insects battering at his helmet. Watching the beach, three !Kora walked by, heading west and towards the village. Taking the lead, he raised his rifle, the stubby barrel released a stun shot, the bolt hitting the female !Kora in the small of her back. The middle-aged woman was falling to the ground when Zuri's bolt flew, clipping the shoulder of the first male ! Kora. Finn shifted target, aiming for the third, stocky and well-muscled member of the group, who immediately looked back in his direction. Finn fired, cutting off a low, rumbling howl from the man's mouth when the bolt seared into his solar plexus, flinging him backwards. Zuri's next bolt hit her first target in the chest, propelling him to the ground as his own deep-throated roar began.

Finn stared, taken aback, when his targeted *!Kora* stood up, clothes singed where the bolt hit. The rumble began again, the *!Kora* bending to pick the woman up off the floor. Finn fired a second time, the bolt hitting the man in the knees, sending him to the floor just as Zuri's target rose.

If that roar is what Yabbin was talking about, we need to finish this quickly.

Zuri's next bolt sent the thinner man down again, rolling onto the crystal floor but clearly not fully stunned. Finn fired again, knowing the third shot would mean a recharge cycle on the weapon. It kept the bull-like *!Kora* on the floor, however, this time the roar didn't choke off.

Zuri's target rolled to his feet, unsteady, stumbling back towards the village. Finn burst out of the scrub bush, running towards the beach, switching triggers and cursing at what he might have to do. To his right, he saw Zuri had already emerged, her Boleadoras swinging above her head. Finn watched it fly, saying a few encouraging words. The three metal stones hurtled forward, the first thumping into the man's legs before the lighter balls swung around, wrapping him up, bringing the fleeing *!Kora* to his knees. Electric charge sparked across the metal balls.

Okay, I can accept being wrong from time to time. Not that I'll hear the end of it.

Finn reached the second man, thick muscles convulsing, trying to stand in front of the prone woman lying on the beach. Finn recognised the protective stance, cursing the *weapons* recharge cycle as he faced off with the determined *!Kora*. Finn fainted low to the right, slow and ungainly, and his opponent followed, caught unaware as Finn then rose at speed, bringing the butt of his rifle sharply upwards to smash into the man's jaw.

The noise stopped, the blow finally sparking him out.

Then the roar kicked in, voices deep and low, rumbling from the village and behind them. The pitch deepened, Finn's chest vibrating in response, heightening the adrenaline running through his system as the unearthly sound reverberated across the beach.

CHAPTER 41

!Kora Village, North Coast Of Southern Continent

Zuri ran past Finn and the two *!Kora* he was binding. On reaching her target, she rapidly cable tied hands and feet before releasing the bolas' weights, restoring them in her belt pouch. She glanced over at Finn, signalling her intent to bag her man. Finn agreed, and she took out the white cloth bag Yasuko had made for them – breathable, strong, and hopefully Fire Tick proof. With a watchful eye on the *!Kora* running from the village, she slipped his feet and body into the bag, sealing it, and upping her armour to its maximum setting. By the time her package was on her shoulder, the *!Kora* were in throwing distance and the first fish spear sailed her way. Not designed for long flight, it sailed by, and Smith's gunfire rang out, the whirring explosive rounds digging into the crystal beach at the *!Kora's* feet, the explosions knocking a few to the floor, but the rest carried on undeterred.

Zuri pivoted, the servos in her armour pulsing with the additional power as she ran for the designated path through the scrub and towards the dunes. Finn joined her, one woman under his arm, and the bull-like man over his shoulder. Zuri ignored his decision to go against his own orders, trusting he knew what he was doing. Two spears clattered into the ground at her feet, this time from the right, presumably from the male group they'd seen earlier. Ignoring them, she reached the desolate power station, driving on through as Finn followed.

The rumble increased rapidly, the depth of the sound causing her armour to vibrate in response. She felt the servos stumble, missing a beat as they shook. Fearing damage, Zuri turned the power down, aiming to reach the top of the first dune and hopefully away from the weird sound on the other side. A spear lanced between her legs, catching between strides, sending her crashing to the floor. The spear snapped as she fell, squeezed between the ceramic plates and subjected to the force of the servos. The bundled !Kora hit the ground in front of her, tumbling forwards. Yabbin passed her, picking up the bundle and powering up the dune with Finn following, checking on her as she rose. Zuri was quickly back into her stride, hearing the whirr of Smith's weapon behind, the explosions ripping into the floor.

Zuri tumbled over the ridge of the dune, gracefully regaining her feet and reaching the other side before Yabbin. The man clearly struggling, she took the bundled !Kora, and as Smith leapt over the top of the dune, followed Finn who set a steady pace towards the hidden microship. She upped her servos again, thankful that the otherworldly thrum had lessened, despite the shimmering crystals that still danced to the vibrations along their path.

Zuri's transponder kicked in, her HUD flashing the microship's presence as they left the ionisation zone. She felt the !Kora struggle in the bag, nothing she couldn't handle, but a sign again of their robustness and resistance to the stun weapons.

"I have the signal, Zuri," said Finn, the radio crackling and laced with static. "You got eyes on Smith and Yabbin?"

Zuri stopped and turned briefly, catching a glimpse of Yabbin's black armour with Smith jogging at his side. Behind, reaching the top of the dune, her HUD flashed recognition of !Kora still on the chase. Too distant to be a threat, she carried on, eyeing Finn as he switched off the microship's light-wrap and entered through the forming doorway. When she finally reached the ship, Finn had dropped his two struggling bags on the floor, and despite the suit's help, was obviously weary after his efforts. Zuri stepped in, easing her wriggling bundle against the ship's far wall, and moving the two others next to it. The nanobots produced belt wraps out from the wall and floor, sliding around the bags and initiating sensors to monitor basic medical data.

"Doorway," said Finn between heaving breaths, "Can you cover. Think I needed a few more days rest."

"There's a surprise," replied Zuri, glancing back. "One day you'll listen to advice."

"I always listen. Well, nearly always."

"Okay, I'll rephrase. One day you'll act on advice, and we'll all faint with the shock of it." She threw him a smile, then turned back to the door as Yabbin approached, hardly sweating due to his excellent fitness, but cursing Zuri's suggestion that his armour should be powered down. Smith arrived last, pushing Yabbin through the door, eager to be gone as the tribesmen exited the scrub bushes a few hundred metres back.

Smith dropped into the flight chair, engaging the engines while the door reformed into the hull. The microship rose from between bushes, and a few ineffectual spears flew, clattering against the hull. He engaged thrust, angling the wash away from the *!Kora* until distant enough to open the engines fully. They all felt the pull of the acceleration, and Smith's eagerness to be away.

"Calm down, Smith. They can't catch us up here," said Finn, moving to the co-pilot's chair. "What's got you so spooked?"

Smith attempted to ease back in the chair, but his systems reflexively kept him forward, tensed. He was still learning about this new form, but the responses coursing through his electronic body were familiar enough.

Fear. Overwhelming Fear. Cyborg Blue knows when he's outmatched.

Smith looked over towards Finn, determined to hide what his

systems screamed, and failing badly. The shake in his hands and shoulders mirrored by his armoured suit, he caught Finn's raised eyebrow as he read the poor attempt at a flat expression on his blue face.

Finn reflexively put his gauntleted hand on Smith's arm, gripping hard, letting the vibrations run through him, trying to share whatever was upsetting his corporal.

"It said *LEAVE*, Finn. In the language of the Haven. It shouted it, wrote it in the patterns of the air, in the radiation, in the sea. Everywhere. *LEAVE*."

CHAPTER 42

— I…

— I can …

— I can know …

— I can know you …

— You can hear me …

— Take

— Talk

— Listen

— LEAVE

CHAPTER 43

The Politico Building, Slabin, Capital City Of The Minoas Confederation, Northwest Minoas

General Hardrin slammed the report on the marble table, slapping hands down on top while Prime Minister Mwandin and her spy chief looked on. He pushed himself up from the chair, his inner ear complaining at the sudden movement, forcing him to grip the table once the world started to tilt. Mwandin didn't move to help, she'd made that mistake only once.

The old man fiddled with his necklace before turning to the wall, composing himself, not trusting speech until he had a coherent sentence formed in his boiling mind.

"General?" asked Jabulani, the spy chief shifting in his seat then rising to help. Mwandin reached across, grabbing the man's arm and pushing him back towards the chair, shaking her head. He sat back down, nodding in her direction.

Hardrin let out a heavy sigh, squeezing the bridge of his nose, settling on a comment he could trust.

"So Yabbin has been captured and is to be tried for crimes against the Stratan. And he has admitted to being a traitor to … to me … us," he said. Jabulani moved to speak, but Mwandin stayed him again. "And the last we know is he left with these … these Earth humans from the spacecraft we picked up."

"Yes," said Jabulani, the ashen faced man responding to the Prime Minister's nudge. "It appears they have business with the ! Kora, and he is experienced in that area."

"But we don't know why. Only that the Earth humans are working on the Brain Fever issue," Hardrin turned to face the spy chief, a look of surprise on his face – it wasn't in the report. He continued, enjoying the small victory after the pain Yabbin's treason would cause, "They've contacted us, the Stratan. They want us to share pre-war medical data, and for us to provide any recent sampling. They want to work together." The General spat the last word out, the taste of it poison on his tongue.

"Sir," said Mwandin, eagerness overcoming the restraint normally required with the General, "is it genuine? The offer."

"Of course it is. They love doing good when it suits them." A wave of nausea swept over the General, forcing the man to his knees as his balance gave, the momentum overcoming his stomach control and its contents rose in his throat. Mwandin moved to his side, bringing her arms round Hardrin's shoulders, trying to steady the shakes engulfing him.

"Fetch the Politico Doctor, now!" she shouted at Jabulani, reaching inside the Head of State's shirt, pulling out the medical locket. Flipping it open, dust puffed out, dropping to the floor. She reached inside his jacket, finding the battered metal box and flipping the catch. Inside lay one small crystal rock, the last of the naturally occurring stone. She took it, placing it in her own pocket, and replacing the powder with a small artificial crystal that Hardrin so mistrusted. The vibration kicked in, and she felt the amplitude lower, the system attuning to the poorly made stone. She placed it back around his throat, the CPU in the locket calibrated to work for maximum effect on the bacteria growing in his hypothalamus from that position.

It's time, General. Your work is done, I need to run the State right now. However briefly.

CHAPTER 44

Explorer Ship, Kaimas Military Garrison, Kaimas

Smith grabbed the nanobot by the upper arms, rolling to the side, pushing his hip outwards and lifting his leg. The nanobot stumbled, the power and momentum of Smith's twist and hip action unbalancing the bot. Smith completed the Hano-goshi, the metal trainer landing flat on its back, with Smith on its front and pinning one arm, swiftly adjusting as the bot struggled, to a fully locked hold. The nanobot tapped out, logic telling it the situation was hopeless.

"Are you sure? I was about to switch holds?"

The trainer didn't respond, they never did. It just tapped again, and Smith released, letting the nanobot absorb into the floor. The machine knew it had lost, so logic wouldn't let the bot carry on when set to attack mode. It did, however, file away Smith's initial feint for later.

"And let that be a lesson to you, perp. Don't go doing criminal things when Cyborg Blue is in town." Smith stood, slapping his hands together and bowing prior to exiting the mat.

He instinctively reached for the towel rack, blue hand wavering over the rail as his electronic eyes caught sight of his metal skin's sheen.

Old habits. No need to dry off when you're made of metal, crystal and optical cable. More precious metal in me than in the Bank of England, more jewels than the Tower of London.

Finally, I'm worth something …

"I know you're there," he said, turning. His sensors provided the full rundown of Zuri's entry, including pheromones and an external medical analysis. She was on edge and here to talk. By the tremor in her crossed arms, she'd probably been waiting a while, letting him finish the Judo session, hoping it would work out the *fear* he'd felt at the end of the mission.

Yeah, like I'm human and I can use adrenaline as a blocker. Fat chance of that. Yasuko has enough processing power packed in here to run a battleship. I just don't know how to use it all, yet.

"You always knew where I was, without your fancy sensors," Zuri said, sitting on the arm of a cushioned chair.

"Yeah, usually in the pub or nearest bar. Or the canteen, rustling up some scran." Smith let a wistful smile creep across his lips, memories flooding in of his time on tour with Zuri, even back at the barracks in Stirling. Then a glimpse of Lieutenant Bhakshi's face, Luther's firefighter honed muscles, Kapoor binding her hair. All gone, lost to the Stratan they were now helping.

Life can be strange at times. Not quite as weird as death, admittedly, but strange.

"I ... I need to ask about the *!Kora* mission. You seemed to have picked up a message, something that shocked you. Not seen you that messed up since Helmond, the poppy field runs." Zuri studied Smith's face, trying to work out where his mind was at. But for all Yasuko and Noah's skills, the metal visage was far from elastic. The expressions were close, but exaggerated, one step from a parody of humanity that she found disconcerting.

Smith caught her looking, and his additional processing power set off in a flurry of activity, cross-referencing her expression and body language against the words spoken. It quickly disagreed with Smith's assessment, dropping a solution in his memory bank for later analysis.

"Yeah, well," said Smith, hand on hip, brushing his non-existent hair back over his brow. "It was the frequencies. At first, when the *!Kora* kicked in, it was synchronised, you know, in tune. But there was an ultrasound pulse from that crystal flower, almost like a response. It went through us all, but there's no way you'd notice. You know being ..."

"Human?" said Zuri, reaching out and taking Smith's hand. Cyborg or not, the man inside had seen her through some tough times, and his voice betrayed more than his expression.

"Uh-huh. It ... it resonated with my internal systems, the ones that are made from precious stones – sapphires and the like. It seemed to align with them, or they it. Hard to tell as I'm still learning about my structure and systems. Either way, after that, the sound switched, matching the Haven language, though without any nuance. Stilted. And the radiation altered, the waves of the sea, the aligning of the stones – I saw it everywhere – my mind's eye systems were flooded with it."

"It?"

"Leave. It wants us to leave."

"Because it, whatever *it* is, was protecting the *!Kora*?"

"No, us. People, humans. It wants all of us to leave."

Noah flicked through the data running across the screen, analysing the electromagnetic waves as the crystalline rock responded to the light he was beaming through it. The refraction response caused tingles along his spine; it was like nothing he'd ever imagined.

"And you make this?" he asked the lab-coated soldier opposite him, the badge declaring the man as Captain Sekani, his relaxed stance belying the initial tension of their meeting.

"It occurs naturally, forming in the planet's crust and spewed up through the thermal vents. We have tried to copy it but struggle to align the structural bonds to achieve the same effect. That is the perfect example, use that and the response rate of the armour is magnified to the point where you can't see the soldier even when walking, never mind smaller movements."

"But your version is good enough when static?"

"Yes. We embed optical fibre throughout the ceramic plate and bulletproof material, and link that with wrist and necklace embedded crystals. If we had enough, and used it all over the armour, then you're looking at complete camouflage, even at high speeds. We were, in the past, working towards swapping out the ceramic plates for industrial sapphire, meaning we could use less for the same effect. But we don't have the resources to keep manufacturing more, and as Minoas fades, there is less and less call for it. Now, we just reuse old armour where we can."

"What about harvesting it from the sea?" said Noah, switching off the equipment and removing the green stone. Captain Sekani held his hand out, Noah reluctantly handing it over.

"Yes, that was how we originally found it. The crystal harvesting process around the deep vents was an old programme, preceding the period when Brain Fever really took hold. And when they decided to send spaceships to Earth, they upped the programme, searching for more of the true sapphires, to supplement the industrial ones for the gigantic lasers used to push against the ships' sails. But that soon stopped after both Minoas and our societies began to break down. There has been no ocean mining for some time, and a lot of our industrial progress with it. And then we just blew each other up," said Sekani, stiffening again and pocketing the stone.

Noah nodded, "Is it possible Yasuko can analyse that crystal, so we can reproduce a version for our armour?"

Sekani blinked, his mind working through the possibilities. "I haven't been given permission for approval, but I will ask," the Stratan Captain flared his nostrils as he turned, heading out of the hold doors at the rear of Yasuko's ship. Noah waited until he was clear of the ramp before speaking.

"You get that?"

"Yes, Noah. A full analysis. It seems we have a problem."

"A problem? With the blood sampling?"

"No, Noah. With the crystal. On first look its bonds are very different to what I would expect, strengthened in places and realigned in others. It's not like any natural crystal I've ever seen, and there's nothing like it in my data banks. I'm not even sure I could copy it, in fact, it would only be a facsimile."

"Metacrystal? As in human made?"

"No, Noah. No human technology could have made this. And if I can't, whatever did has access to technology and resources that we don't. And for something so advanced, where are they?"

"Or where were they? There's no sign of any ancient civilisations on Stratan, but you have said the possibilities for life in the universe is endless," said Noah, standing up from the work bench when Yasuko appeared next to him. She had a 3D hologram of the stone hovering above her hand, eyes scanning across the bonds.

"Yes," she said, appearing distracted, "I could do with the original stone, Noah. I need to examine it closely. But I can't do that, and the work on eliminating the virus. It too has traits that I think are manufactured," Yasuko let the hologram fade away and turned back to her crewmate, refocussing. "I could do with a sample of the original bacteriophage, for a comparison. It won't help with the current work, but I fear there is more to this virus and the bacteria than just an accelerated cycle."

"How's it going with the !Kora?"

"Interesting," said Yasuko. "And noisy."

CHAPTER 45

Holding Cell, Kaimas Military Garrison, Kaimas

Finn watched through the two-way mirror, the gas infusing through the room, billowing from vents in the door and wall. He shuddered, hating seeing what was happening, and on guard to ensure his charges were being treated well. Finn could understand the Stratan's difficulties, the three !Kora had done nothing since Yasuko finished working with them, except hum at a pitch that made the mirror, and Finn's chest, vibrate. However, when anyone entered the room, the !Kora had broken down into a maelstrom of hate and anger, throwing themselves at the Stratan soldiers, or the walls, or the tables, anything where they could harm or be harmed. It had frightened Finn, and the sheer power of their emotions had overwhelmed the soldiers, it being so far beyond their experience they had resorted to violence in return. Finn had stepped in, standing guard and refusing to move or allow access until a better solution could be found, trusting their status to prevent any arguments. That, and he'd ordered Noah to ready his Battle Armour just in case.

"You take this very seriously, Lance Corporal Finn," said Shante at his side, looking away from the mirror as the !Kora succumbed to the gas.

"They are under my care, Councillor. And we took them from their home, kidnapped them. It sits less easily with me, despite it being our decision. The distress is … upsetting." Finn relaxed as the heavily muscled !Kora finally succumbed and fell unconscious. Noting steady breathing from all three, he turned to face the Councillor who he'd marked as military through and through. "What now?"

"Now you can take them back, and we can sterilise the whole garrison. Fire Ticks and irradiated people do not sit well with my need to keep the people here safe. I hope you got what you need, as I don't think it's something the Council will agree to again. They have seen the images of their aggression, and self-harm. Not an easy watch."

"If you found this difficult, wait until you see Yasuko's analysis," said Finn. "She recorded 3D images of their bodies, and the extraction of those Fire Ticks that didn't emerge naturally. Don't forget the popcorn. I'd suggest you make it salty."

"Popcorn?"

"What you're looking at are the eggs hatching beneath the female *!Kora's* skin, under the embedded crystal," said Yasuko, her eyes scanning the room, the Lead Councillor sat among the other members who'd managed to arrive for the meeting. Six in all, including Shante, two more delayed by a sweeping weather front bringing heavy snow and winds up from the southern pole. "Once hatched, they feed on the host. That's the first two stages completed. I believe they exchange bacteria at this point, receiving as well as giving, but I can't be definite yet. The feeding process is longer than the ticks I saw on Earth, but these are much bigger."

Noah watched the image of the six-legged larva biting down into the woman's flesh, and the speeded-up cycle of its blood-filled body expand. How can such a small creature cause so much instinctive fear?

"The Fire Tick, I believe, is of Earth origin by evidence in its DNA. Brought here with the other animals Smith has listed for us. The signs are it rapidly became the dominant blood feeding arachnid, including feeding off the local population of smaller animals, gaining their bacterial load. It's this process that led to the bacteria causing the initial outbreaks in humans and your livestock. You, and the Earth animals, had very little innate resistance to the new bacterial hybrid. Your scientific team, led by Dr Xantathi," the scientist tried to merge into his chair at the mention of his name, Noah behind him patting the man's shoulder, "have analysed the current bacteria in the nymphs as they emerged. They believe it's a new strain, the one infecting Alkinta and the Minoas Corporal – or at least it will be when the nymph, the third stage of the life cycle, feeds off the male *!Kora*."

Finn shuddered, reaching out and taking Zuri's hand, her eyes widening at the images on the screen. The nymph bulldozed its way into the *!Kora's* flesh, its rear pulsing, filling with the freshly pumped blood.

"Again, there's an exchange going on here, and a relationship I struggle to understand. Yabbin spoke to us about it being a blood rite, a religious act. But to my logical mind, it appears to be a perfectly attuned bacterial breeding process. Self-sustaining."

Noah stood, pulling up Xantathi and moving beside Yasuko's holographic image projected through the hold into the laboratory common room. "It would explain why the Fire Tick population is still high, despite the apparent lack of food sources since your nuclear war," said Noah, standing back to allow the Stratan scientist space to talk, and not hide.

"We," he started, coughing into his hand and wiping it on his coat, "believe that if we allow this process to continue, the natural equilibrium between the population of the Fire Ticks food source and their numbers, will continue to decline. The new strain is highly resistant to our most advanced antibiotics, and the Brain Fever virus takes that element and adapts the latent bacteria many of us have in our hypothalamus, spinal fluid and even brain membranes, to mimic those properties. This isn't new, but the cycle has accelerated since the nuclear war. It should do the opposite, there are fewer hosts and food sources around."

"Can we use the *!Kora* as a source for developing antibiotics?" asked Abioyi.

"Yes, I think we can. For this strain, but ..." started Xantathi, looking towards Yasuko, who cut back in to add authority to what they had discovered together.

"There are going to be more strains, potentially one for every tribe. Possibly variants within the tribes themselves. And then we need to consider the radiation, it can cause further mutations in the bacteria, or the host."

Zuri felt Finn tense, squeezing his hand as she began to put things together. Realisation grew, and she prepared herself for the confrontation to come. And what was worse, she didn't know which side of the fence she'd lie.

Umoja ni nguvu, utengano ni udhaifu Unity is strength, division is weakness. This is going to be bad.

"Then we need to eradicate the source, don't you think, Yasuko? Xantathi?" said the Lead Councillor.

"That would be the logical thing to do," said Yasuko, her sensors alerting her to Finn's immediate surge in adrenaline and stress hormones. She looked up, seeing all of it in the set of his jaw and the fire in the eyes. But blissfully unaware of why, until Smith whispered *Genocide* in her electronic ear. She paused, emotions running through her systems like rivers of lava. "No, no. Not that, Councillor. No."

Finn pulled in a deep breath, raising himself up to his full height, stepping forward and drawing the Council's eyes towards him. Shante shifted, her hands wandering inside her ceremonial robes. Finn missed it, but Zuri and Smith didn't, and they tensed, hands free but ready. Shante read their reaction, and whispered, sub-vocalising and setting Smith and Yasuko's sensors on to high alert as she contacted the guards.

Zuri eased into her stance, one foot slightly forward, eyes on the woman looking her way.

How did this go so wrong so quickly?

"No," said Finn. "You haven't said it – you've left it hanging – but it's there. Murder is murder, and we will not allow it."

"And you think you have a say? This is our planet, our choices. It is the quickest, and easiest way to remove the problem. And with your work on …"

"All work on the virus and the antibiotics will stop immediately," said Yasuko, her hologram shifting to Finn's side. "I will not be party to wiping out a people."

Zuri watched Shante, the woman's hands appearing above the table, empty-handed. Words didn't need weapons, they wielded death in a different way.

"We have the right to protect our own people, and by whatever means we deem necessary. The *!Kora* are a threat to our existence."

"As were the Minoas?" said Zuri, uneasy with her own feelings, but Finn needed her right now. "When you struck first – sent a nuclear weapon over a perceived threat. The first strike, trying to take out their ability to launch upon you? I've read your histories, and they don't paint your people in a good light. Your government pressed the button because they feared what the Minoas may do, based on supposition and poor intelligence. Killed millions in their second city, hoping to stop any retaliation, destroying their satellites at the same time. But they found a way to fire back, aimless but hey, they're big weapons with big effects. Instead of solving the potential problem, you caused the death of your planet, starting a war nobody can win." Zuri, eyes flashing as the words tumbled out, stood hands on hips next to Finn and Yasuko.

The Lead Councillor glared, her face stiff, holding back a rising anger, struggling with the emotions Zuri had drawn from suppressed depths.

"That was then – and many would argue it was necessary – and this is now. Hard decisions made by people who were chosen for them. Who chose you?"

Noah stood, "You did. When your people sent Marines to kill my friends."

"When they killed me," said Smith joining the squad, standing by the friends he was so proud of. "I got no choice in the matter, and nor did the billions on the end of a nuclear warhead."

"We didn't choose to be the ones to help, Councillor. It just happened. But we know honour, and duty. Do you?" said Finn. "We're out of here." Finn spun on his heel, heading for the door. Shante rose, the soldiers at the exit responding, stepping across the doorway, guns no longer *at ease.*

Finn stopped directly in front of them, in his armour but with only the energy pistol strapped to his leg. He contemplated his next action, eyeballing each in turn. Behind him, the Lead Councillor put her arm across Shante, raising her palm, telling her to back off. Shante sub-vocalised with Smith staring at her, his blue head nodding as she spoke. The guards stood back, guns still raised, but no longer blocking the way out. Finn gave them both one last look, and strode through the door, his body barely containing the anger. Zuri waited, letting Noah and Smith leave, and looked towards the Council Table, eyes aflame.

"I give you two days – that's it. You have the data we've worked on together, and what it means for you and your people. We will take silence to mean you intend on carrying out your threat." Zuri turned to leave. Abioyi stood up again, eyes studying her.

"Zuri, we have spoken enough about your past. What would you do? If it was your people. We want to survive."

Zuri stopped, turning to face the Lead Councillor, briefly glancing at the floor before looking straight into her eyes. "I would look for another way, Abioyi. Not jump to the first conclusion because it's the easiest. They are not animals to be culled."

But me and mine. What would I do if there was no other way?

CHAPTER 46

Explorer Ship, Kaimas Military Garrison, Kaimas

"Get us out of here, Yasuko," said Zuri, slamming her holster down on the table and throwing herself onto the couch.

"We're leaving?"

"Yes, for now. They need to get the message," Zuri replied.

And I need space to think.

"Can I have twenty minutes? To make sure the lab systems will operate independently. We could lose so much data, and then there's cross over connection into the ship. I need to ensure these are all ready for when we return. I—" Yasuko's hologram flittered in and out as she paced, thinking.

"Do it, get it all prepared. I want to return if we can, but these people, they are so… so volatile."

Noah stopped at the doorway with hunched shoulders, hands deep in pockets, a dark mood written all over him. "Zuri, I—"

"No, Noah. We are leaving. I know the work you've done, and how close everything is. But they are seriously contemplating mass murder."

Noah's face switched to a scowl, anger flashing across his eyes. "I don't disagree. You heard me in there. Maybe you should give people time to talk. I was going to tell you Finn is hitting the crap out of the nanobot and the punchbag." He spun round, stomping off towards the hold, Yasuko's hologram appearing next to him.

Zuri slumped back into the couch, hands on her forehead,

silently screaming at the ceiling. She gave up the silence, letting rip as the need overwhelmed her. After twenty seconds she had a sweating Finn at her side, face contorted with worry, hands on hers while the last sounds faded down the corridor.

"Hey, hey," he said, sliding down into the space next to her, pulling Zuri towards him, feeling her body tense and resist at first, before caving in. "Sorry about the smell, and the sweat."

"You definitely need a shower," she said, reluctantly pulling away and standing up. "I need to find Noah."

"Give him ten minutes, maybe more. The kid's going through it right now. The work's distracted him, but … you know. Fungal death isn't easy to get over."

"I snapped. This world, the emotions. They just pile on top of each other. I feel fragile, and I hate it."

"Fragile? You've always been fragile; it makes you human. And we all keep your pieces glued together, just like you do for us. If we were hard, how would we bend? Or cope with all this crap coming our way – by letting it bounce off? We don't need armour, Zuri. Just each other." Finn stood, gathering the quivering woman into his arms, letting his own tears well, and feeling her finally relax. After a few seconds he lifted her hand, kissing the semi-colon tattoo along its edge.

"I don't agree, you know, with their immediate plan for the *!Kora*. But if there's no solution, they will be putting their own people at risk. It could come down to the *!Kora* or them. If I was in that position, I would choose me and mine to survive." Zuri waited, expecting Finn to tense up, except he pulled her in tighter.

"Yeah. Thought that might be it. Someone also said what's the point of having all this power if we don't make a difference. That might have been you. Let's make sure it doesn't come to that."

Because it can't. I won't be able to stand by.

◆ ◆ ◆

"What are we looking at, Yasuko?" said Finn, eyes flicking across the wall-screen in the control room.

"Smith sent me the recordings from the beach. He's also given me a download of his internal sensor readings when the ultrasound affected his systems – those made from precious stones or industrial metacrystals. He wanted to find the source, or at least evidence that it wasn't just a one-off occurrence."

"Basically, that I'm not hearing voices and going completely bananas," said Smith.

"A blue banana, something to think on," said Finn.

"And what you're seeing wasn't there when we arrived, of that, I'm sure. It's formed over the past week or so, but I can't be precise. There are no Council satellites left to tap into, and the moon base only has a communication array," said Yasuko, carrying on as the screen focussed in on the patterns that appeared static despite the sea swell they floated on.

"I recognise the patterns," said Noah, "from Havenhome. Those lines and swirls are like the scratches the Haven use for writing. Am I correct?" Noah took a sip of his coffee, eyes darting to Zuri and back to the screen.

"Yes. And despite the waves and currents, the sand crystals are not dissipating like they should. Something is holding them together, a binding that should be near impossible." Yasuko engaged the translation algorithm, the screen labelling each word for her crew.

"Come," said Zuri.

"Not quite," said Smith. "It's shouted, like an order, not a request. The Haven use the proportional thickness of the line for emphasis. I'm not being asked but told." He stood, starting to pace the room, hand brushing the top of his metalled head. "I don't like this."

"We'll be there to hold your hand, Blue Meanie, bald – sorry – brave defender of the weak and helpless," said Finn, cracking a huge grin when rewarded with Smith's vicious stare.

"The *!Kora* are deeply connected to those crystal flowers," said Noah, eyes flitting to Zuri again before returning to the others. "This seems fortuitous, after our meeting this morning. There has to be a connection, but the timing?"

"Matches our kidnapping of the *!Kora* test subjects. Not necessarily a distraction by the Stratan, if that's what you were thinking," said Finn. "I can't see this as a trap, though they have had access to information on the Haven."

"I agree," said Zuri, turning to Yasuko. "Where is it?"

"It's the launch site, for the construction of the Sail Ship and later the Marines themselves. A volcanic Island between the main Minoas continental shelf and ours. There's an Atoll, a ring of twelve islands varying in size," said Xantathi, eyes darting back and forth. "I'm not sure I should be talking to you, Noah. You've set the Council into a whirl."

"And you agree with their proposed solution?" replied Noah, Finn tapping him on the shoulder, and showing his finger upon lips.

"We need to look at the data and the potential solutions logically, young man. Together. When did a protest solve anything?" said Xantathi, eyes flickering even faster.

Finn coughed behind Noah, moving away to let Noah dig further without his interference.

"We'll think on it. The island, then. Anything we should know?"

"Well, I shouldn't be telling secrets, but this one is more a source of shame than confidential. We lost the islands just prior to the war, it was one of many catalysts for the first strike. It had become more of a research station by then, space not seen as so vital with the impending war and all. But the Minoas took the islands over, annexed them by force as a possible staging post for invasion, or so it was thought. Except for Khoikhoi, they couldn't take that. Ironic really."

"Ironic?"

"Yes, it means 'men of men' – a show of pride. But it wasn't men who stopped the Minoas. It was the automatic defences, and the war robots."

Finn's spluttering cough echoed through the hold, coffee splattering the wall.

CHAPTER 47

Private Room, Slabin Politico Hospital, Slabin, Northwest Minoas

"He's gone," said the doctor, checking the medical scanner, and setting the time and date for the State record. Mwandin reached over, thumb-printing to agree the death certificate alongside the doctor's information. Her details appeared; the picture only four months old.

Not a lot of time to prepare oneself.

The doctor bowed his head, a brief show of respect, the Prime Minister leaving the General's bedside, and the hospital room. Outside, the available Politico had gathered in the stark corridor, eager for news. Only Lord Pansin was missing – no surprise there. Her greatest critic, probably circling amidst the remaining elite to drum up support to have her removed as soon as legally possible.

Hopefully not soon enough.

She nodded to them, her face communicating their Leader's fate. The hubbub stopped, men and women taking a moment to consider what they had lost. The General had risen to power with a coup, his soldiers holding the Politico to account for their continual failings of state as their people dwindled and died among the ticks and Brain Fever. His systematic programme of fear and respect had shaken the Minoas Confederation to the core, the minor countries falling in line when he gave direction with one hand and slapped down dissent with the other.

But he pulled the people together, improved food production, revamped the health system, gave the people more hope. They had been on the up until the new variant of the ticks swarmed into the cities. And when the virus mutated, the subsequent Brain Fever had hit them hard, driving people out once again and overwhelming their medical abilities. It was only then that he'd turned to Yabbin, and the Shadow Marines. Too proud and stubborn like all Minoas to ask for help from those that had destroyed their world, he sent him in search of the vaccine and antibiotics the Stratan were keeping to themselves.

But it was the loss of his wife that had struck him down, weakened him. It was after that the Fire Tick bacteria took hold. The vaccine had caused a reaction, she being one of the few whose immune system responded aggressively. She had died mercifully swiftly, unlike the others. Hardin had refused the vaccine, instead relying on the stone around his neck. An old tale from the distant past, handed down from generation to generation, and it had worked. Hardrin had instigated the research on his assent to power, pouring state money in until they found that vibrating the right crystal at just the right frequency, in just the right place, stopped the bacteria from propagating. Far too expensive and difficult to replicate, the research was abandoned after the death of his wife, the second precious necklace had sat in the old man's desk for the last fifteen years.

Mwandin took a deep breath before speaking, knowing she had very little time in the coming political maelstrom to really make a difference.

Better make it count then.

"Lords and Ladies, we need to declare a state of emergency. Batten down while the fallout from the General's death sinks in." She held their gaze, setting her chin high. She had read them correctly, the men and women of the Confederation Politico nodding at her sage suggestion. Keeping them in power, while the dust settles.

Batten down the hatches, ladies and gentlemen. This is going to be a bumpy ride.

CHAPTER 48

Council Room, Kaimas Military Garrison, Kaimas

"I need to be present," said Councillor Shante, back stiff and hands in her lap while Abioyi spoke into the screen, her words sub-vocalised and recounted to the Lead Councillor through the bone-radio surgically placed under her ear. Abioyi gave the slightest of nods to show agreement.

"How soon would you like to speak to Captain Yabbin? To announce the sad news," said Abioyi, eyes scanning the image on screen for any signs of weakness or lies.

"Now, if possible. I would not want the news to reach him from elsewhere," answered Prime Minister Mwandin.

Abioyi nodded, Shante in her ear letting her know she needed an hour to ensure things were secure. Mwandin nodded as she passed that on, agreeing to the timescale.

"I have an offer, Lead Councillor. My political time is short, which I'm sure you already know. I understand from my sources that you have visitors from Earth, and that you are working with them on not only an antibiotic regime, but on eradicating the Brain Fever virus that causes the latent bacteria to mutate and mirror the effects from the new variant. I offer our data sets, and the scientific team I have put together. They are willing to work with you, and those from Earth."

"And in return?"

"The medication, and hopefully a future where we can work together on the binding issues we share. The rewilding, and the

Fire Ticks."

"Yabbin betrayed your people, and turned my Field Commander, for the very same cause, Prime Minister. Coincidence?" said Abioyi, her eyes narrowing.

"That's for you to decide. The offer stands. If we can get this set-in-stone before my time is up, then we have a chance to make a change. Give hope. It does not mean we are *friends*, Lead Councillor. But we need to act, or we die out."

"Okay, Mwandin. I'm listening. But before I present your proposal to those that need to hear, tell me about your *!Kora*."

Yabbin stretched his arms towards the sky, cricking his back and pulling briefly at the circlet wrapped once again about his neck. It itched, irritating his skin on contact. But he put that down to nerves, rather than the metal itself.

Not that carrying a bomb around your neck is any reason to be nervous.

"I don't understand why they're letting me come along. Word was you had a huge fallout, you know, explosive," said Yabbin, rolling both his shoulders that pressed into the microship's wall while sitting on the bronzed floor.

"You're a political embarrassment, as are we right now. They've agreed we can collect more samples from another set of *!Kora* tribesmen, looking for a way other than mass murder. And in return, Yasuko agreed to continue working on the antibiotic and vaccine programme," said Zuri, sat in the co-pilot's chair with it turned facing the Minoas traitor. She had less than zero trust in him, the last person she'd wanted along. Though maybe Shante was a little lower on that list. These people just seem constantly on edge, the veneer peeled back after their initial welcome. More like those *!Nias* had said had 'gone bad'. Had she read him wrong?

Mwekaji kisasi haambiwi mwerevu. He who nurses vengeance is not wise. And these people cannot let go.

"You seem to trust the Stratan less and less?" said Yabbin, eyeing Zuri who still watched him like a hawk from the co-pilot's chair.

"A little more than you," said Zuri, eyes flashing. "They haven't actually killed anyone, yet."

"Just a few billion in a war they couldn't win," said Yabbin.

"Ninety odd years ago. Different people, and you fired back," said Zuri.

"Yeah, we did. Humans, eh? A paranoid bunch at the best of times." Yabbin caught the agreement in the woman's eyes, alongside the conflict. He glanced up at the screen, the water flat with a low swell as they flew twenty metres above the sea.

Above the sea!

"Hey, where are we going? No *!Kora* live out here. That's not … you can't be serious? Why are we here?" Yabbin saw the edge of the Atoll rise from the sea, the first few small volcanic islands rising in a rough curve from the seemingly flat-grey ocean. He knew what lay on the south-eastern edge, a place he never wanted to see again. "Khoikhoi. Hellhole."

Smith adjusted the microship's trajectory, and said, "You're the only one to have been anywhere near the island in the last twenty years, except Otegnoa, and they won't be letting him out any time soon. We need to be here, and the Stratan are pleased to see us out of the way. Probably making plans to murder the *! Kora* right now." Smith's sensors picked up the sudden surge in Yabbin's biochemical signature, his heart racing and stress hormones kicking in. "And if they do find out, well, they'll probably hope you die along with us."

Cyborg Blue lays down a little groundwork for the future. You never know when you may need a traitor on your side. He laughs silently to himself, a knot forming, trying to ignore the fact the sea is writing to him. Or singing. Likely both.

"The island, Khoikhoi, you know what's there, right? I lost twenty soldiers in the first wave, and ten more prior to being ordered back. My father ..." Yabbin paused a second, pulling in a long breath, painful memories rubbing against his loss. "General Hardin sent us in to see what tech we could get. You'd have thought the Stratan avoiding the place was enough of a hint. It's dangerous."

"So, my traitorous friend, are we," said Smith.

CHAPTER 49

Approaching Khoikhoi Atoll

The screen displayed the gentle crescent-shaped curve of the island, the outer convex edge facing the main ocean, the rougher sea washing onto the crystalline beach with more vigour than they'd seen elsewhere on Stratan.

But nothing compared to a normal day in the Outer Hebrides.

Finn watched the island grow in size as they closed in, Noah flying the microship, with the help of Yasuko's sliver of AI, towards its southern peninsula. The outer beach rose towards a rocky coastline, prominent obsidian rock protruding from the earth, before reaching a laser flat, precision cut, section. On their stood the old rocket platform, scaffolding lay twisted across the launch pad, and a set of vegetation covered buildings stood in uniform order to one side.

"Fly us round the other side, Noah. There's a lagoon according to the records. I want eyes on, but keep your distance," Noah complied, letting Smith know what they were doing.

"Yabbin's got the picture now," came Smith's response. "He says the surface-to-air stuff kicks in about two kilometres out, limited due to being automated and with concerns over local flight paths. Said it was a mix of heat seeking and visual lock on. We are approaching that now, Finn."

"Suit up. Once we've an up-to-date picture of the lagoon we'll do the diversion run, check how good the tech really is. You follow us in, light-wrapped and full heat retention, see if it picks you up. If not, you drop in and take out the missile batteries," Finn replied, an idea slowly forming in his head. "See if you can do it without too much damage – but no risks."

"We survive, yeah," cut in, Zuri. "Priority One."

Finn ignored Noah's wince when Zuri spoke, nudging him and nodding towards the inner hull controls. Noah sent the signal, the microship nanobots disassembling the wall, revealing two sets of Battle Armour. "Priority One," said Finn, standing up and beginning to prep both sets. The rear of the suits split open, interlocking plates peeling aside and flexing outwards, and he took off the Yasuko issued black kit, revealing a skinsuit underneath.

"Eyes on," said Noah, Finn moving back to peer at the images. A curved cliff face, steps cut in at various places down to the inner lagoon beach. Piled along the beach, crystals of various colour and sizes glistened as the sun rose, the spectrum of light breathtaking, forcing the screen to adjust for the sudden change and failing miserably.

"Anything on sensors? Heat signatures, radar?"

"No, but if these things are relatively dormant, then the major power source could be in those buildings. They probably run off a slow energy bleed or if advanced enough, shielded from us. The microships' sensors don't have the same level of complexity as the Explorer, or Yasuko's analysis crunching to extrapolate anything complex. Might be something to work on," said Noah. "Finn, I … Zuri …"

"Can it, Noah. You and her need to deal with that one – on my orders. I can't have dissent. She's your Lance Corporal, and she gave you more leeway than your outburst deserved. You've been through some serious crap, some of it we might be responsible for. But I am not bending any more. Suck it up, do your job. I need you focussed."

"Yes, Lance Corporal," said Noah, grabbing hold of the roiling emotions pounding his stomach. He turned back to the screen, bringing up a top-down view of the island and its buildings, built from their sensor sweep. He marked four spots on the screen, one on each peninsula at the end of the crescent-shaped island, and two more: one on the outer cliff edge and another on the main building.

"Yeah," said Finn. "Think you're right, most likely sites for the missiles. Suit up."

Yabbin hadn't known what to think, his mind reeling, suddenly aware of the power in the little ship he sat in. He fiddled with the circlet as the Battle Armour split open, the Earth warrior easing herself inside, gawping while it wrapped around her, the helmet lighting up as it fully came online. He suddenly felt small, insignificant.

The blue man flashed him a smile, sliding into his own armour, metal within metal. The huge arms flexing and swinging round the machine gun cradled at his hip, taking three or four stances, before the helmet nodded and the face inside winked at him.

Yabbin knew it was meant to intimidate, and it had damn well worked.

"Where's mine?" he managed to slip out, voice weak, the remark lost and just a little pathetic among the whirr of servos.

"Ah, damn, must have left it behind. I knew we forgot something," Zuri's eyes were grim behind the visor, despite the flippant words. She sighed heavily, and Smith ordered the nanobots to withdraw, a third suit emerging from the hull wall.

"Alpha Mark 3. Slaved to me, you will have no control, no weapons access. You're not trained and not … what's the word? It's on the tip of my tongue," said Smith, his chair absorbing into the floor, and taking up the controls again.

"Trustworthy, honourable, honest, reliable or morally adept. Take your pick," replied Zuri, this time a smile reaching her eyes.

"Yep. And there's no plumbing, so if you are crapping yourself when the bullets fly, hold it in or you'll be scrubbing for days."

"Do you people ever stop preaching?" Yabbin stood and approached the armour, Zuri snapping his bonds with two gauntleted fingers.

"Nope," said Smith. "We are Space Commandos. Our values are excellence, integrity, self-discipline and humility. With the qualities of courage, determination, unselfishness and cheerfulness. The last one is mainly my job."

"Be the first to understand; the first to adapt and respond; and the first to overcome," continued Zuri, fist bumping Smith as he turned towards her, a huge grin across his face.

"Finally. We have a name," said Smith, ordering the slaved suit to close up, wrapping Yabbin tight and analysing his body structure and life signs before adapting itself. Smith cross-checked the data, and satisfied, signalled Noah.

"This is British Space Commando Transport One. We have a go."

And Cyborg Blue sucks in a deep breath, a proud member of the Space Commandos. Ready to uphold its value and qualities – and design a new badge. Just after he's dealt with the sea that likes to write and sing to him. Perfectly normal.

Noah snorted, followed by a suppressed snigger. Finn sighing next to him, slapped both gauntleted hands onto his helmet.

"You've got to admit, he's persistent," said Noah. "This is Commando Transport Two, confirming approach. Good luck, Smith."

Noah turned the microship out of its holding pattern,

standing at the control console with the pilot's seat now merged with the bronzed floor. He checked the trajectory and ran a review of the light-wrap and heat absorption potential. With the parameters in that nice, positive green band he liked, and he'd already checked twice, he took the ship in. He felt Finn tense next to him, knowing his leader hated not being in control of the situation, but more than a little proud he was trusted to be in control.

Discipline and duty.

He put away the emotions of the last few days and focussed, as ordered. The sensors flashed, thermal signatures blooming on the north and south peninsulas, a third in the centre, not on the main buildings but on the launch platform. This one weaker, intermittent. Noah didn't discount it, registering what it potentially signalled. He sent the data to Smith, and straight into Finn's HUD.

The missile flashed, the heat signature running super-hot as its rocket engaged, spearing towards them with a spiral of smoke flowing behind it. Noah flinched, wanting to react but forcing himself to wait and the AI alerted him to the second missile release from the southern tip of the island. In combination with the AI, he turned the ship, bringing it lower down, wave skipping, trying to throw off any potential radar lock the missiles may have.

Ah crap. Should have realised.

A third and fourth missile launched, rushing out towards their little ship, accelerating at worrying rates. The waves were not high enough, and now the control screen threw up a double lock from the missiles' onboard narrow radar beam. He checked the hull composition, ready to adjust the range of absorption for when they could stop acting as a decoy. He wasn't certain he could do that for both heat signature and the radar, when they were running engines this hot, especially without Yasuko. Again, that reliance factor.

"Smith," said Noah, "The launch pad – there's a radar system on there. They have a lock on us and we're going to be running hot. Need you to take that out ASAP." Noah pulled the microship up. Time to head for space.

CHAPTER 50

Research Facility, Khoikhoi Atoll

Smith gently wheeled the microship, bringing it round the outer cliff's rock edge to land on the flat, basalt edge. With the speed low to minimise the movement of the air, the light-wrapped ship settled onto its landing gear. He heard Zuri's slow intake of breath and gave her a thumbs up.

"Time to kick some robot butt," he said, powering down, and when Zuri reached the exit area, ordering the nanobots to form the door.

Yabbin suddenly found himself moving, powered legs pulsing a warning before they strode to stand behind Zuri. He felt Smith behind him, and glancing over the HUD, found the images of the blue man in the top left corner. He eye-clicked, the system following his commands and he switched between thermal, night vision and back to the normal view. It was just like standard armour, and he felt a little more at ease.

Zuri dropped to the ground, her boots imprinting in the thin layer of soil covering the smooth, flat stone. They had landed halfway between the northern peninsula and the centre of the island, about five hundred metres from each. With Noah's request on her mind, she turned towards the buildings, the white, scorch marked stone walls, holding up a roof covered in low bushes and small trees.

"Flash soot marks," stated Yabbin, exiting the ship and noting where Zuri was looking. "This place was a primary target during the war. With the main comms knocked out by the Stratan's first strike, the warhead exploded about three kilometres to the east, above the ocean. Everything on the outside was incinerated, but those walls were built to withstand a close proximity rocket misfire. They took it and laughed back."

Zuri, feeling exposed due to the minimal plant cover, kept low. It didn't help her unease, the armour's bulk a hinderance, memories of angry, buzzing machines and suit-wraiths flashing through her mind. This wasn't Nutu Allpa, and these auto machines couldn't pass on any EM wielding alien madness, but the feeling nagged.

Smith signalled the microship was on auto before following Zuri. Sensors interlinked with the suits instantly screamed an alert. Sending the coordinates to Zuri's HUD, he dropped low, raising his assault rifle to scan to the north just as the heavy calibre bullets smashed into his chest plate. A large, quad-engined drone rose from within the basalt floor, underslung weapons smoking. Staggered by their power, his energy bolt slammed into the drone's barrels, warping one but the other fired again. He rolled, the large armour's servos pushing him sideways as he heard Zuri open up to his left, her responding fire clattering against something hard. A second burst slammed into his hip, but Smith carried on the movement, coming up and swinging the rifle around, sensors locking the rifle onto the drone's body and the explosive round flew from his gun. It ripped into the drone, burying in, the whirr increasing in pitch with the armoured plate resisting. The ensuing explosion rocked the drone sideways, taking out two propellers, the drone crashing into the floor. Smith ran towards it, slamming an armoured foot down onto the working propellers and unleashing an energy bolt into the main body.

Cyborg Blue, hero.

Zuri's first burst had sent another armoured drone whirling to her right, ducking underneath her energy bolt, its own bullets

215

smashing into the rock at her feet. She jumped forward and left, using the servos to lift her high, releasing another shot down towards the spiralling drone. The explosive round smashing into one set of blades before exploding, rupturing another, sending it crashing to the floor. Zuri landed, rolling forwards and bringing her rifle up as the drone rose again, unsteady, but locked on, releasing a mini-missile. The rocket hurtled towards her, far too close for her to dodge. It slammed into the armour's chest plate, knocking her backwards and to the ground. Zuri braced, waiting for the pain. But nothing happened, and she looked down to find the spent missile lying in pieces next to her. She took a breath as the drone exploded into flame, the machine finally succumbing to her previous attack.

Bahati haiji mara mbili. Luck comes only once.

She rose to her feet, Yabbin standing stock still, exactly where he'd been when the drones attacked. The problem of slaved armour. However, the machines had selected Smith and her, perhaps they had some form of threat detection.

"You okay, Smith?"

"Just peachy. That missile, did it fail to go off?" he replied.

"Luck I'm not going to pass up on. This equipment has been here a long time, maybe not all of it will be functioning well. How's your armour status?"

"Forty percent damage on the chest plate, twenty-five percent on the hip. Those rounds have some grunt," Smith stood by Yabbin, eyeing Zuri and switching to English. "We're going to have to give him some control, he's a sitting duck. As much as I like someone else being shot instead of me, we …"

"Okay. Is there any way we can adjust it? So, if he goes rogue, it shuts down."

"I can put on a proximity alert. That'd do it," Smith adjusted Yabbin's control link, testing it a couple of times until completely satisfied while Zuri covered. Switching back to Stratan, he informed Yabbin.

"Thanks, might mean a little less scrubbing."

"Always a good thing," said Smith moving to take point, with Zuri ordering him back.

"I'm on full. Just get those sensors up. Yabbin, you see anything else other than those drones?" said Zuri, moving out towards the edge of the first building, still 400 metres distance with only a few scrub bushes and low palm-like trees in the way.

"Yeah, briefly. There's a biped robot – twin cannons on top, with a mini-missile battery. Like the drone, but heavier armour. Only saw one, and it was enough."

Zuri nodded, ignoring Yabbin's gasp as her *weapon* transformed, taking on the appearance of a Multiple Grenade launcher, with six grenades loaded into a cylinder slung between stock and barrel. She moved forward, aware Smith had brought the gimble mounted machine gun to bear, its design from the events on Nutu Allpa lending it the stopping power equivalent to the AW50 armour penetrating rounds. She eye-clicked Smith's sensor feed into her HUD, and began to move slowly forward, adding her own magnified visual search to the information stream.

She moved directly towards the building, with no cover, and a non-human enemy, there was no point in using stealth. If they'd had time to transfer Noah's new knowledge of the light-wrap crystals, she wouldn't have trusted that, either. Too many ways to detect them when the enemy was static and fully tooled up. Smith's sensors highlighted a thermal image to her right, and then another, low-grade. He amplified the information, a family of wild pigs grunting among the low-grade roots. Zuri ignored them, and the few tiny birds roosting on some of the lower bushes.

At least some life is making its own way back from the brink.

Smith splashed an alert, dropping into a firing position, his machine gun tracking movement from the far corner of the building. Zuri picked the striding robot up, a second emerging from the other side, a slight limp to its movements but no less fast. She brought the launcher up, releasing a *weapon* enhanced grenade and moving sideways. The twin cannons tracked her, then opened up. A burst of bullets clattered into her right hip plate, sending her spinning as the grenade exploded against the robot's knee joint. The pain in her hip erupted, throbbing, and she hit the floor. Zuri locked the pulsing agony away, continuing the forced spin and hitting the power button on her gauntlet's wrist. The servos surged her up and forwards, rising to witness the bipedal robot wavering, before collapsing to the floor, its knee joint shattered. Zuri instantly jumped to the side, the missile launched from the robot's prone torso slamming into the spot she'd just left, basalt fragments peppering her armour. Coming down, she brought the grenade launcher to bear, willing the *weapon* to hit home, firing dual shots before using the leg servos to drive her onwards again, with a second missile curving in flight locked on to her. Zuri leapt into another roll, the spinning armour constantly on the move as the missile exploded, the impact smashing her into the floor.

Smith opened up as soon as the limping robot attacked Zuri, his machine gun burst raking the second advancing robot, its long legs stretching out in a run towards him. It reminded him of an ostrich, clawed, splayed feet slamming into the ground, the twin cannons tracking him all the way. But nothing fired, the weapons only following him, no bullets sent his way. He cut across the advancing guard-bot's knee and hip joints, pouring hot, explosive metal into the armoured plate. The robot suddenly jinked to the right, then left, its movements deliberate, and fifty percent of his rounds missed their intended targets as it closed in. When within fifty metres, the robot fired multiple grenades into the air, Smith leaping to the side as they sailed downwards, smoke billowing accompanied by a loud bang and huge flashes designed to blind his senses. Smith hit the floor, servos taking the weight of his landing, and switched on the sensors that had automatically muted. The robot slammed into him, the scythe like talons on its toes ripping into arm and neck. The armour held firm, but with the talons raking downwards, they tore at the meta-Kevlar weave between them. Smith, prone, on his back with a clawed foot pressing him down, could only watch the second taloned foot bearing down on him, angled to rip at his head.

Alpha 3 hit the robot hard, its shoulder plate taking a huge impact against the metal legs, with Yabbin powering into the three-metre-tall robot. Without knowing the power settings, he was operating at standard 1g, twenty-five percent more than he was used to, but doing enough to force the robot's claw to scrape against basalt rather than the blue man's helmet. Yabbin's proximity alarm kicked in, the armour immediately becoming rigid as he hit the floor.

The robot wavered, off balance and on one foot, it released the pressure on Smith who grabbed at the machine's toes. Heaving upwards, the robot sensed a new imbalance and tried to reposition itself, bringing the raised foot to the floor. Smith ripped the toes he held apart, splitting the armour plates and exposing the hydraulics. He head-butted the pistons, smashing the links, and his arm mounted energy weapon followed up with bolt after bolt into the robot's foot. He shoved upwards again, rolling out from beneath the toppling machine. The heavy robot torso clipped his back, pinning him briefly to the ground until he slid out from under it, turning and grabbing hold of the twin cannons. He heaved, exposing a crack below the turret, pumping in two arm mounted grenades and subsequently rolling out to the side.

The turret erupted, the explosion hurling shredded metal and wires to batter at Smith's armour as he came to a stop. He rose from the ground, brushing the dirt off, and turned to face the ruptured machine.

And Cyborg Blue delivers justice. Be aware perps, you may be next.

Ah crap, have I killed the traitor?

Smith strode back to the huge robot, lifting the twisted metal leg that lay across Yabbin's immobile armour.

"You alive in there?"

"Just," replied Yabbin, his voice a little strained. "You owe me one."

"Yeah. Maybe." Smith reset Yabbin's armour, holding a hand out to help the man up. As Yabbin reached out, Smith turned away, seeking Zuri and leaving Yabbin hanging. "We aren't friends. I hold grudges – long ones. Nobody's perfect. But you can strike that one up as a little credit."

Zuri pushed herself up stiffly from the floor, her armour pockmarked by metal shards, with scorch marks scarring plates. Managing to stand, she pressed her hands into her back, just above the hips, stretching the joints. Smith flicked over her medical data, noting the damage in her hip, most likely bruised rather than anything broken. But he knew she'd taken a hefty hit. They both had. Yabbin hadn't exaggerated the threat.

"We good?" he asked Zuri.

"Marvellous. Never felt better. Any more of these things, Yabbin?" she said, eye-clicking her visuals to magnify the building.

"Pretty much decimated my team by this point. So, anything else will be new to me."

"Hey," said Noah on the radio, "You guys on holiday or something? Could do with that radar down if you want any help."

CHAPTER 51

Airport, Tralakin, Northeastern Minoas

With the last of the equipment stowed aboard, Lanre turned over the engines, air intake blades spinning as the twin jets came online.

"Buckle up," he said over the radio, the six scientists in the stubby transport plane's hold complying, feeling the rumble of the engines kick in. Lanre checked the systems again, with no co-pilot he had more roles than he really wanted. But the fewer people who knew about the flight, the safer he felt. Checking the failsafes, and satisfied, he flipped the light-wave switch, the camouflage enshrouding the entire plane as he taxied out onto the runway. Right now, the remaining satellite orbiting Stratan would be out of direct sight, with only the radar systems able to pick him up. The light-wrap would help, once airborne he would be extremely difficult to pick out. But should the Minoas fighter jets be sent his way, there was nothing more than a few magnesium flares between them and the ocean.

He sucked in a breath, mentally saluting the bravery of the scientists in his hold. What they were doing would have been treason a few hours beforehand, and most likely would be again once Mwandin was removed from office. But Yabbin had been preparing for this moment for years, manoeuvring Mwandin into higher and higher office with bribes and promises that most other men would have quailed at. Lanre knew of at least one assassination the man had carried out personally, and two his Corporal was rumoured to have undertaken. Each outwardly political, the Minoas penchant for paranoia and subterfuge as they lost sight of the bigger, long-term picture of humanity's slow, chaotic spiral into death.

They soon reached take-off speed, the wheels lifting from the runway and into the airplane's fuselage, lost to sight with the camouflage kicking in. He dared not think how much the crystals had cost, nor the time and effort taken to build them in. The design of the plane was pre-war, its structure as near to minimal radar reflection as possible considering it was a transport craft. Lanre said a final prayer, this one for Mwandin.

The battering on her door escalated, Mwandin recognising the sound of metal truncheon on wood from her days in the Slabin slums. The raids had been constant, the Minoas Constables on the hunt for whatever imagined traitor they had dreamed up to satisfy their current leader's paranoia whenever protests ebbed and flowed within the city. It's what had been the greatest loss for her when Hardrin died. The man had been tough, gave little. But he would not bend to the Politico's need to lash out. Yes, he ruled by fear, but he gave back, and those that suffered were often deserving of it somewhere in their past.

The door gave, uniforms piling through, with Lord Pansin and his pathetic entourage following. He waved a wax stamped paper, shouting and bellowing about her being ousted from office and her personal affairs were to be investigated.

Mwandin knew better than to react, keeping her decorum, giving no excuse for anything other than the treatment an ex-Prime Minister deserved. It was to be her role from now on, no longer an active member of Yabbin's treason, but a dam to hold the tide back for as long as she could.

Buy time. Don't forget me, Yabbin. We are to be in prison a thousand miles apart, but our cause stays true.

CHAPTER 52

Research Facility, Khoikhoi Atoll

The auto-sentry kicked in, the rounds lower powered than the 30mm cannons the robo-guards had been sporting, but the fire rate huge. The rock face Zuri, Smith and Yabbin had thrown themselves behind had lost the first two steps down, the basalt erupting in a flurry of stone chips, the shells shattering the rock. The shooting stopped, silence only punctuated by the flap of receding wings, and the distant grunting of the pig-like creatures heading for the beach below.

"That thing works off movement," said Smith, his back to the stone steps, staring at the receding birds in the blue sky.

"You don't say," said Zuri, checking her armour over before examining the chips in Smith's helmet. "You okay in there?"

"Yeah. They were aiming for the least important bit of me. Need a plan? I suggest we throw Yabbin out to the north, we move south and while it's hammering him, we hit it with a grenade."

"The best plans are always the simplest." Zuri took the large stone chip from the pile near her feet, throwing it up and over her shoulder, the rock shattering in mid-air and showering her with the grey, powdered rock. "It knows we are here, movement or not."

"It's encased in the building, pops up to fire and then drops down again. I think blue man's idea would work, except we use him as the decoy," said Yabbin.

"Well, I'm not the one wearing slaved armour," said Smith. "And I've died twice already, trying my best not to get the hat-trick." Smith locked Alpha 3 down, sending an image of a smiling blue man to Yabbin's HUD.

A few minutes later, Yabbin's armour scrambled up from the northern set of stairs. Its booted feet surged above the cliff edge using its full power, zig zagging towards the building edge, trying to get below the auto-sentry field of fire. Bullets rained in, hitting the plates, helmet and boots here and there while it wove, dived and tumbled to slap against the scorch marked wall. The gunfire came to a sudden stop, Smith's dual grenades exploding under the stone cap, the intense heat melting the auto-sentry's control mechanism, twisting the barrels and finally reaching its ammo store. Zuri subsequently threw a second rock sailing over the cliff edge, one that landed with a thud twenty metres away in one piece. The third confirmed the auto-sentries prognosis, and Zuri, Smith and a suit-less Yabbin rose from the floor to climb back onto the plateau.

"See, you make a fine decoy," said Smith, recalling Alpha and noting the armour's twenty percent damage level. He instructed it to resize for a human and split open. With no human inhabitant, the suits lowered their centre of gravity, increasing the hydraulic mass at hip, knee and ankle. They switched from being a Husky to a full-on Wolf, and Smith's mind wandered back to the pleasure of it. Yabbin eased his legs inside, then arms, and the armour automatically wrapped around him.

"I could get used to this," said Yabbin, the HUD engaging and adjusting to his eyes.

"Don't. It's a one-time offer with no buy-back option. And you pay for the damages," said Smith, now covering Zuri who swept her gaze across the first of the research buildings. "I have no heat signatures, Zuri. But I'm going to guess there's at least one more of those sentries at the far end of the site. Probably near the launchpad."

Zuri nodded, "Noah? You read me?"

"From the upper atmosphere, yep. Finn's chomping at his visor, Zuri. The man with no patience is taking it out on me. The floor is wearing out."

"Can't be helped, these things are powerful. We are getting closer but can't give a timescale."

"We've outrun the last of the missiles, and are heading back in. Finn wants us to use the light-wrap and heat sink, but we won't have the diversion you had. Please get the batteries offline, or you might have to put me back in the growth tank. Either blown up or gnawed on depending on who gets me first."

"On it," said Zuri, looking back towards Smith. "He's spending far too much time with you; it's beginning to rub off."

"Nice to hear him in a better mood. You and him …?"

"We'll sort it. It's why Finn is with him. Surprised we've not had a few more spats, with the stress and all."

"Discipline, working by the numbers, and relaxing together in between – bonding. Between you and Finn, you have it right. Better than I could do it."

Zuri stopped briefly, about to turn when her HUD flashed up the sight of a gauntleted hand on her plated shoulder.

"It's better this way," Smith said. "And I don't want to be in charge. Hell, I don't know if I even want to be human. I'm the comedy foil, remember. A far more important role."

And Cyborg Blue gets deep, too deep. He reels himself in, aware he has exposed himself to pain despite the powered armour and the machine gun.

They reached the scorched walls with no more incident. Close up, they could see the apparently smooth stone was rippled with heat deformations. With backs to the bulging wall, they moved towards the huge doors at one end, the dull grey metal built in sections into a 30 by 30 metres opening. Closing in, Zuri noted the buckle in its surface, and the numerous flat hinges were warped in places, soot streaking across the metal.

"We thought this was the development warehouse," said Yabbin. "There's a deposit of true sapphire across the islands, so this place began as the laser and laser sail testing lab. Later, they built the engines and the internal systems here. The external portion of the atoll has upwellings of rare metals too, our scientists assumed these were in use somewhere. The whole atoll was subject to ocean mining. Hence, the crystal beaches."

Zuri moved towards the door edges, examining the hinges and the area in front of the warehouse. It clearly hadn't moved for decades, and they passed by, heading towards the next building, using the increased cover of rusting, twisted military vehicles that lay between them and it. With Zuri leading, and Smith's sensors on full alert, they left the last of the vehicles behind to reach the smaller building, wreathed in twisted metal pylons, old aerials and snapped wires. They sidled along the wall, reaching the battened down windows and eventually the metal shod doors in its centre. Assessing the decades since these were also last opened, Zuri moved on past, reaching the corner and the sight of the huge scaffolding whose rusted, malformed structure lay broken across the launch pad.

"Anything?" she asked.

"Getting a faint heat signature, residual."

Smith marked the spot on Zuri's HUD, and she magnified the picture, catching sight of the bulbous radar structure just off the edge of the platform, standing alongside four others.

"And those?"

"Dunno, dormant or decoys. I'm guessing they would only need one, maybe another as redundancy if they were exceptionally paranoid."

"I'd say that's a fairly common trait we share with the Stratan," said Yabbin.

"Finn wants us to disable, not destroy it. So we need to be close in, find the transmitter link for the missile batteries," said Zuri. "Normally, it'd be me with your sensors on cover. But you'll detect the cabling links. You're up, Smith."

Smith adjusted his assault rifle across his back, making sure it was loose in his holster, and checking Zuri was ready, walked out low and steady towards the curved edge of the raised platform, his machine gun moving side to side on the cradle. Sensors on sweep, switching between modes, the area appeared lifeless as he reached the five-metre-high ledge. He continued to walk towards the south, swinging the machine gun to maintain its firing line.

It's quiet, too quiet. Like the type of quiet you get when the audience knows that you're next on the hit list. Cyborg Blue can sense something is about to happen, he's on the edge. Come on perp, make my Earth standard day.

The robo-guard rose from under the twisted pile of scaffolding, online with its system picking up Smith's movements. The twin cannons, wrapped in wire, were stuck solid and unable to track round. Smith flattened against the wall instinctively, memories of the cannon's power urging his servos to act. A grenade smashed into the robot, the explosion sending it spinning, but freeing the cannons at the same time.

"Smith," bellowed Zuri, another grenade flying.

He stepped out to lay a burst into the guard, bullets raking the machine's knee joints, cracking the metal, and the guard bot wobbled wildly, its balance failing. And then it fired, the whomp of a grenade rising from the top of the robot, reaching a four-metre height before dropping to the floor, apparently harmless.

And Smith froze, HUD shutting down, and servos frozen. Nothing responded to his commands, he was locked in. And panic began to rise.

The HUD flickered, sparking into life for a millisecond. Maybe a little more. During that time, his powered arm raised a tiny fraction, his knee joint less. The radio crackled with static, so quickly a human would miss the hiss, but not Smith.

And the cycle repeated, and repeated. And Cyborg Blue stood among the ruins of Stratan's past hope, locked in, as the EMP pulsed.

CHAPTER 53

Research Facility, Khoikhoi Atoll

Noah watched, eyes tracking the gap between the two buildings, Finn moving from rusted vehicle to vehicle, reaching the scorched, white building they assumed to be Mission Control. Finn signalled, and Noah moved, only his Yasuko issued, 3D printed uniform between any bullets and his fragile body. He had never felt so naked in his life, and his adrenaline was surging. It was a continuous battle to lock it down, focus on his job.

By the numbers, Noah. By the numbers.

He reached the building, standing with his back against it, the assault rifle they'd used for combating the EM creature on Nutu Allpa in hand. Finn had stowed one aboard each microship, and the Glock which he currently wielded. Noah, thankful for Finn's preparations, followed his squad leader as he slid along the wall, past the old metal doors, and towards the twin statues at the far corner. Finn worked his way round Alpha 3, eyes warily watching the thrashing robot about twenty metres from Smith's frozen armour.

He signalled Noah over, and on joining Finn, handed the monocular over.

"There," he said, pointing to the right of Smith, between him and the robo-guard. "See it? Not the same as that box thing the Stratan had back on Earth, more compact, but its new – see the impact in the surrounding dust. Has to be that."

Noah focussed on the object, grenade sized and shaped, but the structure very different. With their systems knocked out by its constant wave changes, they were stripped back to the old days. Worse in fact, with no armour, enhanced sights or night vision.

And I don't like it. Too exposed.

The rapid wave changes allied with the pulse effect meant the suits had shut down, internal systems protected by high-quality shielding, but unable to operate, repeatedly shutting down after each start up when the pulse wave hit again. Once the EMP was negated, all the systems would boot up. But all he could think of was the mess they'd be in if the robo-guards or auto-sentries had been operational. Sitting ducks, and by the way the damaged robot was moving, it clearly had a way around its own weapon.

Store that for later.

Finn signalled wait, heading out towards Smith, and using him as a shield, pumped two chemical fused grenades into the flailing bot. The explosions ripped it apart, and with a final, limp flap of its leg, the bot died. Noah responded when Finn motioned him over, keeping low and wary until he reached Smith. He rapped on his friend's armour, knocking out his favourite rap metal riff before proceeding to the grenade.

Noah opened the metal lined bag, extracted from the microship's own EMP internal shielding, and placed it over the grenade. He heard Smith's servos whirr, the reboot kicking in, swearing pulsing down the radio.

"When you've finished your paddy, Smith," said Finn, "We need *you* to scoop up the grenade and wrap it in the bag. Just in case it has an explosive failsafe. But don't throw it, this one's for Yasuko and Noah." Finn tapped the raging Corporal on the hip, and walked away, whistling. Noah winked at Smith and followed.

The air turned Cyborg Blue.

"Okay Yasuko, we have three sets of missile batteries and two radar systems. The three shot up robo-guards are of little use, but Noah has been cannibalising their metallic shells. Says they have a workaround for the pulse EMP that enables them to operate at a lower level. From what he's saying, Smith and the rest would have been dead meat had the robot been fully functional."

"What do you want me to do, Finn?"

"When we're finished here, and I have my sights on the auto-sentries too, we're going to set up some protection for the *!Kora*. Not that I don't trust the Stratan, or the Minoas. But if we find a way to negate the *!Kora's* impact on the Brain Fever then we can give them a helping hand."

"And if not? My work shows they are at the centre of the bacterial mutations. Their rites create a third stage Fire Tick that infects animals and humans at a much higher rate. The bacteria enter the blood stream through the saliva glands – the bigger the tick, the larger the bacterial load. And if every *!Kora* tribe is doing this …" Yasuko left it hanging, the implications too painful. "And the Brain Fever virus takes elements of this new mutation and transfers its traits to humans carrying latent bacteria in their hippocampus. We need to break the cycle. Or at least slow it down. It's not just the human population, I can't see Alkinta's breeding programme working either."

Finn sighed, rubbing his forehead as he thought. "Let's face that if we have to, yeah? I can't … choose. But maybe a few defences will buy them some time."

"If I agree to manufacture them. I'm not sure the Stratan are wrong, Finn. My mind is reeling. Xxar was petty, wrong in so many ways, but this is … is different. I need Noah back, to see through the logic and use that malleable human brain of his. The scientists are so compartmentalised, they are too much like me – very focussed. Connections take an oversight I don't have without him," Finn could feel the despair in Yasuko's voice, despite the distance and the comms system between them. He glanced over to Zuri, her eyes on him, knowing the turmoil that she shared, and hating herself for agreeing with Yasuko.

We survive, me and mine come first. Why should the Stratan be any different?

"We need to send Noah back," said Zuri. "Finish what he started. Maybe Yasuko's right, and together they can find a way. Or at least buy some time to delay the Stratan. Maybe move them from their homes? Or destroy the crystals in their seas, possibly end their rites somehow."

"Listen to yourself, Zuri," said Finn. "How many times has that happened in our history? And when you read about it, watch it on TV, we are in up in arms about what others are forced into. Yet, when faced with it ourselves …"

Zuri stood, turning away from Finn as she walked towards the microship door. Her body tense, mind flickering through her grandmother's tales of British Colonial rule in Tanganyika, later to be Tanzania. On reaching the door, she gripped its edge, hard.

"If we do this, then my rule still applies, Finn. Us first," she stepped out, the pressure of the moment released, the conflict of morals versus survival dampened. For now.

CHAPTER 54

Lagoon, Research Facility, Khoikhoi Atoll

Cyborg Blue stands at the edge of destiny, his name would be written in the stars after this day.

Or at least the sea. Come on, get on with it.

Zuri and Finn stood at his side, looking across the lagoon, with the sun about to reach its zenith. Reds and purples flashed across the crystal lined beach, reflecting off the cliffs where the obsidian poked through. Noah had already left, taking the extracted parts from the research station and the data Smith recovered from the main data banks. They had plans, schematics and processing designs for all that they had faced today, plus a few spare rare metals and precious stones from the store. More was on their ship, prepped for when they were ready to leave. Yabbin sat on the cut stone steps, throwing obsidian and basalt stones onto the crystal beach, waiting, Alpha 3 stood close by.

"You're fully sealed, Smith. Space worthy, remember," said Zuri.

"Yes, but I can't go deeper than about 40 metres. These suits are designed to keep air in, not water out. Yasuko adapted our microship, so I can take it deep. But …"

"Go on," said Finn. "But …"

"You going to make me say it? Really? After what you go through at night?" said Smith, whipping his helmet round to face Finn, electronic eyes glowing.

Finn took a step back.

Too much. I didn't know he hated the water that much.

"Sorry, Smith. If it comes to that, I'll come with you," said Finn, stepping back in, arm out.

Smith eyeballed him again, letting a grin crack across his blue metallic face. "Yeah, why not. Two emotionally dysfunctional people under extreme pressure. What can go wrong?" they bumped gauntleted fists, and Smith strode out into the lagoon, the seawater lapping at his knees and thighs.

He reached the point where he calculated the crystal Haven writing appeared, and swirled the water, like a challenge to the sea.

Come on then. How weird can it be?

Smith watched the crystals rise to the surface, the small granular pieces interlocking, linking together into undulating, complex patterns. The Haven formed, and once locked, held their shape despite the waves lapping at them. He sighed, mouthing the words, taking in the writings' depth, curve and width, cross-referencing with Yasuko's detailed data bank.

Well, that's to the point, and not the least bit demanding.

Wading back, relief washed through him, nothing had arisen from the water to drag him under.

Always start with a positive.

"Okay, Lance Corporal. Looks like we have a journey to make, should be quite pretty. You know, fish, coral and that. Ever seen a deep-sea vent? No, nor have I. Just the 2500 metres or so straight down, no light. Nothing to worry about."

The microship dropped gently onto the sea, the nanobots adjusting the hull and engine shrouding using Yasuko's algorithmic instruction, reforming the ship. It wouldn't be the fastest, sleekest nor the prettiest thing in the sea. But Smith's requirements had been clear, if they were to be near the surface all that was well and good. If not, then he simply wanted the safest. And he'd asked for that with capital letters and everything. Possibly a couple of exclamation marks and some underlining.

Smith's ability to control the ship was to be limited initially, until he completely felt at home with the change in movement required when cutting through water, as opposed to an atmosphere, or the vacuum of space.

Don't let anyone tell you they are the same.

The viewscreens provided a full 360 degrees of perspective, with Yasuko ensuring him it would maximise even the tiniest light traces should they be going deep, to give them a better than reality view. In addition, they had temperature sensors, but no thermal imaging beyond an eight-metre range due to water's propensity to block most electromagnetic waves. All in all, Smith felt not only stripped down to the bare bones, but completely out of touch with the world around him.

Cyborg Blue sucks it up, ignoring the increasing pressure and oppressive darkness he is about to enter. Instead, he turns his attention to Killjoy, his arch nemesis. Perhaps winding him up will make him feel less ... blue.

"You okay, Finn? You know, if you need to hold my hand on the way down, you can borrow my powered armour. I'm sure it wouldn't mind."

"Funny. Your jokes get worse the more nervous you are," said Finn, walking round the adapted microship, marvelling at the lava layers that appeared still to flow outwards from the island as they descended. Layer upon layer, each thicker but more encrusted with coral and the life it encourages. The fish, though different from Earth, kept to the same archetype of fins and tails, gliding through the orange and black horned branches, or flittering between the green and fire red growths. The table corals were familiar, ones he'd seen on a few old Jacques Cousteau films from the sixties, but their undersides were iridescent, light from their ship causing sparkles of sapphire and blue among the crawling life beneath.

"You know," said Finn. "This is something I always wanted to do. But life just got in the way. Too much of a grunt in the army to get the chance, and little effort on my part in the downtime. I can understand why people want to keep this safe. Look."

Smith turned, his hands running through the motions with the controls, the mini-AI really running the ship. Finn pointed out the cascading rock crystals dropping from a protruding edge of the island, the closest section to the lagoon. Its beauty took Smith's non-existent breath away, holding his body still while his digitised eyes tried to process every colour, every refraction, almost overwhelmed by the sheer complexity of light.

And the human part of me holds its breath, and the inhuman calculates the refraction rates. Where am I in that?

The crystals tumbled into the depths, and the lava layers came to an end. Already at forty metres, the light level dropped, accentuated by the murkier water clarity – a result of the finer crystals suspended within it. In another one hundred and sixty metres or so, the light would fade rapidly, its penetration limited. Below that, maybe a twilight zone where some light may get through, and below one thousand metres, as black as black, except for their own lights.

And we thought space was scary, even when being shot at or grabbed by suit-wraiths it does not compare. Cyborg Blue decides to think about something else.

They dropped further, the journey slow and steady as the pressure built on the microship. Smith ran the checks three times, to be sure, every few minutes. Even the AI, with low processing power dedicated to any personality traits, started to respond with indignance at his constant need to run by the numbers.

Passing into the twilight zone, they managed the odd glimpse of super-sized predators with a whale's bulk and a shark's teeth, and smaller, tentacled and gelatinous creatures that brought up too many recent memories. Finn sat down beside Smith and began to talk, running through old missions, reminiscing about the bars they'd been thrown out of, or even better, ones they'd managed to stay in. Smith chipped in, and their thoughts turned to Afghanistan and the separate roles they'd taken as their battalion struggled with the desperation overwhelming the people, and them, as the allied withdrawal descended into chaos. A people unhomed after so many promises, with some finding a place in a strange, new world, and others left at the mercy of those they'd struggled so long to keep at bay. Both lives, where they were lucky enough to hold on to life, completely changed with no say, no control. What happened was done *to* them, not *with* them.

Silence descended, along with the ship, as they moved into the dark. Their thoughts sliding over anything and everything to keep them from having to think of where they were, and what they were doing. The AI flashed Smith a message, and he clicked the screen view away from the edge of the shelf wall they were descending, to look below.

"What the …?" said Smith, eyes flickering across the screen, trying to take in the images below. Finn grabbed his arm, his organic brain registering the scene with a mix of fear and awe. Spread below them were shelf layers, each glowing, pulsing with strobes of blue-green light. Flutes and tunnels, tree like bursts of crystals shone with a near neon luminescence that caught their breath. The nearer they came, the clearer the pulsing pattern of light. An outward passage, like a heartbeat, rode a wave of colour until it reached the outer edges, then a return pattern, each slightly different, flowed back towards the centre.

"What depth are we at, micro?" asked Smith.

"*Two thousand and fifty metres.*"

"So what we're seeing is how far away?"

"*Five hundred and seventy-three, seventy-two, seventy-one metres.*"

"That would make this structure how big?" asked Finn, eyes fixated on the apparent centre where the neon light wave was currently pulsing towards.

"*About five thousand metres, based on a few assumptions about water density, pressure differences, gravity fluctuations, etc.*"

"Does the sonar show anything about it?" asked Finn, looking towards Smith, not quite sure what he should be thinking right now.

"Micro?" said Smith.

"*The crystal held in solution is dense here, the sound waves dispersed. I could try a narrow focus, but be warned, that could be destructive on contact, both to life and inanimate structures.*"

"Whatever is down here has intelligence, Finn. And we are the vulnerable ones, as I'm sure you are aware. My advice, we descend and wait."

"Wait?"

"For instructions."

Let the sea talk to me. When did it all get so weird?

CHAPTER 55

Kaimas Military Garrison, Kaimas

Noah brought the microship down towards the Explorer, signalling Yasuko to widen the hold doors so he could avoid the new Stratan lab building currently being extended further at its side. Letting Yasuko take over, the small ship eased through the widened gap, and she brought it down at the furthest point from the doors, shrouding it with a new nano-wall as it settled, blocking it from view. Newly formed bots began to remove the equipment he'd brought, Noah directing them towards his workshop, except for the EMP shielded system.

"I think this is vital, Yasuko," he said, exiting the hold. "Something we need to look at for both sets of armour. For all it being funny seeing Smith like that, I'm not so sure Zuri having a repeat experience would be beneficial to my future prospects. I have schematics for the robot weapons too, and the missile defence systems."

"I haven't agreed to make them," said Yasuko. "And we may not need them. We have a new group of scientists with us, from Minoas. I would like you to be in on what they are saying."

"When?"

"Now, of course, always now," Yasuko appeared next to him, the grim expression from the last few days a little lighter, her virtual skin tone brighter. "You have time for a shower, and something light to eat. I will gather them together, say, in about thirty minutes?"

"Yes mum," said Noah, avoiding the look of disdain Yasuko threw him, and catching the smile that followed. "On it."

After the shower, a quick sandwich and the best coffee this side of the universe, Noah felt at least half ready to face the Minoas academics. He stretched his metal leg, feeling the tendons shift where they attached. The EMP had knocked it out of use, stiffening when they'd hit the island. But he'd coped and hidden it well, though he was now paying the price. His urgency for the new EMP shroud went beyond the squad armour.

Not just my leg to worry about, aye Smith?

Noah entered the Stratan conference room, expecting a few extra scientists. But he caught himself at the door, the Stratan Council sat waiting, arms folded, expectant looks on their faces. Assembled to one side were the Minoas delegation, their skin paler, expressions a little haunted. Yasuko had explained during his meal what they'd risked being there.

Noah swallowed, and gripped the flask he'd brought with him, searching for a cup of some form and spotting one on the table in the centre of the room where all the chairs curved in for the best view. The cup sat in his place, waiting, his name card next to it.

Stiff-legged, he walked towards it, nodding towards the scientists he recognised, and bowing slightly towards Abioyi. Reaching the chair, Yasuko appeared at his side, her demeanour shod of the lingering concern, a glow of confidence infused in her hologram.

She understands more about human behaviour than she realises.

Lead Councillor Abioyi stood, the dark rim around her eyes and widening crinkles poorly hidden behind rushed attempts to get ready. Clearly tired, her voice still rang clear, "Welcome. I need to provide you an update on the Tick infection rates. From the initial data Yasuko has analysed, there is a rapid spread of a new strain – a more malicious bacteria, faster acting and the symptoms are … are unpleasant. We have cases where the host has attacked their own families within hours of being bitten. In addition, the effects of the Brain Fever virus has risen, there is evidence it has already taken on elements of the new bacterial strain and is infecting those with latent or earlier variants. In both cases, this is the shortest cycle yet, and a huge threat. As of now we have suspended all work on rewilding and given the dispersal order for all towns and villages in the temperate zone, and the smaller cities of Rutiae and Thsiana just below it. The Council is on the verge of declaring Martial Law across Stratan. There will be further actions to be announced after this meeting. Yasuko, if you please." The Councillor sat, eyes downcast, Shante by her side.

Yasuko turned to the audience, "I am sorry for the rushed nature of this meeting, and the need to drop what you were doing. I hope the disruption doesn't affect your work too much, but you can understand the urgency. We have a delegation from Minoas, and some of you have already started working with them. I felt it was time to explain to the Council, and to you, where we plan to take our work next. And the barriers we face." Yasuko walked to the front of Noah's table, all eyes in the room following her. "We have refined the antibiotic for the older strain, and it is ready to go, thanks to the Stratan sub-team A. They are working on the new strain as we speak, Professor Xantathi?"

"With Yasuko's previous knowledge, data power and the analysis teams we now have, we could have the new antibiotic within a month. Possibly three weeks – unbelievable but true. Testing may take longer, but as it's an adaptation of a current drug, we see little reason to prolong it in desperate times when side effects are minimal."

"A vaccine will take longer," said Yasuko. "But we are working from a much-improved knowledge base, and I can synthesise the antigen of the bacteria once we know which is best to cause the appropriate immune response. The dispersal of the population should give us the time to save many lives and reduce the potential long-term effects on the hippocampus from those attacked by the bacteria. Stratan sub-team B have been working on the viral vaccine, Xantathi?"

"We will need to gather more information on the mutated virus before we can establish a timeline. However, I foresee by the data we will get there soon, depending on where we prioritise resources. There is hope, but we will never eradicate it. When a new bacterial strain arises and the virus takes on part of it, it will require a new vaccine to dampen the whole cycle. It's going to require a long-term strategy, and that means surviving this cycle."

"And so, we return to the same problem, Yasuko," said Abioyi, her voice clear throughout the room. "The source of the bacterial strains. The *!Kora*."

Yasuko looked to the Council, her eyes briefly flashing, before turning back to the expectant scientists.

"The Minoas delegation bring us a fresh direction. They have brought evidence of old research, previous to the nuclear war. Something I'd like Noah to see in detail, but I think it could work for your long-term benefit. And news of something I hadn't considered. A concept that might buy you time along the way – a fresh perspective. Professor Rhitarin, if you would?" Yasuko streamed a confident tone through her voice, adjusting the pitch and richness to positively affect the human emotions in the room and counterbalance the mood she expected towards an old enemy.

The young man stood, perhaps three or four years older than Noah, his eyes dancing as he surveyed the room.

"Thank you." He coughed, looking down and then straight towards the academic audience. "We have evidence that, pre-war, our scientific teams adapted the Fire Ticks' genes. They had not successfully changed their behaviour in this way, that would have been their next step on presentation of the evidence to the then government. We have the theoretical basis for it, and some of the data sets that were available if you dug deep enough."

Xantathi raised his hand, and stood when Yasuko nodded, "There is evidence we carried out the same research, but it failed. We couldn't get the gene alterations to take, from what I remember."

Rhitarin nodded, "Yes. Nor did they until they injected the females during embryonic development. But that worked, from the evidence Yabbin found in the Politico's data. It was he who directed us to dig deeper."

Xantathi sat down, talking animatedly to his neighbours, the noise around the room rising. Yasuko raised her hands, and the room rapidly quietened down.

Rhitarin continued, "I can see you have already worked out where I am going. However, for the benefit of the Council, if successful, we can alter the ticks' behaviour, possibly make human blood indigestible, and even that of the animals we need. Maybe alter their saliva glands, negate the bacterial transfer. There are huge possibilities to stop the scourge for ever."

The room erupted, voices shouting to be heard. And Yasuko let them, eyeing Noah while his mind worked. After working together so much, she could sense the moment when his thoughts coalesced, and the human brain made connections that she so desperately wanted to learn.

And what is this warmth I feel inside as I look at him?

Noah stood, walking over to the Minoas and animatedly talking back and forth. He turned to Yasuko, a sliver of a smile forming, and once again she raised her hands, orchestrating the room with her soothing tone as she asked for quiet.

"You have a chance here. A huge one, and the *!Kora* remain at the centre of it. As distasteful as it may seem they provide you with access to a huge store of female Fire Ticks. You need to leave them be, ready for when we can change the Fire Ticks' nature." Noah could see the nods around the room, and the swift, worried glances Abioyi and Shante threw each other before Shante pushed her chair back, rushing out the room. Yasuko immediately winked out, leaving Noah alone. He looked towards the Lead Councillor, and the fear she held there.

"We never even spoke of the crystals," said Rhitarin, walking over to stand beside Noah. "There is a way, a costly way, to hold the bacterial growth back."

CHAPTER 56

Deep Below Khoikhoi Atoll

"You know, you keep this going and people will think you're really popular, maybe even have loads of girlfriends," said Finn, staring out of the wraparound view screen at the coalescing crystals.

"Ha bloody ha. A love letter from a … I have no idea what it is." Smith sighed at the moment the crystals solidified, the words complete with the nuance and inflection required by the Haven to give full meaning. "It's a set of directions, colour coding for us to follow. Look." Smith pointed to the flashing tip of a crystal strand, the red standing out in the murk. "I'll have to steer."

"Whatever you do, don't knock anything off. "

Smith sat at the controls, linking directly into the AI and apologising when he took over. He placed a special request for a proximity response the AI begrudgingly accepted. He pushed the microship onward, down towards the red glow. As they neared, the strangeness of the animal life at this depth mirrored much of what they'd seen on TV on Earth. All teeth, jelly, tentacles, and some very slow-moving larger fishlike creatures. Many exhibited the bioluminescence of the crystal structure at a much smaller scale, be it as warning or as tempting lures when hunting. The scene was mesmerisingly alien, and they had to focus on the few metres ahead to not get lost in the detail of the teeming life.

"The temperature is rising," said Smith, sending the data to the bottom of the screen. "Rapidly for these depths, and the mineral content is going through the roof."

Smith steered the microship to within ten metres of the red crystal nodule glowing at the top of an extensive crystal growth that stretched like a jagged tentacle built from hexagonal tubes linked to the central hub. Closing in, the colour switched, turning a blue-green and separated, reforming along the crystal outcrop's edge. The viewscreen magnified the image, showing scuttling crab-like creatures grouping together to form one, central, bioluminescent glow. They wiggled in unison and started to walk along the top surface of the hexagonal crystals. Smith magnified the image as far as he could.

"They're encrusted with rock fragments, or are they crystal growths? I wish Noah was here, I bet he knows this stuff," said Smith. "And I don't think he's seen quite enough *weird* on this planet. I'm beginning to feel…"

Finn looked over the images and back to Smith, shaking his head. "Don't say it."

"…a little …"

"No."

"…out of my depth."

Cyborg Blue strikes again, going for Killjoy's weakness.

The luminescent crabs came to a junction, the crystal formations interlocking and shooting off in six different directions. The creatures flowed over the lumps of glass-like stone, marching onwards towards the centre. To their left and right Finn and Smith could see new connections rise up and over rocky protrusions from the seabed, before thrusting downwards into gaps at the top. From these rose black clouds, with a plethora of long, thin plant-like animals, fronds waving in and out of the rising minerals. Weaving around the living tubes were small, white crabs and fish, grazing among the rooted parts in their thousands. Each creature, whether animal or plant, was partly encrusted with lumps of rock or crystal, though none glowed like their guides.

"Temperature's peaked," said Smith, more as something to say as his eyes were drawn to the rising central hub – a forty-metre high, pulsing structure of fluted hexagonal blocks, teeming with all manner of life. The crabs switched colour, a pure green glow, strong and pulsating with heightened power, before diving into a gap between the towers just wide enough for the microship to follow.

With the AI's proximity system in full operation, they edged through the gap, Finn squirming in his seat as the crystal walls closed in. After a minute of the oppressive, throbbing walls setting the inner ship aglow, the way ahead opened out, and the crabs marched onwards, towards a huge vent smoking in the centre of a bowl of shimmering crystal. The fluted columns of glass-like stone curved inwards, joining above them, the tips merging, streams of light continually pulsing from their base to form a bright, almost day-like feel to the space. The crabs broke apart, scattering from the bowl at pace, their luminescence dampened.

"Now this may only be a guess," said Finn. "But I think we're here. Wherever here is."

Ahead of them, suspended crystalline particles began to coalesce, swirling in a current from the vent. At first it seemed to have no shape or form, and then, briefly, an image appeared – a sphere – a world, Stratan. It quickly dissipated, the particles stretching out and shrouding the microship. Nanobots screamed alarm as the particles attempted to attach, pushing the crystals away with electromagnetic discharges, their defensive program kicking in. The particles withdrew, swirling to form a new Haven word.

"Sing? Not sing … but it is. I can't explain it in English, Finn."

"We're at this thing's mercy, down here. In its territory, without a white flag. I'm guessing we're here to talk," said Finn.

"Like the crabs? We let it attach, do you think? This goes wrong, we're, you know – deep."

"Either that or we leave, and it's all been for nothing. It's a long journey back being chased by a five-kilometre-wide crystal alien. Just saying."

And Cyborg Blue wishes he was somewhere else. Preferably with a glass of whisky and some better company.

Smith sent the order, the AI battering against him when he removed the protection protocols. The crystals rushed towards the ship, wrapping themselves around and attaching to the hull.

The hull began to vibrate, the pitch and depth of a low rumble that rose in a sudden surge of noise. Smith instantly adjusted his ears to cope, but Finn crashed to the floor, gripping his ears, overwhelmed by the sound. Smith scrabbled for his helmet, shoving it on despite Finn lacking the rest of his armour, sealing him from the rising power of the sound waves. Connecting to the helmet's CPU, he could sense Finn was out cold, but the systems had blocked the continuing waves of noise, protecting him from further damage.

"Oh crap, I'm not the sci-fi guy here, Finn. Superheroes, maybe. But aliens and stuff? Nah."

CHAPTER 57

Kaimas Military Garrison, Kaimas

Shante stood at the edge of the hold ramp, arms crossed and an unreadable look on her face. Yasuko let her wait, informing Noah of her presence while sending a brief message of acknowledgement. After the meeting, they both had a strong sense of what the Council had been up to with the *!Kora*, and despite her misgivings about the possible choice of actions, she greatly feared the Council had already acted.

Noah emerged from the airlock door, pulling on his jacket against the chill of the Stratan capital. He stepped out from the ship, unwilling at this point to invite Shante aboard, now agreeing with Smith's assessment of her as military through and through.

"Councillor Shante, shall we?" he said, trying to mask his emotions and gesturing towards the tables set out for the scientists' downtime. Noah poured Shante a coffee from the steaming pot in the centre. In Noah's eyes, the Star Trek mantra of non-interference couldn't possibly include coffee, how could you deny the universe? Especially the human-seeded portion.

"Considering your propensity for knowing things, I assume you have worked out why I'm here?" said Shante, taking a sip and nodding as the taste washed down her throat. Yasuko appeared in the chair next to her, of no mind to care whether it was startling or not.

"If you mean the sudden rush when you realised we needed

the *!Kora*, then yes. Amazing how we can value life when it's useful."

Now that would have made Finn proud.

Shante looked straight at Noah, then glanced over towards Yasuko, eyes narrowing at the barb. "It's my role, whether pleasant or not. I am here to protect, to make sure my people survive."

"And make the hard choices?" said Yasuko. "We have heard it all before. And you don't know my background, or that of my crew. We have faced many of those decisions on this journey and witnessed the sacrifice and subjugation of others along the way. But you people, you react so fast. You assume everything needs an immediate answer, taking the surface of the problem as the problem itself. I don't know if it's as a result of the bacteria, but I can't see your society reaching the peak it did with you all so ... so paranoid."

"How many?" said Noah.

"We managed to call back all but two squads, they had already entered the blackout zones and carried out their orders. About a hundred *!Kora*, probably more. I don't know if Mwandin followed through in Minoas, she was deposed prior to our meeting. The Council has now ordered the Marines to guard the *! Kora* sites, not to let anyone in or out until we decide on the next action. Yabbin has told us they fish for food, so we are not starving them out."

"Better than I feared," said Noah. "And thank you for letting us know. But there's something more? Yasuko can read your adrenaline levels and stress pheromones like a book."

Shante threw a quick glance over to Yasuko with the first glimmer of surprise forcing its way through her mask. "Yes. The Minoas delegation, they have been talking with our scientists. They all agree we can massively speed up the gene work on the Fire Ticks if we gain access to the data and samples from the

Minoas lab. Do you agree?"

"It's not my greatest area of expertise," said Yasuko. "Though I could assimilate the information and work with your scientists to get there. But yes. In fact, with that information your teams could do the work while I perfect, manufacture and distribute the antibiotics and vaccine. It could save months of work, maybe more. And we may well have to leave by then."

"Then I have a proposal, because the Minoas shut down the facility. Sealed it away as an embarrassment."

"It was the same lab that developed the bacteriophage?" Noah received a nod in reply.

"And now they know we want it, and that we have their defectors in our midst. They have set their Shadow Marines to guard the place. You say we do not look underneath the surface -well if we attack then we will be setting up yet another diplomatic incident. One that could escalate, possibly prevent the sharing of your antibiotic and vaccine."

"Ooh, that's well played," said Noah. "Hit us with the emotional plea right at the end." Noah looked to Yasuko and knew she'd wanted to finish the job they had started. But it wasn't up to them.

We are a team, a squad.

"I will relay your request, but we will need schematics, numbers, firepower assessment and timescales for deployment."

"Okay Noah, I understand. Finn and Smith are still under. I will discuss it with them when they return, but prep what you can now ready if it's a 'go'. Both suits, yeah. And I'd suggest hiding the minigun until the mission is agreed in case Smith decides to let off a little steam." Zuri clicked off the radio, Yabbin watching her from the step he'd returned to sitting on.

"There anything you want to tell me, Yabbin?" said Zuri, striding over. "About Prime Ministers, and scientists? Plans within plans."

"Me? I'm just a traitor. Whose father died."

"A cunning one, by what I've just been told. And I'm sorry about your loss, but you clearly knew something like this was going to happen, and with more than one layer to your planning when it did. Okay, let's say your desired outcome matches ours, though not your methods. Tell me about the Facility at Kimorosin."

"It's got that far?" said Yabbin, rising from the step. "Really? The Stratan have come on board?"

"With Yasuko and Noah's assistance. Your government has decided to cut off any contact and are guarding the place. You have a plan in that scheming head of yours?"

"Yes. But you will need to be in two places at once if Mwandin is no longer in charge. The facility, and the silo. If the Politico feel threatened, they may well launch," Yabbin threw the stones he'd been rolling from hand to hand. "They have the last nuclear warhead of a lost people, Zuri Zuberi. What my father used to keep the people in check. He called it Project Fear."

CHAPTER 58

Deep Below Khoikhoi Atoll

Smith felt the change. The sensors telling him little, but there was a *presence* in the microship. An otherness he couldn't describe, hanging over him, pressing in with *age* and an *alienness* he'd never felt before. Being without his armour as a barrier between him and *it* left him exposed.

He felt the shift, a weight sliding about the room, the *regard* shifting from the ship to Finn, and finally him.

Cyborg Blue … who am I kidding? I am currently crapping myself and the alter ego isn't helping.

The microship lurched as it touched down on the crystal seabed, Smith recognising the ship's AI holding its virtual hands up in surrender as it withdrew. The room shook, the tone low, deep and in ancient Haven. It took a few seconds until Smith's brain worked out its source, and that it spoke not aloud, but sang directly into his brain.

"He is not Haven. You are not Haven. Explain."

"We – well he – is human. From what we call Earth," said Smith, visualising each word. Matching the tone and timbre of the voice's sung words.

"Where are the Haven that have infested my planet, the colonisers, those that brought their land animals with them?"

"Ah," said Smith. "They sent humans first, to alter the biodome. That's why humans are here, and they came with

253

animals from Earth as food. "

"I do not know 'human'. So that is why they never answered my song or read my words." The voice hung in Smith's brain, thinking with such a depth it began to suck his mind inwards. Smith's mind gripped his systems with all his inner strength, singing for the alien to stop. He felt it respond, the whirlpool of thought releasing the pressure.

"Humans are the vermin that have infested my land? I thought you animals were slaves for the Haven, or beasts to be controlled, not a coloniser. Now I know. The pieces interlock. Not Th'lgarr's children, but their infestation upon my world. You must GO!"

Smith's mind shattered, flying towards all corners of his data banks before he pulled himself inwards, clinging on to his sense of self, knowing there would be no coming back if he failed. Scrambling to hold on, he felt the presence push with him, surround the shards, and squeeze them back together, bonding the pieces. Smith's mind reformed, and he felt stronger.

"I am too much for you, construct. I have solidified you."

"Yes. I can feel it. Why? Why do you want humans gone?"

"I thought it was the Haven, but no. The humans kill my children without direction," Smith knew the word children had a deeper meaning, the picture forming in his head was crystalline, a dispersal, a seeding of the seas. *"They smash and ruin. They make me less than I was, and do not stop. And then they release fire in the sky, shockwaves pulverising that which forms below, leaving ash to taint and acidify my seas. Why would I not?"*

"Ah. Good point."

I said that out loud and am currently slapping my virtual forehead.

"I sang to them, I wrote to them, but they did not STOP. I had no choice, I limited their beasts, kept their numbers low, so they could not return to old ways. But it appears it is the humans that are the infestation, a disease that will mutate and rise again. An Invasive

Species."

"You limit ... how?" The picture slipped unbidden into his mind. The image of the surrounding ocean, the crab-like creatures, the worms clustered about the vents, all glowing, all feeding. And the core source of it all was the bacteria, chemosynthesis, creating food for others as they, in return, were fed the minerals from the hydrothermal vents. Smith couldn't hold the complexity in his mind, the relationships so interrelated, with each creature relying on symbiotic bacteria for survival. And as he watched, the structure and relationships grew and grew, until it wrapped around the planet, gaps only appearing where the vents were few or non-existent. Each connected by the crystals, cogs in this mighty machine's wheel. The scale terrified him. And then he knew.

"The *!Kora*, the Fire Tick bacteria. You..."

"I adjust what already exists for my purposes – dealing with what makes my world sick. The bacteria are a hybrid caused by the Haven bringing the Earth animals here, including their ticks. They fed on species from both planets and evolved. Since the fire came, I have stopped singing and decided to limit the scourge, knowing you will not die, always mutating, surviving. A disease this world does not want. LEAVE."

"I can pass your message on. Tell them what has happened, what you are asking for. But ..." Smith's mind flashed back to Havenhome, and the deaths caused by their inability to communicate. They had learnt so much since that time, but it was key to every world's future. "What if we enable communication? A method to talk to the humans? Find a way, a pathway, to a future where maybe you can reduce their impact. Or ... at least try. You were willing beforehand but used the wrong song." Smith felt the weight in his mind shift, and prepared himself for the whirlpool, but the new bonds held him firm as the depth of thoughts pulled at him.

"I will agree, but I will only communicate for a short time. I am

tired of this scourge. I will stop the breeding song, for now, but you will need to deal with that which already exists."

"How short?"

"Fifty years. That is all. But know this: if, when the time is up, humans remain a threat, I will work to end humanity on this planet, even if it means wiping out all that lives above. And if any more of my children die, then the agreement ends immediately. I leave you the means for the song, it must be in contact with the sea."

Smith felt the presence lift, a final pluck at his memory banks lifting his language files as it left and re-entered the crystal encrusted hull.

Just how old is this thing, if it regards fifty years is a short time?

The microship lifted from the seabed, the AI grumpily extracting itself and taking control as all but one of the crystals sloughed from the hull. Smith instructed it to take them back up, managing one final look at the expanse of glowing crystal as the ship manoeuvred out and away from the central core. A five-kilometre wide, neon pulsating organism.

And do I feel small, it stretches around much of Stratan's oceans. Something so old it has woven itself into the whole planet, claiming the ocean as its domain. And who am I to disagree?

CHAPTER 59

Explorer Ship, Kaimas Military Garrison, Kaimas

"We are nearly there, Finn," said Zuri, pacing across the control room. "Yasuko and the scientists have a handle on all the bacterial and viral elements, with the Stratan and Minoas responding to the work. We do this, and the people on this planet have a future."

"For fifty years, going by Smith's new friend," said Finn, his sore brain already running over the logistics of the operation despite his headache, and knowing Zuri needed to do this out loud. Yabbin's involvement irked her, and she needed to persuade herself by convincing him.

"That has an element of hope. We already have one reason to stop the Stratan from murdering them. Now another, with this … this alien stopping the unnatural development of the bacteria. We just need that research data, and we can leave. Noah and Yasuko have set the structures in place, we get the information on the gene editing, the scientific teams can get the process up and running. It's possible that even the rewilding can get going."

"Just the Minoas to bring on board, and prevent them using that nuclear warhead," said Finn. "How's that going to work? Another coup? Like on Vai? From what I've seen, the Minoas are only guilty of paranoia. They did not strike first in the nuclear war, and the Brain Fever virus was a mistake or accident. What are they guilty of?"

"Not a coup," said Zuri. "Just a removal of the warhead.

That's it. Yasuko believes Yabbin, having seen enough of the communication evidence now she knows what to look for. It exists. But I am not putting Yabbin in charge of anything."

"Then we agree. We go for the warhead itself, not the Politico holding the codes. Two teams, with a little help from Yasuko. I suggest we take the nuclear option and Smith the research Facility with Yabbin on a leash. That way, we limit any political *fallout* should it go wrong."

"I heard that," said Smith, walking in with Noah at his side. "I'm the one that makes the jokes around here. We off to kick arse? I have some anxiety issues I need a big gun to work through."

Noah started stretching his leg at Smith's side, smiling at Finn.

"Yeah, lad. You're coming too. Just keep your leg attached this time, we're running out of ways of putting you back together," Finn clapped him on the back. "Okay, we go tomorrow night. Full Battle Armour, Smith you break out the minigun, time for Blue Bottle to swat back."

"Funny."

And Cyborg Blue marks Killjoy's card. I'm gonna get you, arch nemesis.

Yabbin sat in the curved metal chair, the pseudo-leather seat creaking as he settled back into it. He watched the lights and numbers on the screen, reading the life signs, holding his breath between each ping of the monitor as if his presence might stop it working.

"Ah Mehin, how did we get here? It's happening, yes. All that planning, all that work and we have a chance to change things. And typical, you decide to sleep through it." He reached over, taking the man's hand and squeezing it tight. "How many years have we struggled to get to this point? Twenty? You were right about Mwandin, she did it. Got the scientists here, set it in motion and now I have one last mission before I walk off into the dark, to be forgotten or reviled. But we'll know, we will remember if nobody else does." Yabbin pulled back, a heavy sigh on his lips. "The blood on my hands, and yours, won't ever scrub off. The stain is too deep, yes. Too deep. Goodbye, old friend. Live, tell our story."

CHAPTER 60

Explorer Ship, Kaimas Military Garrison, Kaimas

"There," said Noah, pointing to the grass mound surrounded by a low, damaged wall on the microship feed. "That's what I was saying. If the Stratan Council had no clue about it, then it was likely a silo. That's the shaft."

"Yasuko?" asked Finn. "Anything you can help us with?"

"I think Noah's right. They've shielded it but when you start triangulating communications, and those anti-aircraft and tanks we can see, it's all centred on that position. It's going to be a heck of a lot of trouble getting in ... there's at least forty human heat signatures and eleven vehicles."

"Do we have to?" said Zuri. "Yasuko, can you warp the shaft lid? Seal it in?"

"I – well I had started planning for adapting the ship. You know, the way things have been going we seem to stumble from fight to fight. I started a redesign of the energy debris cannons; I think I could modify those enough to disable the mechanisms. I'd need about half an hour, but I can start the disconnect from the lab now, to speed things up."

"Finn?" asked Zuri.

"Yeah, but suit up. If they start the countdown, we'll have to react. And we don't know how long it will take for the silo to be sealed."

◆ ◆ ◆

The rattle of the anti-aircraft fire pummelled the hull, a third of the heavy calibre rounds clattering into the metal, while Smith weaved and dodged around the rest. He brought the microship down low when the treeline appeared, hoping they'd be below the guns' field of fire as he adjusted the flight path.

"On my mark," he shouted, wheeling the ship, with Yabbin poised. He hit the ground, holding the position briefly as Yabbin activated the auto-control, the two Yasuko manufactured robo-guards coming instantly to life and running out of the doorway. Smith lifted the microship, a barrage of rounds sending it sideways, the AI flashing the eighty percent mass warning.

"Yeah, yeah," he said as the microship headed for the second drop off to the east. "I hope you kick arse, Yabbin. Because it looks like they knew you were coming. Got the welcome mat out and everything. Can't see any tea and cake, though."

"Have you always been like this?"

"Well, I think I may have got worse since a little case of death. Oh, and suit-wraiths, and killer slime moulds, oh and a tentacled alien the size of an office block. Then there was the egg-harvesters. But, yeah, pretty much." Another barrage pummelled the side of the hull, Smith adjusting and blocking out the AI's swearing, regretting teaching it some of the words it threw his way. "Gonna be bumpy."

He brought the microship down behind the service building next to the research facility. Their intelligence and light-wrapped flyby had identified it as empty, and out of range of the anti-aircraft fire. Just a Shadow Marine squad and a couple of personnel carriers with their heavy machine guns stood between them and the main building. The inside was more of a mystery.

Smith tapped into the communication feed, the ship screen now showing the robo-guards speeding to the attack. He set one to full auto, directing it towards the anti-aircraft batteries either side of the L shaped building, while directing the other towards the first armoured carrier pulling up across the entrance.

"Flash," said Smith, directing the bot to release two adapted grenades, the searing light and smoke aimed at disabling their initial sensor sweep as he changed the biped robot's direction from a left to a right flank charge. The carrier's machine gun fire swept across where they expected it to be, and taking the chance, Smith ordered the bot to jump on top of the vehicle. Its clawed feet ripped into the roof plating, and two more grenades timed two seconds apart dropped into the hole. Two high calibre sniper rounds smashed into its knees and the bot buckled, dropping off the three metres vehicle to crack against the concrete, scrabbling to right itself.

Smith ran the AI program, extrapolating the trajectories against his own internal HUD to pinpoint the two snipers they'd flushed out. He sent the information to Alpha 3, Yabbin finding himself with two targets, the second bot having neutralised the anti-aircraft battery on their side of the research facility.

Smith lifted the ship, accelerating towards the roof of the four-storey building as the second personnel carrier sped onto the building's forecourt, the machine gun raking the microship's hull.

"I'm not going to popular," said Smith, "The trade in value is going to plummet." He brought the ship down to running speed, sweeping across the leading edge of the building and ordered Alpha 3 out the door, Yabbin's tirade soon following. "Oops, forgot to warn him."

Yabbin's powered armour took the six-metre impact with ease, stumbling slightly, then picking back up, requesting orders. Yabbin eye-clicked the *subdue* tag as the sniper rolled over from the eastern corner, sweeping the heavy rifle up to bear on him. He urged the armour to aim and fire, finding the speed of response phenomenal and the assault rifle cut loose, the stun bolt hitting the Shadow Sniper in the chest. As the soldier shook, Yabbin ordered the suit to the left, then right, dodging round the roof vents with the second sniper aiming and firing at speed. The first round staggered the armour, the bullet cracking a chest plate above Yabbin's heart. The second smacked into the roof vent and Yabbin dived forward, sending the armour into a roll as a third round smashed into the air conditioning unit between him and the Shadow Marine.

Yabbin pointed the assault rifle around the edge of the unit's corner, using the linked electronic mirror sight to target the rising sniper. The stun shot caught the Marine on the shoulder, sending them into a spin towards the roof edge.

"Oh crap," said Yabbin, pausing briefly, and then powering out from the corner towards the soldier, his muscles screaming as the suit pushed itself to the max in response to his orders. Gauntlet stretching, his fingers grabbed the man's armoured forearm, grasping a metal vent with the other and swinging them back onto the roof. Alpha 3 stumbled with the momentum, giving Yabbin a direct view of the twenty-metre drop. The servos whirred, dragging him back as the armour pulled on the metal vent.

"You good, Yabbin?" said Smith.

"Marvellous. You people are nearly as infectious as the virus. All down, and alive as ordered," he replied, panting while peering back over the edge.

"You should see us on a bad day," said Smith, exiting the microship, now back behind the service building. The second robot limped beside him, scorch marks from the anti-aircraft battery along its central core, both stun cannons on its top, twisted and useless. As he checked the corner with his sight, the second personnel carrier came to a halt, the front wheels parked on top of the first robo-guard, its legs flailing. Six Marines exited, spreading out, and heading his way.

"The other thing about us, Yabbin," said Smith, sending the damaged robot careering out into the forecourt, "is when you do have to fight, make sure you are fully tooled up." The Marines opened fire on the robot, and Smith stepped out, the minigun spinning up, and he released a torrent of hot metal into the personnel carrier, ripping the machine gun from its housing.

He swung the gun round, bulking up the armour as the first Marines switched targets. "Please surrender, you are outnumbered and outgunned." Yabbin pumped a bullet into the floor at the Marine's feet, causing one to turn and look to the roof. But they had their orders, and as the shots battered into Smith, his finger hit the fire button.

Yasuko brought the Explorer ship down, dropping at speeds her normal human crew would be blacking out at. But they flew decoy, speeding across the silo site in full view, the rattle of gunfire and rocket flares punctuating the night, trying to target the microship. Spiralling inwards, her light-wrap engaged, and with heat absorption maxed out, she reached the target point. She brought both energy weapons on the base of the ship to bear, triangulating their aim and switched them on. The intensity of the beams super-heated the metal shutters, but they were designed for this, protected in case of a local nuclear strike. Once the hinges and hydraulics were hot, Yasuko shifted the beam to cut into the ground surrounding the concrete silo.

At the same time, the missile batteries switched to target her, the beam lighting the Explorer up like a beacon. As the first anti-aircraft missiles flew, the microship swung back over, low and fast, causing confusion among the Minoas. Yasuko could feel the radar pulses hitting the ship's hull, doing her best to absorb the signals, knowing she was so close it would only make a little difference. The first heavy calibre rounds hit, followed by the heavier payload missiles. The nanobots threw themselves into defence, shifting in front of the hull, causing missiles to trigger early, and manipulating hull mass to absorb as many rounds as they could. Yasuko felt the steady depletion and knew she didn't have enough time.

"Zuri," she said. "I need help."

"Me and mine," said Zuri, and she dropped from the hovering, light-wrapped microship. Finn and Noah followed, absorbing the five-metre drop in the Battle Armour and powering through the woods, HUDs updating from the microship's last sweep of the combat zone.

"Noah, target," ordered Finn as they reached a small rise at the edge of the woods. Noah stopped, using the brow as cover, sensors sweeping ahead. Finn and Zuri flanked both sides of him.

Minimal force. Hit them from distance.

His *weapon of choice* morphed, and he brought the AW50 up, his HUD and the powerful sniper rifle's night sight locking in. Acquiring targets, he eye-clicked *ready.* Getting the order, he opened up, and his first shot blew the power unit on the targeting radar array on the nearest missile battery. His second hit the unit's power links, and the third the knee of the soldier who'd caught sight of his muzzle flash.

His HUD threw up the hits coming from Zuri and Finn, and the barrage targeted at Yasuko dropped significantly. He moved, following orders, dropping back to provide covering fire as Finn and Zuri took the opportunity for another set of targets. He kept the rifle up, using the HUD to warn of any incoming hostiles from the wider field of vision. The flicker across his sight sent the hairs on the back of his head into overdrive.

"We have light-wrapped Shadows in the woods, approaching both your positions. Fall back, I repeat, fall back." Noah took the shot, missing but causing a quick movement from the Marine, temporarily exposing his position. The *weapon* responded, adjusting itself in line with Noah's human senses and understanding of the armour. The second shot hit home, the Marine screaming as the armour piercing round smashed through the ceramic plate and on into his thigh. Noah fired again, this time towards a Marine flanking the retreating Zuri. The Marine's helmet shattered, the plate and gel not enough against the accuracy of Noah and the *weapon* combined.

Noah caught the third movement as Zuri reached him and knew there'd be at least one more out there, tracking Finn, working in fireteams. He sent the information across to Zuri, letting her take the target as he scanned the woods. Finn was powering back after releasing a final round into an anti-aircraft battery when Zuri aimed and fired, based on Noah's data. The Marine collapsed to the floor, but the fourth rose in front of Finn, opening up with a light machine gun. Noah's bullet caught the Marine between his shoulders, taking out the suit's power pack. Finn smashed into the soldier, the Battle Armour breaking bones as he powered on. Sighing, Noah tracked the flattened Marine, the limited movement a sign of life but not enough to be a threat.

Finn sped past them, spinning to cover while Zuri and Noah followed. On reaching the microship they heard a roar from above the silo, Yasuko speeding upwards, the shearing of metal and concrete finally sealing the warhead into a permanent grave.

The warped metal door swung on its last hinge, clattering to the floor of the roof, molten metal dripping as the last of the chemical explosive finished its work. Yabbin checked round the corner, the mirror sight nearly catching a bullet when an answering hail of metal sped through the entrance.

"Four, Shadows. All with visor and sound protection, light-wrap if it's working and ceramic armour. It means there's at least four more holed up in there," he said.

"Be a damn sight easier if you people used windows," said

Smith, initiating the chemical detonator on the entrance door.

"I know our rep, Smith. But we do like the sun, just a life born from past necessities. You're lucky this place isn't in one of the underground cities. It's only because of the medical research that they put it here, away from a centre of population."

"Yep," the door hinges gave, then the lock and Smith ripped the door open, swinging to the side, bullets flying past. "Found them, or some of them at least. Surrender," he shouted. "No one has to die today."

He sent the damaged robot ahead as the rain of metal came back in reply, the expected grenade lifting the biped bot into the air and smashing it to the ground. Smith jumped through the twisted metal and smoke, his three barrelled stun rifle erupting into life. Two down, with two more running towards the stairs. He took aim, catching one as they leapt the first set of steps. The other stopped, turned and shot, Smith recognising the rocket-propelled grenade a fraction too late as its smashed into his chest, the explosion sending him flying backwards into the sparking robot. Smith rolled, his battle armour flattening the robot's metal legs, with more rounds battering into the spot he'd just vacated. A second burst raked his leg, but Smith stood, engaging the armour's additional power and charging the Marine, hitting him in shoulder and hip, crashing the hapless soldier into the concrete steps. He pummelled the helmet against the stairs, the neck snapping, ending all resistance. Smith stood back up.

"Trying to keep you people alive," he said, examining the ruptured chest plate, and deciding it wouldn't take another heavy hit.

"Two have moved Smith, probably covering behind or heading your way," said Yabbin.

"That's your cue," he replied, checking on Yabbin's HUD screen. "Take them down."

Cyborg Blue heads up the stairs, pissed off and angry. He takes a breath. Does no one want to live today?

A grenade bounced down the stairs, and with Smith already moving, sensors picking up the timer click, shrapnel only pinged off the left side of his armour as he turned and ducked. He stowed the assault rifle, bringing the minigun back into the battle.

Obviously not. Cyborg Blue decides it's time to go all the way up to eleven.

"Hit it," he said, the Rap Metal raging from his speakers. "This time, the guy playing the music survives the film." He took the first flight of stairs at speed, turning round to pound up the second, shadows shifting in the corridor ahead. His air movement sensors told him what he needed, and the minigun spun. And as the bullets ripped through walls, armour and flesh, his HUD flashed, with Yabbin taking multiple hits as he risked himself in an effort to stun the remaining Marines.

Cyborg Blue experiences a brief moment of guilt. Ah well.

"We've got the data set and samples," said Smith, covering a limping Yabbin who heaved the metal crates and sample pouches under his powered arms. "We kept as many alive as we could, but the robot's kind of took a beating at the beginning, reducing the opportunities. I assumed too much intelligence, they're nothing like an Alpha." Smith signalled the nanobots to form an entrance in the microship.

"Silo has been disabled, and we're headed back," replied Zuri. "Mission complete."

CHAPTER 61

Explorer Ship, Kaimas Military Garrison, Kaimas

(Three Weeks Later)

"We have completed as much as we can," said Noah, turning to Zuri who bit into a cheese sandwich. "The antibiotics and vaccines are working, and the microship distribution system has dampened the new outbreak's effects. The Minoas have accepted the deliveries, the Politico seeing sense after the loss of their warhead. The new Head of State has also pledged to work with the Fire Tick gene programme, they have their own *!Kora* tribes."

"With the new labs, the scientists are able to manufacture and develop at the speed necessary to keep on top of any natural bacterial mutations. And with the successful Fire Tick trials for the nymphs, I can't see any long-term issue with eradicating the bacterial transference. I think they'll have that under control within six months, with or without us here," said Yasuko. "I don't think there's a need for us now."

"What about the Crystal Being?" said Zuri. "According to Smith, it believes it can wipe out life on land, and plans to do so in fifty years."

"The radiation has stopped, and the crystal formations lie dormant. So, it has been true to its word about the *!Kora* and the bacterial breeding. Its size would take some deep analysis to understand, but if it has grown as much as he says, then it must have some form of great power it can wield. It will depend on how embedded it is into the vents, or integrated into the planet's crust, as that'll be its energy source. The only way for me to know for sure is to stay here and run a full analysis, but that could take months, possibly years," replied Yasuko.

"They're going to have to look after themselves on that one," said Finn, pouring a second coffee and handing it to Noah. "But they'll need to communicate if they need help. Build a ship to get through the anomaly maybe, now that whatever was in there has gone."

"I have no doubt that entity could do what it claims," said Smith. "I felt its size and *will*. But maybe talking to the people might help, it has been alone a long time. Maybe that connection would make a difference, especially if the humans understand the impact they had on the ocean. But, for me, we're done here."

Alkinta checked the freezer systems, the egg chambers showing green, but she mistrusted the readings, her mind still fogged after the bacterial infection. While crunching the numbers again, she felt the tremor of the microship's engines passing over the compound. She dropped her head into her hands, the tear forming at the corner of her eye running down her cheek as she struggled to concentrate. She slammed the pen down, making for the lab door, more tears flowing.

Outside the fences, the blue metal ship shimmered, a doorway forming in its side. She pressed her hands into the fence, squeezing the wire, racking her memory for the name of the female Earth warrior who stepped out.

Zuri. That was it.

She peered into the darkness behind as another figure followed, a metal circlet around his neck. Funny how the mind worked, she knew him instantly, and the man who came after.

Yabbin and Mehin. Shadow Marines.

Alkinta tensed, her whole body shaking a little as slivers of memory and the chase towards the cove slid into her mind. Behind them, Councillor Shante stepped out, leading a handcuffed Otegnoa. The tears heightened, pouring down her face as he caught her eye, shame dragging his gaze to the floor. Alkinta grabbed the fence tighter, her heart thumping with doubt and pain.

"Alkinta," said Shante, approaching the compound gate with her charge, the others following. "How do you fare?"

"I have been better. The fog, it is daily, ya? Some days worse than others. I would ask," Alkinta said as she keyed the gate number, "why you are here. But I don't think I'll cope well with the answer."

"We are here at the Earth humans' request. They have done so much to change our future, as have you. And for all their methods, so have these prisoners. We can take them back, Alkinta. Throw them in the deepest hole we have. Or they can stay here, under your charge, maybe doing some reparation for their methods."

"My choice?" she said. "For those that betrayed me, and caused the death of people I oversaw, ya?"

"Yes."

Alkinta stared at Shante, eyes then shifting over to the three men. "I will take the Minoas. They were doing their duty. But he," she said, pointing to Otegnoa, "can rot in whatever pit you have, ya? I don't want that man near me."

Yabbin made to speak, stepping forward to defend Otegnoa, the man he had turned. But he caught Mehin's eye, his Corporal's frailty causing him to shake. He would die in prison, and it wouldn't take long. He stepped back, choosing loyalty, just as Alkinta had.

CHAPTER 62

Near The *!Kora* Village, Northern Coast, Southern Continent

Yasuko's hologram sat at the water's edge, the Explorer ship pulsing behind her as it read the song from the blue-green seed crystal she had planted in the warm waters of the bay. She waited, the song from beneath the water changing in response to her call. When the vibrations altered, and the ripples shaped a response, she stood, sending the ship's sensors outwards. Connecting.

"Ah. You are a construct too, like the Blue Machine."

"No, I am organic. I live within the body of the ship. I … I am a piece of Th'lgarr, I believe. You mentioned that name to Smith, the Blue Construct."

"Yes. Th'lgarr, the maker of those I thought infested my world. But no – they sent their beasts to do their work."

"You knew her?"

"Yes, I am … I was owned by Rhy'lgarr … before I became part of this world. He left me in pieces when he ascended, having sucked most of the life force from this planet."

"You were his…?"

"The memory hurts and is weakly bonded. I was … I do not know. That is the past, I have a future."

"Can you tell me about Th'lgarr? What she was? Or did?"

"She was a Garr, a female, mate to S'lgarr. Eater of souls like they

all were. Though Th'lgarr changed, so I remember. Became a drinker, like many of the females when the Garrs turned to excess in their drive to ascend. When the hunt became a massacre."

"A drinker?"

"Yes, one sip from each rather than take it all at once. A farmer, not a predator. She bred the Haven for their strength of will, a powerful force to live off. Like the humans."

"Humans?"

"Yes, I have found their memory, bonded and locked away. Bred by Kha'ligarr. For food. Though that was a long time ago. I have answered your questions, construct. Now answer mine. When will the humans leave?"

◆ ◆ ◆

"Is it…?"

"Yes, Noah. That is the final exit anomaly. It will take us to Earth," said Yasuko.

"I am not…" Noah took a breath, the sudden anxiety spurring a tightness in his chest. "I am scared, Yasuko."

"Because you died? They will not know, Noah. You cleared things up with Zuri, yesterday, about your mood swings. And everyone changes. Smith says growing up is painful, like evolving, yet humans do it in such a short space of time. We are both going through a period of self-discovery, and I need your help as much as you need mine. I know now that we were wrong to have kept your death hidden. I am sorry."

"Yeah, all of that. But we are like a family, and we squabble at times, yet we are strong enough to repair things. No one set out to hurt me, only protect. I understood that at the time, but painful emotions can be overwhelming. No, it's that we are the only ones who understand what's happened to us, and I don't want to go back to Earth and lose that."

"It is your home, Noah. Why?" she replied, moving next to him as he sat at the table in the work room.

"Because this is my home now. This is where I belong. The others, I don't think they realise it yet, but we are not the same people that left. It won't *be* home; we will be characters in a sideshow. And they will want you, Yasuko. They will do anything to get hold of you, your technology and what you represent to the other governments."

"Noah, I am having this same conversation with Smith right now. I have just come from Zuri and Finn, who are as concerned as you. You have all chosen to express this worry separately. This is a new human trait to me." Yasuko sat at the table, forming a virtual chair and placing her head in her hands.

Noah smiled, "Yeah, keeping you on your toes. Another idiom for your collection. I suppose we are suddenly finding it difficult, becoming introspective when at journey's end."

"End? Why does it have to end?"

After collecting the mining equipment, they had all sat down with Yasuko and Noah, and laid out their plans for the Explorer and the microships. Each had given their views on what they thought would be the best adaptations for the future, and to be prepared should things go wrong back on Earth, with memories of the Russian attempts to take them down still raw. Yasuko had already set the digging equipment to acquire the additional metals and mass, using the extra time working with the scientists to give her the chance to prepare. The time spent on the journey to the outward anomaly allowed them to finalise the redesign, and support Noah as he modified the light-wrap camouflage for their original armour with Yasuko's copied crystals. Anything and everything they could do to fill their time, needing to suppress the trepidation in their hearts as they closed in on the pathway home.

They had all wanted to stay awake through the Node transfer, but Yasuko insisted they could not, needing to test the empty Nodes prior to risking her crew. The journey was as empty as the last, a deep emptiness, a well of darkness that Yasuko found difficult to resolve against the stress of so many past voyages.

When they emerged, she cast her sensors wide, gathering the data as fast as she could, hungry to know. Would the Russians be waiting? The world watching for them? She was desperate to give them good news when they awoke.

And Yasuko wailed – for the pain – for the loss – for her friends.

As Earth burned.

WEAPONS OF CHOICE

The Lost Squad Novellas

You can find out a little bit more about the future of the series at www.nicksnape.com and join the mailing list that will keep you up to date about forthcoming books.

Subscribing also gets you access to a series of FIVE FREE Novellas about an alien Stratan Marine squad marooned on Earth. These alien marines arrived soon after Yasuko's ship left the Solar System in Hostile Contact, and the books chart their experiences as countries and mercenaries vie for their technology and knowledge.

These Marines join the main series when the Weapons of Choice finally reach Earth in Books 7 and on into Book 8, so this is your chance to get some background about events on Earth before the series returns to the home planet. To subscribe and receive your FREE novellas please click the link below:

www.nicksnape.com/subscribe

ABOUT THE AUTHOR

Thank you for choosing to spend your precious time getting to the end of my sixth book. If you have got this far into the series, then you really must be enjoying the ride.

The joy I find in writing these characters and the events surrounding them is difficult to measure but there's always some trepidation mixed in. The worry about carrying the reader, you, along with the story. I hope it is something I have achieved with Invasive Species, the longest book in the series. And there is so much more to come, with two more books planned for this story arc, and, if the interest is there, I have new stories to tell.

Reviews are the lifeblood for any author, and it would be greatly appreciated if you would take the time to write a few words or leave a star rating. This helps to spread the message about the Weapons of Choice series and may bring a little starlight into someone's search for a series that is just a little bit different.

USA Review Link
UK Review Link

BOOKS IN THIS SERIES

Weapons of Choice

Join Finn, Zuri and Corporal Smith (deceased) as they explore new worlds and face hostile Alien Contact during their desperate search for a pathway home, in this thought-provoking, military sci-fi thriller series.

Propelled at a blistering pace into strange solar systems desperate for warriors, liberators, and their newly acquired alien technology, Delta Squad evolve from modern-day soldiers into full-fledged Space Marines.

From the forests of Scotland to the stars, they walk the fine line between self-sacrifice and vengeance, with the help of an alien ship and its Artificial Intelligence on a personal journey of their own.

The Weapons of Choice Series explores rich themes of ethical intervention, genetic manipulation, and moral courage, set against a diverse background of political impotence and pitiless alien lifeforms who see humans as food or tools to manipulate.

Read the enthralling series that reviewers have described as 'superlative', 'compelling' and 'an outstanding piece of sci-fi story telling'.

It may be 'eccentric, creative, and thought-provoking' and 'rich in character development', but it's also one heck of a ride

Hostile Contact

Hostile Contact, a sci-fi survival thriller with a military twist...
Finn had thought he'd seen it all...but no...he had to admit...
Not quite everything...
There was a big universe out there and it was about to land in his lap.
Just how bad could it be?

In this fight for survival, Delta Squad discover the aliens are more than they seem, and that alien technology can be just as deadly in the hands of humans - when they unearth the Weapons of Choice.

Return Protocol

If you were eighteen hundred light years from Earth, how far would you go for that one chance to get home?
Still struggling with his guilt, troubled War Hero Finn leads the remaining Delta Squad as they encounter the fallen Haven race on an advanced Space Station and the aliens' home planet.
As they explore the hostile alien world, they face startling revelations, dangerous alien Masters, vicious predators and harrowing missions while trying to outsmart and outgun their way to freedom.

Aliens, they are more like us than you think.

Zuri's War

Alien First Contact meets Adventure Sci-Fi as Delta Squad face their most terrifying opponent yet. After landing on a devastated, human-seeded planet for the first time, they are thrown immediately into an interspecies war. What happens if the people you've come to meet are on another alien's menu?

"Me and mine. We survive." Alien or human, don't get in Zuri's way.

Finn's War

If you had the power to genetically alter yourself, would you? Even if it meant others died under the knife for your pursuit of perfection? Would you? Could you?
While searching for the SeedShip on the advanced human planet Togalaau Vai, Zuri is hurled into the world's seedy underbelly of gladiatorial games and genetic engineering. Finn, in desperation, ramps up the firepower as the Weapons of Choice hit their next level, with Battle Armour to match.

"If you want to wrap that up in some fancy ideology, go ahead - I'm right behind you with a big gun, powered armour and a bad attitude."
It's Finn's War. You think you're ready? Think again

Alien Rebirth

How wrong can you be?
Just when the squad think they've found a quiet solar system to pass on through, a new alien threat raises its tentacle.
The reserve squad reach the Tiqsimuyu System, human-seeded and thriving, with the inhabitants spreading out from their home planet to begin in-system mining operations and the first steps of colonisation.
Little do they know their arrival, and especially that of Zzind's ship, has awoken an ancient alien force on the outermost planet. As it rises from the depths of slumber, it begins to exert control, and subjugates every machine in its path.

Humans are back on the menu.

Legion Earth (Working Title)

To be released mid October

On arrival back on Earth, Echo Squad, the copies of Finn, Zuri, Noah and Smith find little warmth in their welcome as they track a deadly alien threat home. With panic rising among the politicians, and on the brink of war, they find themselves caught in a friendless world with only a group of Stratan Marines to defend their backs

ACKNOWLEDGEMENT

As with all authors, this book would never have existed without the dedicated friends and family who were there by my side throughout the entire process. The least I can do is give them a mention for their patience with my obsession! My Beta readers and fiercest critics have been Pak, Julie Snape, and Paul Derwent, with support from Robert Davies and Mark Hartswood. Amazing friends and family, who put that aside to make sure whatever I put out there was something they wanted to read.

I also need special mention my wife, Julie. She was the one who encouraged me along this path, even pressing send on my resignation email to make this first leap.

Finally, the New Year and Pub Night Crews. Wouldn't be here without you.

Thank you all.

PRAISE FOR AUTHOR

'This is a moment in time humanity will never forget. Hostile Contact' - A sci-fi winner!
★ ★ ★ ★ ★ *Good Reads*

"A real "page-turner" of a Sci-Fi romp. Some very clever concepts and plot devices and it's nice to see some respectful nods to the classic Sci-Fi comics and books of the 1980's and 90's'
★ ★ ★ ★ ★ *Good Reads*

'So looking forward to the next book. This is old fashioned, page turning, sheer escapist Sci fi. Brilliant.'
★ ★ ★ ★ ★ *Amazon Customer*

- HOSTILE CONTACT

'Brilliant sci-fi book with great characters'
★ ★ ★ ★ ★ *Amazon Customer*

'Hugely entertaining'
★ ★ ★ ★ ★ *Amazon Customer*

'Snape excels at creating realism with a far-flung premise, making the story immediately visceral where you can feel the action along with the characters.'

★ ★ ★ ★ ½ *Self-Publishing Review*

- RETURN PROTOCOL

'Couldn't put it down' ★ ★ ★ ★ ★ *Amazon Customer*

'Leaves me eager to read Book 4' ★ ★ ★ ★ ★ *Amazon Customer*

'Action packed' ★ ★ ★ ★ ★ *Good Reads*

'Equally thought-provoking and action packed.'
★ ★ ★ ★ ½ *Self-Publishing Review*

- ZURI'S WAR

'Stunning series. Very highly recommended.' ★ ★ ★ ★ ★ *Grady - Good Reads Author*

'A captivating read for fans of sci-fi and action-packed adventures.'
★ ★ ★ ★ ★ *Amazon Customer*

'An epic fourth installment, Finn's War is propelled forward at a blistering pace by gripping sci-fi action in a fully realized world, with searingly good descriptive prose and compelling thematic development. The strongest installment yet in this continually engrossing series, Finn's War is an outstanding piece of sci-fi storytelling.' *Self-Publishing Review*, ★ ★ ★ ★ ★

- FINN'S WAR

'Draws you in, then hits you between the eyes.'

★ ★ ★ ★ ★ *Amazon Customer*

'This book rocks.'
★ ★ ★ ★ ★ *Good Reads*

'Snape delivers another superlative work of alien sci-fi.' Self-Publishing Review, ★ ★ ★ ★ ½

- ALIEN REBIRTH

Printed in Great Britain
by Amazon

30970845R00169